NEED, WILD DESIRE
UNCOILED INSIDE HIM

Pent up all these years, his emotions went wild from a mere promise of a hamburger at the Dairy Queen. He wanted her in his arms so much it burned in his gut.

Not just his gut.

As he closed the door, she met his eyes.

There was a question in them. Uncertainty. Need. Heat. Desire. She held out her hand.

It was all the invitation he needed. He stepped close, pinning her back to the wall, placing the flats of his hands either side of her shoulders.

"Annette." His voice came out rough and tight.

Didn't seem to worry her.

The Morgue The Merrier

ROSEMARY LAUREY
KAREN KELLEY
DIANNE CASTELL

ZEBRA BOOKS
Kensington Publishing Corp.
www.kensingtonbooks.com

Contents

Dead Certain

Rosemary Laurey

Chapter One

Ten years hadn't improved things, Annette James decided as she drove into Christmastown, VA. Ten years ago, the town had been rundown and shabby. Now it resembled a theme park on steroids.

Given a choice, she preferred the decayed look. She couldn't quite get the hang of a six-foot elf directing traffic. The illuminated reindeer on the roof of the Ebeneezer Baptist Church seemed a trifle out of place too. Yes, it was the season and all that but when the woman at the Sleigh Bells Inn mentioned the town was festive for the holiday season, Annette imagined a few strings of lights stretched across Main Street and a ten-foot cedar in the town square decorated with tinsel and twinkling lights. She hadn't imagined the twinkling lights would also be draped around the doorway of the public toilets.

Not that Christmastown had possessed public facilities back then, obviously an innovation to accommodate the tourists who jaywalked recklessly across Main Street and clustered, with rapt expressions, around the five-foot-tall mechanical Santa in the window of Barlowe's Drugstore. Admittedly, Santa's gyrating hips had distracted her as she waited for the light to change, but she was quite content to turn left and leave the sight of the grooving Santa Claus behind. She glanced at her directions to the Sleigh Bells Inn. A couple of turns and she was there. And stunned to realize it was the antebellum mansion that used to house the town hall, the library and the Police Department. Dear heaven! It had been in a building behind—the then town morgue—that her parents' bodies had lain after the accident.

Maybe it had been a big, big mistake to come back.

But what the hell? She was here now. All she had to do was sign the papers for the sale this afternoon at Jim Cullen's office, meet Juney Whyte—her one-and-only friend from her days here—for dinner and, first thing after breakfast tomorrow, she'd hightail it out of here and be back in Richmond in time for the Christmas Eve carol service.

She couldn't wait.

The parking attendant, or perhaps it was his red nose and reindeer antlers, yanked her back to the present.

"Welcome to the Sleigh Bells Inn, ma'am. Merry, merry Christmas."

"Thank you." She handed over her keys, to be confronted by a bellboy wearing a snowman suit.

"May I take your bags, ma'am? And a merry, merry Christmas to you."

"You certainly get into the spirit of the season."

"Yes, indeedy. We do!" He sounded positively ecstatic. "Christmastime in Christmastown . . ." he began, to the tune of "'O Christmas tree."

"Business is obviously booming," Annette said, hoping to interrupt the choral interlude.

"It's the Christmas celebration, ma'am. People come from all over. We've even had visitors from as far away as Japan and Europe. Where are you from, ma'am?"

"Richmond."

"Oh, I see. Here you are, ma'am. Mizz Charlaine will take care of you." He nodded to the teenager manning the reception desk. Obviously in-state didn't impress like Japan. He pocketed the tip and smiled under his mask. "Thank you, ma'am. Enjoy your stay with us and may you have a very merry Christmas."

The prospect of Christmas alone, apart from her cats and a couple of likewise single friends, seemed positively delightful.

At least Charlaine wasn't in costume, if you didn't count the holly wreath with little electric candles on her head, and there was a beautiful seven-foot cedar in the corner by the sweeping staircase that, if she remembered rightly, once led up to the mayor's office and the accounting department where her grandfather had worked.

"A beautiful tree," Annette said. She couldn't help smiling at the cascades of tinsel and the twinkling lights.

"Mom and I did it," Charlaine said, obviously warmed by praise of her efforts. "My dad fussed at us to get an artificial one as it was cheaper but Mom put her foot down and said she wanted the scent of a real tree, despite the fire risk. We have to be careful about that. Did you know they had a bad fire in the back of the building years and years ago?"

"Yes." She did. Her parents' bodies burned in the fire.

"You have a reservation, ma'am?"

Maybe not. Charlaine frowned at the computer screen, searching for Annette's reservation. "There has to be one. Jim Cullen made it for me some weeks back."

Dropping the name of the town's top-notch lawyer (and one-and-only lawyer, for that matter) did the trick. After frowning at the computer, Charlaine announced, "I can put you in the Ten Lords A-Leaping Suite."

Telling herself it was only one night and lords a leaping had the edge over geese a laying or drummers drumming, Annette followed the snowman bellboy as he led the way toward a wide door at the far end of the hall. As she turned, she glimpsed a man walking in the front door and did a double take. Jake Warren! Heaven help her! She *was* leaving first thing in the morning. Maybe before breakfast. According to local gossip, Jake left town after high school and had never been seen since.

What were the odds he'd end up here this one and only night in ten years? Jake had been her first, and most memorable, sexual mistake. A mistake she since put down to adolescent hormones and curiosity. He'd satisfied her curiosity all right, and shattered her adolescent soul by ignoring her the rest of their senior year. Her brief glimpse of him showed he'd done nicely for himself, considering. . . .

"Here you are, ma'am. Let us know if there's anything we can do for you."

Refuse hospitality to the man now standing in the lobby? If that was too much to ask, how about a long-handled broom and duster to clear the plastic holly from the window frames and the wardrobe? Better not. "This will be fine." It was only after he left and she looked around the suite that Annette suspected where she was. A glimpse out the French doors that led onto the courtyard confirmed it: the Ten Lords A-Leaping and the next-door Nine Ladies Dancing suites were in what had been the old town morgue.

Annette sat down hard on the edge of the tester bed. Her first instinct was to reach for the phone and demand a different room but decided to go in person. She marched down the hallway and pushed open the door into the lobby, just in time to hear Jake Warren say, "You have to have a free room. I reserved one a month ago."

Poor Charlaine was not up to coping with a Jake Warren. "Yes sir, but . . . Would you mind waiting until my mom gets back? She can sort this out for you. You could have a drink in the bar and lunch on us, while you're waiting," she added, seeing him hesitate.

"Okay," he said, "but the minute your mother returns, I want to see her." He turned toward the oak-paneled and greenery-bedecked bar and Annette did a quick reverse and shut the door hard behind her.

So, no other rooms. She was stuck with hers. At least Jake Warren hadn't seen her, that was one small mercy. Quite a massive one actually. Much as part of her longed to snub him in public and turn a dramatic heel, she really had far more important things on her mind.

'She's here, Bob. She's here. I never imagined it possible. She's really really here: Our little girl!'

'Yes,' Bob James replied. 'She's lovely. Looks just like you when I first met you.'

'Oh, honey.' Katy James couldn't sigh without living lungs but she felt the sadness all the same. 'She grew up and went away. I never thought she'd come back.'

'I bet she's come to sell the old house. She won't stay.'

'But what if, while she's here she could . . .'

'Now, don't get your hopes up, Katy. Maybe we're meant to stay down here as spirits.'

'Piffle! I don't intend to spend eternity wafting back and forth over this tacky hotel. Annie's come back for us. You wait and see.'

'Katy, honey, she doesn't even know we're here.'

'She will!'

'And what do you mean by that? You're not haunting her, Katy, I won't have it. The girl needs a life.'

'And by the look of things, has a nice one. You commented on her car. Said she had to be successful to afford a Volvo.'

'This isn't about her car!'

'Of course it isn't! It's about our little girl and releasing us.'

She sounded wistful but Bob wasn't buying it. *'Whatever you have up your sleeve, Katy, forget it."*

'Forget it? Robert E. Lee James, I cannot forget the last

twenty years wandering. Your interfering old father anchored us down here, why shouldn't our daughter release us?'

'And how do you propose she does that?'

She couldn't snort without breath, but did her best. *'It's not going to be as hard as you think. All I have to do is convince Annette what to do.'*

Bob shook his spectral head. Katy Willow had always been hard headed. Dying hadn't changed that one iota. *'Look here, Katy . . .'*

'Hush! She's coming back. She'll be here soon. I'm going to watch her.'

Annette seldom indulged in the overpriced goodies in a minibar but today the expense was justified. She reached for a tiny bottle of gin and another of tonic and stirred both with a green swizzle stick topped with the seemingly de rigueur holly sprig. She took a deep taste, settled herself into the poinsettia-covered sofa, inhaled the sweet perfume scent of gin and took an even deeper drink, letting the liquid rest on her tongue before slowly swallowing.

Running into Jake Warren, or rather *not* running into him, was enough to drive a teetotaler to drink. What was she going to do? Halfway down the glass, she knew. Simple, really. She was meeting Jim Cullen at four, having dinner with Juney at seven, staying out late to talk and catch up on news, getting up very early and heading home. Heck, if she left early enough, she might just make it to Richmond in time for a late lunch.

Good plan! She topped up the glass with the remaining gin.

'Annette?' a voice in her head whispered. 'Annette, honey? It's Mommy. Please listen.'

Annette set the glass on the side table with a clunk. This was what happened when she got maudlin and indulged in overpriced gin. She hallucinated. But, damn, it sounded like Mom's voice. Yeah! Right! She remembered so well after twenty years. Shaking her head to clear it, Annette stood, walked back into the bedroom and unzipped her case. She didn't have much to unpack: just night things, toiletries and clean undies and a sweater for tomorrow. She looked around; apart from the over-the-top decor, the suite was actually rather nice. The sitting room and bedrooms had separate doors to the hallway and French doors to the courtyard. Pocket doors, decorated with the inevitable Christmas trees and wreaths, closed off the two rooms, and the bathroom connecting them had a vast whirlpool tub and a spacious shower. The red and green tiling took a bit of getting used to and the plastic mistletoe suspended over the tub was quite beyond the pale.

She was tempted to try out the tub, but it was cold outside and she was due in the lawyer's office in twenty minutes. Might as well leave her car parked and walk. It would be nothing if not interesting. She changed her driving shoes for boots and reached for her coat.

'Annette,' the voice said. *'Please listen, honey. I need your help. We need your help. Daddy and I can't . . .'*

Yes! She needed a walk in the crisp air to clear her head. Either that or . . . There was no 'or'. Annette grabbed her bag, pulled on gloves and marched out.

'I warned you, Katy, she won't listen. She's too rooted in her world.'

'She will, Bob, you wait and see. She will. Our little girl will set us free.'

It had been a well-seasoned hamburger, cooked to a perfect medium, the Bermuda onions and blue cheese a touch he'd never have credited to Christmastown, but Jake Warren hadn't come all this way to eat a hamburger in a plastic holly-decked bar. Having his food served by an elf didn't help his mood in the least. He wasn't about to snarl his frustration at a slip of a girl who was obviously doing the best she could but, dammit, he'd booked the room—or rather his PA had—weeks ago when they set the closing date. Once Charlaine's mother—who presumably ran the place—showed her face, he was getting a room for the three nights he'd booked, or know the reason why.

What wild impulse had given him the idea to come back here for Christmas, Jake would never know. But it was distinctly satisfying to drive a Porsche into the town he'd left on a Greyhound bus. And he rather looked forward to tomorrow morning when preppy Jim Cullen learned who was behind the Warren Corp. that was buying the old tool factory, the pumping house, and the old James place. The latter, he admitted, was sheer, sentimental indulgence. He'd loved Annette with a wild, adolescent passion that had never quite faded. And broken her heart. He'd once harbored dreams of finding her again but when a search some years back found her married, he shelved that fantasy. She wasn't meant to be his. Her old bear of a grandfather had been right there. Trouble was, every woman he met, and they were quite a few willing to snap up the owner of Warren Corp., didn't touch his heart the way Annette had.

Enough maundering. He was here for business, not sentimental indulgence.

It was a good hour later that Charlaine's mother, Melanie, returned, proffered abject and profuse apologies and frowned at her computer screen for a good ten minutes. But the upshot was he now had a room, or rather half a suite with a sofa bed, and the promise of free use of the minibar for his delay and inconvenience.

Once settled, he had time to review the contracts, spend a pleasantly sweaty hour in the Sleigh Bells gym aka the former sheriff's department garage, and enjoy dinner: onion soup, locally-raised lamb chops, parsnip puree and fresh asparagus. He declined a dessert menu—no point in putting back on what he'd just sweated off—and settled in for a quiet evening reading sheaves of legalese before treating himself to an early night.

Chapter Two

'Do you see that, Katy? A man sleeping in our Annie's bedroom! Oh, if I just had a body I'd have it out with him.'

'Hush! He's not in her bedroom. He's on a sofa bed next door.'

'And there is a difference, my dear?'

'Big difference. If he were in her room, she'd notice the minute she walks in.'

The meaning of that wasn't too hard to grasp. 'What in tarnation have you been doing, Katy? And how the hell did you manage it?' Katy Willow had stunned him when they first met in eighth grade geography and still made a habit of it, even dead.

'It's not too hard. A little distraction is all it takes. Did you know if you cause the electricity to flicker at the exact right moment, it takes things off the computer?'

'No, Katy, I did not and neither should you. We're not supposed to mess around with the living. And what in heaven were you thinking, luring a strange man into your daughter's room? Honestly, woman!'

'Don't 'honestly' me Bob James! Besides he's not a 'strange' man. You may not have eyes but you can still see. Take a good look at him.'

Bob wafted lower, looked at the sleeping man and almost dropped onto the bed in shock. 'It's that Jake Warren!'

'Yes, it is.' Katy smiled fondly, or rather did the nearest incorporeal equivalent of a benevolent maternal smile. 'He was a handsome boy and he's sure grown into one good-looking man.'

'He was a randy lout who couldn't keep his hands to himself! Have you forgotten how my father had to warn him off and threaten he'd be arrested if he as much as spoke to Annette again?'

'No! I most definitely have not forgotten. The old bigot broke Annette's heart in the process.'

'He was just looking out for her. Young Warren was far too hotheaded and nowhere near good enough for her.'

'Right, just like I wasn't good enough for you. I'll never forget what he said when we told him I was pregnant.'

Even after all this time, Bob James shuddered at the memory of his father's wrath. 'He was wrong there, and said as much later on. He loved Annette. Thought she'd hung the moon. Nothing was too good for her.'

'He meant things for the best, Bob, but he was wrong about you and me, just as he was wrong about Annette. She loved Jake.'

'She got over him and married that Philip what's-his-name.'

'And had her heart broken a second time. No, Bob, this time it's going to come out right.'

Annette stamped her feet and brushed the snow off her shoulders as she walked into the lobby. She'd been glad of a ride home from Juney's husband, Jon. It had been a bit of a dicey drive too, the snow coming down like great goose feathers and drifting in the driving wind.

Nice to see the blazing log fire in the lobby.

"Would you like a nightcap before turning in, ma'am?" the youth behind the desk asked. "We have carol singing in the bar."

Annette didn't think so. She rather thought that second bottle of wine had been a mistake and she wasn't up to "Santa on the rooftop, click click, click," just this minute. "No, thanks. I think I'll turn in. I've an early start in the morning."

"Better check the roads in the morning, ma'am. There's a bad storm coming up from the south. They're calling for eighteen inches, or more, before morning. Looks like we'll have a white Christmas."

At least someone was delighted at the prospect. She did not share his enthusiasm. He had to have it wrong. It hardly ever snowed that bad before January.

This place was getting to her. Hadn't she imagined her mother's voice earlier? What would she imagine with her head woozy like this? Lee giving his farewell address to his troops? Time she went to bed.

Only the damn key card didn't work. What the heck? Maybe the other door? Bingo! That one worked and her bed was turned down with a Lindt truffle on the pillow.

Lindt chocolate, yum. Maybe the Sleigh Bells Inn wasn't such a bad place after all. If she ignored all the plastic holly and the leering elf perched on top of the TV. Letting the truffle melt in her mouth—it was hazelnut, one of her favorites—Annette kicked off her shoes, turned the elf to face the wall so he wouldn't watch her undress, left her clothes on the snowflake-printed chair, pulled on her nightshirt and decided her teeth and face were going to have to wait until morning.

The sheets were smooth and the pillow down. As long as she ignored the ten lords a leaping over the bed, she'd have a good night's sleep and worry about the depth of any possible snow in the morning.

Annette yawned, stretched and looked up at the clock. Seven forty-five. Later than she'd planned to sleep. Time to get moving. Sitting up, she swung her legs to the side of the bed, stood up and walked over to open the curtains at the French doors.

Damn! Eighteen inches had been a conservative estimate. There had to be nearer two feet and still falling. Damn and double damn. No point in panicking, it might stop in an hour or two and no doubt the state crews had been busy all night clearing the Interstate. All she had to do was cover the twenty miles or so from Christmastown to 81. She had snow tires and a car built for bad winters. She'd be home at her own fireside by tonight.

No prob.

A quick shower, breakfast and she'd be on her way.

Annette crossed the room to the bathroom, pulled open the door and gaped, her voice box paralyzed. A butt-naked man was standing in her bathroom. Very nice firm butt, actually, not that she was looking. With a gasp, her larynx resumed function. "Excuse me," she said, trying hard not to shriek. "What exactly are you doing here?"

"Shaving," he replied, in a crisp voice, as he turned to look over his shoulder.

Dear Lord in Heaven! Half his face might be obscured with shaving cream but she'd recognize those blue eyes anywhere. She opened her mouth to speak but somehow her breath jammed up and all that came out was a squeak.

He did little better. "Good God!" he managed as he reached out for one of her towels and wrapped it around his waist, dropping his razor on the floor in the process.

He gaped at her.

She stared and swallowed.

"Annette?" he whispered. "Annette James?"

"Right first time." She could breathe again and was back in control. Sort of. "Please explain what you're doing shaving in my bathroom, Jake Warren." She'd said his name without a flicker of hesitation. Good for her!

"It just happens to be *my* bathroom."

Indeed! "I don't think so. Whatever sort of smart-ass game you're up to. It leads off my bedroom. It's my bathroom."

"It so happens to lead off the room I slept in last night."

Saints and Angels! "You slept in my sitting room?" This was beyond any sort of pale. How could she have slept all night with Jake next door? It was darn hard to even think straight with his nipples at eye level. Hard nipples, each surrounded with just the right amount of dark . . .

"No!" He was getting a trifle testy. "I did *not* sleep in *your* sitting room. I slept in the only room they had left." He gave an exasperated sigh and shook his head. "Look here, Annette. I did not plan this. I am not playing any sort of game other than trying to shave and get a shower. There is obviously a major mix-up we need to sort out. We can either do it right now, although I'd prefer not going down to the lobby barefoot and wearing a bath towel, or we can both get dressed and take care of it in half an hour."

She was tempted to insist on going right now, he did look good with a towel draped low over his hips, but no way was she toddling down to the lobby in her ratty old nightshirt. Especially the way he was looking at her.

"Get dressed!" she snapped. "But would you mind nipping out a minute. I do need to pee!"

Acting the perfect gentleman, he agreed with a smile and backed out, shutting the door behind him.

She locked it.

Taking care of nature's call, when Jake was inches away, probably listening for the flush, was by no means the most comfortable experience of her life. After all, this was Jake Warren. Apart from one sole, glorious, incredible and soul-shattering exception, encounters with him seemed destined to be utter mortification.

She was out the bathroom in a flash and back in the bedroom, heart racing. Why was she so upset by this? She was not a shy virgin any more, thanks—or perhaps no thanks—

to Jake! She'd cope. He'd dress, so would she, and she'd be gone. *Tout de suite*. She'd get breakfast on the highway. Eating anything, even oatmeal, under the same roof as Jake was a bit more than her digestive system could cope with.

Mind you. He looked damn good in a towel. His shoulders and chest had filled out nicely since he was a teenager. His thighs were more muscular and the brief glimpse she'd had of the rest of him, before he grabbed the towel, hadn't shown any atrophy.

Dear heavens! She ran her hands through her already messy hair. Just when she was tying up all the loose ends of her life, he had to swan back in. It was ludicrous. The whole situation was more fitted to some Monty Python skit than her nicely-ordered life.

Her heart wasn't slowing one little bit and no doubt her blood pressure was sky rocketing. She forced her shoulders to slacken and breathed slowly and deeply to ease the tension out of her body, shut her eyes and willed her mind to calm. She was going to have to face him again. She was not going to be frazzled and keyed up. Calm and totally in control was exactly the way to go.

Once she got her clothes on.

That thought was a dumb one! Oh! Would she have a word or two with the management of the damn Sleigh Bells Inn when she checked out.

Another deep breath, Annette relaxed back in the arm chair, closed her eyes and let her mind and body go slack.

'Annette? Annette, honey, please listen.'

Strewth almighty! She was hearing things again.

'Please listen, Annette. You're not imagining this. It's your mother.'

Mom? It sounded like her mother, but no, had to be her mind playing games. It was just being here. Right where the disaster occurred.

'Listen, love. I know you can't believe it's really me, open your eyes. Please.'

Annette opened them as a nasty chill wafted through the room. She wrapped her arms over her chest and shivered, just as a white misty shape came together in front of her. It was too much. Jake Warren naked before breakfast and now . . . Her mother's face appeared in the mist.

'I'm here, dear, and so is Daddy. Please, please believe what you are seeing. We need your help.'

"Dad? He's here?" Heaven help her! She was now answering the voices in her head and the misty shape that spoke with Mom's voice.

'Yes, I'm here, sweet punkin.'

This time the shudder came from deep inside. No one except her father had ever called her that.

'Listen to your mother, sweet punkin.'

"What's happening?" Other than she was cracking up from seeing a naked Jake before coffee.

'Honey, we need your help. Remember what happened to us?'

"Sure." As if she was ever likely to forget!

'We're stuck here. You need to help release us.'

"You're ghosts?"

'Yes, dear. We've been waiting a long time to leave. Please don't refuse to help.'

"Mom and Dad. If you want me to help I will. What can I do?"

'Find our ashes.'

Now she did swallow hard. "Your ashes?"

'Yes, dear. After the fire, we were mingled with the ashes and ruins of the building. Most of us melted back into the earth or flew off on the wind, but the rest of us was caught up with the ashes of the building and was sealed up. Is there any chance you can find us? Set us free?'

Sounded a pretty tall order, except, she had this memory

of her grandfather taking those jars down to the basement and . . . The voice faded and the misty shape dissipated. "Mom, are you still there?"

'She's used up, sweet punkin. Taking shape like that uses a lot of energy. She'll re-form soon but meanwhile, please help. If you can.'

"Dad, I will. I remember Grandpa keeping your ashes in jars. He scooped them up from the ruins. They're in the basement." Of the house she signed away yesterday.

'Can you retrieve them, Annette? If they're scattered and we can be separated from the building ashes, we'll be free. It's because they're not that we're stuck down here.'

Stuck in Christmastown for eternity wasn't something she'd wish on Jake Warren, much less her own mom and dad. "I'll do everything I can. I promise." Pity she hadn't known this before she sold the house but damn. . . .

'I know you will, sweet punkin.'

'Dear Annette, thank you, honey.' Her mother's voice was back but faint.

"Annette, I'm through. It's all yours!" And just in case she hadn't heard his basso profondo, Jake banged on the door. Hard. My, my he was getting testy. Maybe her presence had skewed him a bit off-kilter. Good!

"Mom, Dad, where am I supposed to scatter the ashes?" If she found them.

The room was once again warm and she sensed her parents' spirits were no longer there.

Darn! This needed thinking about. If the ashes were still in the house after all this time, she might find them but she'd handed over all the keys to Jim Cullen. She could hardly ask to borrow one back. He'd want to know why and try to get her committed if she told him.

Drat and double drat! Maybe inspiration would come in the shower.

Distraction more likely.

Jake had removed all his things and hung his used towel on the hook on the door, but his presence remained, along with the scent of expensive men's cologne. At least the shock of seeing him and conversing with her dead parents had rather brushed aside her worries about road conditions.

Chapter Three

Jake sat on the arm of the sofa bed and smiled. Wasn't often a man had a chance to put right the errors of his youth. It was a long shot, and no doubt he was years too late but . . . the big 'but' was that Annette was married. He hadn't a chance in that direction but at least he could say his piece and wish her well.

Odd though that she was here, at Christmastime, alone.

Talk about wild chances! He'd so often fantasized about seeing Annette waking in the morning, warm from his bed. Forget the bed bit, but she looked every bit as wonderful as in his dreams: hair still all short curls but nicely rumpled from sleep, and a sexy flush on her face. Okay, that had mostly been anger and embarrassment but she still had those wonderful, warm brown eyes and luscious mouth. He didn't need to guess how her breasts looked and tasted. That was something he'd never forget. He looked down. Seemed his body hadn't forgotten either. Better get his thoughts up above his waist if he wanted to look presentable when they next met. Chance had thrown a lucky opportunity his way and he never turned his back on luck. Annette was going to have to talk to him. Didn't they have this room fiasco to sort out?

He reached for his shirt. He'd be ready and waiting when

Annette emerged from her room. She was going to hear him out. She had to.

Was she going insane and hearing voices? Or was she in full possession of her faculties and hearing voices? Seeing Jake *deshabillé* was enough to unhinge anyone's reason. But, unless she really was losing it, that truly had been her mother and father. She had to forget Jake Warren and figure out how to do what Mom and Dad needed.

Pity they hadn't materialized before she signed the house away. But they had! She had heard her mother yesterday, but brushed it off as imagination. Damn! Oh well, couldn't be helped now. She had to figure out how to get into the house she no longer owned and second, how to find their ashes. Even if Mom and Dad were right and their ashes were still in the house. Who knew if the jars of ashes had been broken or tossed away or shoved in a corner . . .

Shoved in a corner . . .

Once the memory struck her, she knew she was right.

Her grandfather, grim and severe as always, walking into the house with several canning jars full of gray and black dust: The remains of her parents scraped up off the floor of the fire-damaged morgue. Her grandmother, protesting saying it was morbid and ghoulish and they shouldn't be shown to the child. Her grandfather replying it was all he had left of his son and goddammit he was keeping them with him. Forever.

When her grandmother insisted they should have decent, Christian burials, they'd compromised. The old man chiseled out stones from the wall in the basement and placed the jars in the thick stone wall and mortared them up.

Annette shivered under the warm water. Just thinking back to her dictatorial old grandfather gave her the jitters.

So. She knew, sort of, where the ashes lay. Assuming the

distant cousins who'd rented the houses the past few years hadn't found and moved them. Given their meager interest in house maintenance, she rather doubted that. All she had to do was break into the house, armed with a crowbar or jackhammer, and hack away at the old stone foundation. All!

She definitely should have listened to her mother yesterday. Too late to worry about that now. Better get going. She had a job to do before she went home.

She dressed fast, dried her hair, almost skipped make-up but decided the effort was worth it. She was not getting out of here without seeing Jake again so why not let him know what he'd tossed over? The silk sweater and jeans were a nice mix of style and comfort and her mother's pearl earrings added the right extra touch.

She almost fancied she heard a little whisper as she put them in her ears but her, "Mom? Dad?" brought no response. She reached for her pocketbook. No point in hanging about here. Might as well get breakfast and go housebreaking.

She was all set to face the morning. Until she opened the door and met Jake's eyes. He'd been laying in wait for her. And he looked luscious. Even with clothes on. Damn! He could still get to her. He was dressed for a day at the office: dark suit, a pale gray shirt that fit his lean body so well that it had to be made to measure, and of all things, a tie with a Liberty pattern in blues and greens. Not that she was looking but it was hard to miss how it caught the color, and the glint, in his eyes.

She was tense as a drum but he, damn him, looked cool and relaxed, leaning one shoulder against the wall, his jacket slung over his shoulder. "Good morning," he said. "Want to sort out the room situation?"

"There's not much to sort out. I'm leaving today."

A lock of his chestnut hair fell over his brow as he shook his head. "That I doubt, Annette. Have you looked outside recently? According to the TV there's more than two feet and the Interstate is blocked. The National Guard has been rescuing stranded motorists by helicopter. Princess, you are stuck here. With me."

She shrugged. Her throat was a bit too tight to reply anyway. Damn and double damn with sleigh bells on! Deep breath. "I'm sure there's a better alternative."

He fell into step beside her. When she walked faster, he lengthened his stride, determined, it seemed, to stick to her like glue. She caught his aftershave, even over the scents of cedar and bacon cooking. Hell! She could all but hear his heartbeat. Even after all this time, she remembered just how it sounded if she rested her head on his naked chest.

Enough! No, far too much! She was not going there again. Ever. Still on the rebound from Jake, she'd married Phillip her second year of college. A major mistake, but all that was behind her now. If only Jake Warren had stayed right back in the mists of her youthful mistakes too.

The Sleigh Bells Inn offered profuse apologies. Annette tried to be gracious. Not exactly easy with Jake inches away, his body heat a distinct contrast to the gusts of frigid air from outside.

"I'm so sorry," was Melanie's reaction. "I know you both reserved a suite, but we did find rooms for you."

"Separate rooms. Shared bathroom," Annette reminded her. A trifle terse but . . .

She shook her head. "Oh, no, both rooms have a bathroom." She looked up at them, seeing, perhaps, something in their faces, she went on. "Two bathrooms in that suite: one off the bedroom, one off the parlor."

"One off the parlor?" Annette echoed, giving Jake a long, hard look.

"If there is, it's invisible!" He said, sounding unconvincingly affronted in her opinion.

Someone was playing games here. And she wouldn't put

anything past Jake. "How about we go back to the suite and check?" And if there was a second bathroom . . .

There was one, as Melanie had insisted, but—pissed at him as she was—Annette understood Jake overlooking the door. It was concealed quite effectively behind the gathered swathes of red and green cloth that covered the walls. Melanie gathered up the fabric and pulled it aside.

"There it is!" she announced, obviously pleased at being vindicated. "The second one! There was no need to share. This one's clearly here."

"Not exactly clearly," Annette was snapping but darn it, Melanie's attitude irked. "More like the Secret Bathroom." Jake's laugh caught her like a warm ripple of delight. She did not want to respond to him but . . . "Hardly matters now," Annette said, "I won't be here tonight." Jake had to be wrong about the weather.

Melanie shook her head. "You will unless a miracle occurs." Her assessment of the situation pretty much echoed Jake's. Damn. "One good thing. The people due today can't get into town so rooms should be all right. You two will be fine here."

"I'm not so sure about that." What was she saying? She was dead certain!

"How about we fight that out after breakfast?" Jake said. Good idea. As long they ate at opposite ends of the dining room. "Just for the record," he continued as they retraced their way back to the lobby again. "I'm sorry if this foul-up embarrassed or upset you, but I'm not sorry it happened."

"Really, your idea of fun, is it?"

"No." Seemed he chose to ignore the sarcasm. "But I am glad to see you again. There's been something I've wanted to say for years."

"And you think I want to listen?"

"Why not? What do you have to lose?"

"What would I have to gain?"

"You'd learn why I never spoke to you again back when we were kids."

That was easy enough. "Because you got what you wanted and had no more use for me."

"God! No!" He sounded almost in pain. "Dammit, Annette! You are going to hear me out." As if to make sure, he grabbed her arms and held her. The hallway was narrow enough that he had her all but pinned against the wall.

"Would you kindly let me go?" If not, she'd ram her knee straight up.

"In thirty seconds, okay? Give me thirty seconds, then you can walk away. I'll never bother you again. Hell, I'll even move out and sleep in my car."

Unwise given the weather, but she nodded. Might as well hear the man out. Before she laughed in his face.

Jake stepped back, letting go his hold on her. He shut his eyes a moment before looking right at her, his eyes as intent and blue as ever but under the intelligence that had always been there, was a shadow, a grief. "Remember that Friday night after the ball game?"

"What Friday night?" Why make it easy for him?

"The one and only Friday night I made love to you and promised to take care of you forever."

"Oh. That one." Good thing Melanie had hightailed it back to her desk in the lobby.

"Yeah! That one!" His face was steady, almost impassive, as if he were fighting to hold back emotion. "The Sunday after, your grandfather came by the house with old Sheriff Byson and one of the deputies. I thought they were coming to arrest me, and was scared witless what Mom would do without me. She was already ill then." Annette nodded. Jake's mother had been more than ill. She'd died a few months later. "Your grandfather said if ever I spoke to you again, ever tried to communicate with you by letter, phone or anything, he'd evict us both."

"He what!" Annette shrieked, cold fury boiling inside. "He told you that? He couldn't just throw you both out like that."

"He could. We were way behind on the rent. Mom hadn't worked for months and what I earned doing yard work and busboying at the Scarlet Parrot barely bought groceries."

Annette looked up at him, wide-eyed. For several hideous seconds, Jake was certain she did not believe him, would laugh in his face, sneer, burst into some defense of her grand-father, call Jake a liar, a seducer, a bastard.

She clenched her fists and scowled. "The wicked old man!" Shut her eyes a few seconds, then looked up at him, her dark eyes brimming with tears. She took a deep breath. "I need coffee. Lots of it. Strong."

She believed him. He read it in her face and voice. Sweet heaven! She believed him.

"Come on," he said. Without even thinking about it, Jake took her hand and pushed open the door into the lobby. "I'll get you coffee." Hell, for believing him, he'd get her the moon if she asked.

She drank her coffee with just a little milk, holding the cup in both hands as she rested her elbows on the holly-and-snowman decorated tablecloth and frowned. Hell, even the little crease between her eyes was sexy. But if she belonged to another man now. He'd be content. Whatever bizarre quirk of fate had brought them together in this way, he'd be forever grateful. He'd never quite realized how it still rankled that he'd been unable to explain things to Annette back then. He was halfway intoxicated on relief and sheer joy.

"You know," he said, "I should thank the management for the mix-up since it gave me the chance to put this right. I've always hated that I couldn't tell you why."

She nodded, eyes distant. "It all makes more sense now. I should have figured it out myself." She took a sip of coffee and shuddered as if remembering. "Saturday morning, after we . . ." She smiled at him. "It must have been written all over my face. My grandfather demanded to know what I'd done and who I'd been with. I did not tell him what we'd done, but I did admit to having a hamburger with you at the Dairy Queen.

"He went off at me and forbade me to see, speak to or think of you again. Gave about twenty reasons, starting with you and your mom being white trash and going on from there. I'm sure you can fill in the details." He nodded. He could. The old man had not minced words and the sheriff had added his share. "My first instinct had been to disobey him. I was, after all, rather emotionally linked with you at the time." She smiled and shook her head. What did that mean? "But the next evening, Sunday, when Grandad went out, obviously to threaten and harass you and your mom, my grandmother begged me not to disobey. Said if I did it would cause terrible trouble. She must have known what Grandad was planning.

"I still didn't much care. I was going to defy the lot of them. Until I got to school Monday morning and . . ." She shook her head. "You know the rest."

"It killed me not to be able to at least explain, write a note, but I didn't dare. I knew he meant it."

She nodded and took another sip of coffee. "Your mother was dying, wasn't she?"

"Cancer. It ate her away. She only hung on by strength of will. She wanted to see me graduate from high school. She never made it."

"I remember." She went quiet. "That old man caused a lot of trouble with his . . ." She broke off. Whatever was on the tip of her tongue stayed there.

"It's done and past," Jake said. "Let's order breakfast and part as friends."

"Okay." She didn't seem too enthused over the idea.

Annette ordered eggs Benedict, unsure she could chew or swallow right now. Talk about thrown for a loop. If learning her parents were earthbound and it was her job to release them wasn't enough for one day, now it seemed Jake hadn't screwed her and tossed her over. She hadn't just been a notch on his belt. If her head started spinning, she wouldn't be surprised.

"So." Might as well find out a little about him. "What are you doing in Christmastown?"

Chapter Four

He actually looked shifty—for about three seconds. Interesting. "Investing in the Christmastown boom." It was the same old grin that had driven teachers batty. "And indulging myself in coming back in style after I left with my backpack and gym bag riding on a Greyhound bus."

"What did you do after high school? You weren't even at graduation."

"You noticed?"

Skip that. "Did you join the military? Everyone said you had."

He shook his head. "I considered it but . . . remember old Mr. Mason?"

"Who taught American History? His sister was librarian at Back Creek Elementary?"

"That's the one. He and his wife let me sleep in his spare room the weeks after Mom died. Then, he found me a job. Some distant cousin of his had a little grocery store up in Lexington. Mr. Beecham was a decent man, paid me a fair wage and let me sleep in a room over the store. He also had a hobby of playing the stock market and convinced me to invest part of my salary. With his help, I amassed a nest egg, even thought of going to college, but hated to leave the old man. He relied on me to help run the store. Late one winter afternoon, we got robbed. We both got shot." Her throat went tight and cold. "Mr. Beecham died. Heart attack from the shock, they decided. My big shock came later. He left me the shop, his house, savings, everything."

Jake shook his head and smiled. "Incredible. He was a millionaire several times over. Lived in a very modest house and opened that store at seven in the morning every day except Sunday."

"What did you do?" Aside from investing in tailor-made shirts.

He gave a rueful shrug. "After I got over the shock, I spent months deciding what to do. Even thought of selling the shop but he had three other employees who depended on him. I'd never forget my mother losing her job when she got ill. Couldn't do that to another human being. So, I kept it all. A woman who'd worked there for years and knew the business, I made manager.

"Then I went on a spending spree, buying up little businesses, another grocery store, a couple of independent drugstores, a small appliance repair shop, a place that did custom mill work, a restaurant and more. They're all part of Warren Corp. Wages aren't great, but everyone has job security, health insurance and a promise of a modest pension."

While he was talking, their food arrived. She barely noticed. "Investing in hardworking people."

"Right! People at the bottom of the food chain. The ones who work long hours for modest pay and are first to get shafted."

"And you're doing the same here? In Christmastown?"

He still had the dimple in his chin when he grinned. "Not precisely." He picked up his knife and fork and cut one poached egg in half. "To be honest, and just between us, I wanted to swan into town in a flashy car and rub a few people's noses in it." He shrugged. "Trouble is, you're the first person I've encountered who recognized me."

"I did see more than most people!"

Sweet heaven! Her laugh was lovely: warm and utterly sexy. Right! Better keep reminding himself she was married. "What about you? You've had my life story. Who's waiting for you at home? Kids? Husband? Gerbils?" Did he really want to know?

"None of the above."

He almost choked. "None?" he asked, after he swallowed and gulped coffee to get it all down. "You're alone?"

"Not exactly."

He should have guessed.

"I own two cats or should I say, they own me."

"No significant other?" This he really needed to know.

"No, thank you!"

That sounded definite enough.

"I was married briefly. Not the smartest thing I ever did." She paused. "I was so in love I dropped out of college to get a job and put Phillip through law school, until I learned he planned on trading up for a 'better' wife once he was established in a good law firm. I moved out ahead of his schedule. He was rather put out about that."

The laugh now was plain vicious. Not that that snake Phillip didn't deserve all he got. "Divorced?"

"Yes!" Her smile was next to jubilant.

Joy was not the word for it. She was free. Single. How often did a man get two chances? "Where do you live? Work?"

"That's changing. Soon. I used to manage a chain book store in Richmond. But always wanted my own shop. I've just sold my grandparents' old house. Now I have the money to set up on my own."

"I'm glad." He reached over and squeezed her hand.

To his astonishment, she squeezed back. "It's a gamble and a risk, but I've spent the past eight years learning the business."

"You'll make a go of it. I know, Annette."

"I'm going to have to," she replied. "I'm sinking all I have into it but," she looked at him, a question in her eyes, "if I don't, maybe you'll be looking to add a bookstore to your empire."

"Annette, you need help. Of any sort. Let me know." He pulled out his wallet and handed her a business card. "I'm serious."

She glanced at the card, but didn't put it away, just left it beside her coffee cup, as if she were uncertain whether to keep it or not. "Thank you."

At least it got him another smile. Not that she'd be smiling if she knew what was happening under the napkin covering his lap. Or would she? She'd definitely thawed toward him and . . . Hell, he was going for it. "Want to have dinner with me? If you can't get home before then?" he added.

She thought about it. That was something. She hadn't laughed in his face.

"Okay."

"You name the time."

"Eight?"

"Here?"

Again a pause. "No, you know where I'd really like to go eat? The Dairy Queen."

Just like last time. He took that as a symbol of hope. Big hope. "It's still here?"

"Yup. I noticed it yesterday. Rebuilt. No longer a shack, it's a brick building now. You can't miss it. There's a lighted sleigh and eight massive reindeer on the roof."

He had linen tablecloths and fine wine in mind but if the Dairy Queen was what she wanted, the Dairy Queen was what he'd give her. "Okay. Doubt I'll need to make a reservation." Assuming they were open Christmas Eve. If not, he always believed in a fallback plan.

That seemed to be it, or was it?

She seemed to think so, placing her napkin beside her place and standing. "Tonight then? I better get going. I've things I need to do."

So did he. Like buying her family house. He'd tell her but . . . "I'll walk back with you."

Things had certainly changed between them in the last hour and way for the better. Annette smiled at him as he stood aside for her. The warmth in her eyes gladdened his heart. She was single, right here, and no longer viewed him as a bastard. Tonight he'd do his level best to convince her to give them both another chance.

He didn't have to wait that long.

He opened the door from the lobby to their hallway. As she walked through he caught her perfume, like flowers in a summer garden, like the pale pink roses that grew wild over the back fence of his old house.

Like Annette.

Need, wild desire uncoiled inside him. Pent up all these years, his emotions went wild from a mere promise of a hamburger at the Dairy Queen. He wanted her in his arms so much it burned in his gut.

Not just his gut.

As he closed the door, she met his eyes.

There was a question in them. Uncertainty. Need. Heat. Desire. She held out her hand.

It was all the invitation he needed. He stepped close, pinning her back to the wall, placing the flats of his hands on either side of her shoulders.

"Annette." His voice came out rough and tight.

Didn't seem to worry her.

"Yes, Jake?"

This was no time for conversation. He lowered his mouth and brushed his lips over hers. She might slug him one or knee him in the goolies but . . .

Annette opened her mouth and wrapped her arms around

his neck. How could he have forgotten the heaven in her lips? The sheer and wondrous heat of her need and the softness of her breasts as she pressed closer? Their tongues met and something deep inside his brain snapped, like need pent up too long, or a dam breaking, releasing a flood of want and sheer physical longing.

Annette kissed him back, her tongue touching his, her lips pressing, as if she were absorbing his need and satisfying hers at the same time. His body went wild. He held her hips against the wall with his and she pressed back, rubbing herself against his erection and giving soft, sexy whimpers as she pressed her mouth hard on his, returning his kiss with a torrent of her own.

Her legs fell apart at a nudge of his knee and as his thigh parted hers, she pressed down rubbing herself against his leg.

It was too much. It was wonderful. It would never be enough.

"Jake," she muttered into his mouth.

That was all it took.

"We'd better get inside." If they didn't he'd have her right here, up against the wall.

Wrapping an arm around her shoulder and pulling her along, he fumbled for the key card. The door swung open. He whirled her inside, kicking the door closed, sweeping her up in his arms and carrying her over to the unmade bed. He yanked back the rumpled covers and laid her down.

Chapter Five

Annette smiled up at him but only for an instant. Her eager hands grabbed his tie, his shirt, his belt, as he unsnapped the waist of her jeans and lowered the zip.

Hot damn! If he'd known she was wearing red lace undies he'd never have made it through breakfast. He just had to know if her bra matched. He yanked her sweater over her head. It did. Very beautiful and all that against her pale skin, but in the way. His hand under her back unsnapped the bra with a twist of his wrist. The red lace hit the carpet moments after the silk sweater.

Not that she'd been idle. He had no idea where his tie and shirt had ended up, and didn't much care; he was too busy running his hands over the sweet soft flesh of her belly and fastening his mouth on her breast while her hands found his belt buckle.

It was crazy, lunatic and utterly fantastic. They were two wild things as they pulled and tugged at clothing. At some point they both shifted and stood, kicking off shoes and yanking down each other's remaining garments until they both stood. Naked.

Annette stepped back, as if to get a better view, her dark

eyes bright with a delicious lasciviousness as she eyed him from face to ankles and everywhere in between.

Especially in between.

Smiling, she took a step closer. Resting her hands on his chest, she rubbed her fingers over his nipples. They'd been hard before, now they went rigid. And they weren't the only part of him standing to attention.

She bent her head and licked his left nipple. He thought he'd explode. Need and heat raced across his skin and, as if to show him just who was running things, she fastened her mouth on his right nipple, pulled with her lips and nipped.

Enough was enough. She paused for breath, so he grasped her by the waist and in seconds, she was back where she belonged: on the bed, flat on her back looking up at him, a little, twisted smile half-daring him to do more.

He'd never in his life resisted a dare.

His nipples still throbbed from her efforts. Now was her turn. Holding her down on the bed, with a hand on her shoulder, he trailed his fingers around the curve of her breasts, cupping each one in his hand and rubbing her nipples with his fingers. It took very little effort to leave them satisfyingly hard. Her little whimpers were just a complimentary extra.

There were going to be one hell of a lot more extras.

Meanwhile.

He licked her nipple. Slowly. Dragging his tongue over every little bump and ripple of flesh, circling the aureole with deliberate slowness, flicking the tip of her nipple with his tongue before closing his lips tightly and suckling her breast as if to draw hope and sustenance from her.

Her hands closed around his head, holding him to her. Just to make sure she understood how things were between them, he lifted his mouth and looked her in the eyes.

"I've dreamed about doing this to you, Annette, this and so much more. Once with you was never enough. We're made for each other, remember what you said?"

She nodded. It seemed speech was a bit beyond her right now. That he took as a compliment and encouragement. "I've never forgotten," she managed with a bit of effort. "Ever."

"Me neither."

"Jake . . ." she began, "this is crazy."

He wasn't going to waste breath arguing. Her smile and the sexy cast to her eyes was all the go ahead he needed. "Yes," he agreed, "be crazy with me," and covered her mouth with his.

It was a slow kiss this time. She wasn't going anywhere, so he took it leisurely, teasing her lips open, finding the tip of her tongue with his. Gently, caressing her tongue, stroking lips with lips as he marked her mouth as his.

Before, they'd been two ardent teenagers, scared but drawn by a mutual passion, now they were man and woman, ready and hot for each other.

There was no hesitation, no nervousness on either part. She'd had other lovers. So had he. All have been rehearsal for this coming together. This renewal.

He broke the kiss. Gently. "It's been too long," he told her, "but worth the wait."

"Why wait any more?"

Why indeed? Except, "What's the hurry, Annette? I want this to last." If he could.

As he hesitated, she acted, wriggling from under him and flipping him. With a whoop of satisfaction, she straddled him. No problem from his point of view, just gave him better access to the parts that really mattered. As she stroked her hands over his chest and shoulders, he grasped her hips, drawing her down on him. If he could just feel himself inside her . . .

She had other ideas. She shifted a little and she rested back, rocking her butt cheek against his erection. She was out to kill him. Torture him. But before she did, he ran his hands over her hips and thighs and down to her pussy. As he stroked the

soft folds open he caught the scent of her arousal. Gone was
the girl he'd loved. Jake had a willing, sexy woman in his bed
and rejoiced in her. Easing his fingers inside her and apply-
ing gentle pressure on her clit with his thumb, he took his turn
at sensual torture.

She threw back her head and gave a long, slow groan.
"Again, please!"

How could he refuse? As he pumped his fingers in and out,
she rocked, caressing his cock inside her until he was ready
to explode.

"You're killing me, Annette!" he said lifting her up by her
waist. "Enough!"

"Nowhere near enough," she replied, shifting off him, but
only to slide down the bed and settle herself between his legs.
Resting her hands on his thighs and grinning up at him. Reading her intention in her eyes, his mouth went dry with anticipation.

Hers seemed to be watering. She licked her lips, slowly,
before brushing them over the head of his cock, covering the
smooth flesh with little kisses, stroking his shaft with her fin-
gertips before opening her mouth and enclosing his cock with
her lips.

It was his turn to throw back his head and groan.

Annette chuckled, her laugh muffled by his erection but it
was a laugh all the same. And he loved it. He shut his eyes to
block out everything but her mouth and what she did to him:
swirling her tongue over him, easing her lips up and down his
shaft, taking him into her mouth down to the root before
easing back to suck on the sensitive head and tease the nerve
endings around the rim, before swallowing him deep again.

He was tempted to beg her to do this all day, all night, until
the snows melted, the skies cleared and spring thaw turned
into summer except he couldn't hold out much longer.

"Give a horny man a break, Annette," he said, reluctantly
easing her head off him. "I'm not made of ice!"

"I had noticed," she replied, gently licking the very tip of his cock. "You are wonderful, Jake."

"You're pretty damn wonderful yourself but now it's my turn."

She didn't make the least objection to being flipped on her back, and when he spread her legs wide and settled between them, she gave a big, sexy grin. "Yes, please, Jake."

Since she'd asked so nicely. "My pleasure, love."

He felt like a kid again.

She was as ardent and eager as ever. But so much more. Annette was all woman. A woman ready and open to her man. Gently he parted her vulva, and gazed at the beauty of her womanliness. Nothing in life had ever compared to Annette and nothing ever would. The sexy giggle of anticipation just about did him in.

"What's the delay, Jake?"

Good point. Pushing her thighs wider, he lowered his head between them and covered her pussy with his mouth. Her gasp was all the encouragement he needed. She was hot, slick, and ready, and he had every intention of making her wait. Just a tad. She was moaning aloud now, her head tossing on the pillow, as his tongue caressed her. She grabbed his hair, her clenched fists pulling, but he barely noticed; he too was caught up in her need and the sheer sexy wonder of Annette soaring to climax. It didn't take long. Just a few strokes with the tip of his tongue and she screamed aloud her climax. He held her tight as the ripples of her orgasm eased and she sagged back a limp, sated mass of magnificent woman.

"Everything okay, sweetheart?" He couldn't resist asking. Her reply was a tired smile. "Yeah! But what about you?"

"Here I come." Pausing only to reach for his pants and take a condom from his wallet, he lifted her hips and positioning himself carefully, entered with one movement.

She cried out, "Jake it's almost too much!"

Almost was good enough by him. "Annette we're only just

beginning." He couldn't hold back, the feel of her slick woman's warmth just about did him in. Gently at first, then harder, as his own arousal surged, he rocked his hips back and forth, making her his own. Her cries and shouts echoing in his ears, as he felt her come again and again around him.

She was fantastic, incredible, wonderful. And his. Of that he was determined. He was not losing her a second time.

Spent and more satisfied than ever in his life, Jake slowly eased out of her loving warmth and snuggled beside her. She was limp, cuddly and sated. What more could any man want?

"I love you, Annette," he whispered.

Her eyes flashed open. "Oh, Jake!" she replied. "You're incredible. I think I had a few extra climaxes there."

"We've a lot of time to make up, honey. Oh, God! I love you."

"I love you, too, and always have." She curled into him, nestling her head against his chest, and closed her eyes. He listened as her breathing changed and she was fast asleep.

Jake glanced at his watch. Damn! He wanted nothing more than to spend the entire day naked with Annette but he had thirty minutes to dress and get down to the lawyer's office. Carefully, so not to disturb her, he eased out of her embrace and stood up. With luck, she'd sleep until he got back.

He scribbled a quick note: *Annette, I hate to leave but have to. Let's make it a late lunch together as well as dinner. Love, Jake.* And just for the heck of it, he drew a pair of entwined hearts and printed their initials inside them. Corny and downright sophomoric but what the heck? It felt right.

Dropping a kiss on her cheek, he went back to his own half of the suite (it was going to all be theirs from now on) and washed and dressed as fast as he knew how. He'd be a few minutes late, but too damn bad. He'd been busy putting his life right.

Chapter Six

Something woke Annette from her doze. The bed was cold beside her. No trace of Jake. And she was darn certain she had not dreamed their wild lovemaking. No way, not with that delicious ache deep inside. She padded across the room, barefoot. Bare butt come to that but, heck, he'd seen it all. Bathroom was empty but hadn't he mentioned an appointment this morning? He wasn't going to be leaving Christmastown any time today and besides, she had an errand herself.

Hoping her parents hadn't been hovering overhead while she and Jake renewed their acquaintance, Annette dressed fast, pulling on both sweaters. The house was bound to be cold. She glanced at her watch. It was after eleven. At least the roads in town would be cleared by now.

Before leaving, she stood in the middle of the room. "Mom? Dad?" She wasn't sure why she was whispering, but . . . "I'm going back to the house now. Think I know where Grandad put your ashes. I'll find them. Promise."

Maybe she heard a quiet sigh.

Maybe she was hallucinating.

Annette shook her head. No. She'd seen her mother's form and heard them both yesterday. And hadn't she heard her grandfather insist he was keeping his only son with him? The old man had no idea what he was doing. Or had he?

No time to worry about that. Chipping away decades of old concrete was not going to be quick or easy.

'She's going to the house, Bob. Annette's going to set us free.'

'Grrreump.'

'What's that for? We've been dreaming of this since we died.'

'That boy! Did you see what he was doing to our little girl?'

'No, I did not. Bob James, you should be ashamed of yourself, watching them!'

'I did not watch them! But I'm not deaf even if I am dead! They were . . . well, you know . . .'

'Yes, I most certainly do! They were making love. Just like we used to. Have you forgotten how it was?'

'Of course not! How could I? But Annette, she's so young.'

'She's five years older than I was when I had her. She's quite old enough to make her own decisions.'

'Maybe . . . but if he does her wrong, he'll have me to answer to!'

'And what, pray, will you do?'

'The same things to his laptop that you did to the hotel computer.'

'You won't need to. He's got it so bad.'

'Know everything do you, Katy?'

'I know this.'

Wilson's Hardware was hadn't changed much since the days when Annette came here with her grandfather. Off the tourist track, their only concession to the season was a dilapidated tree in the window. Made a nice change from the overly seasonal atmosphere of the Sleigh Bells Inn and the center of town.

She bought a heavy chisel, a hammer, a crowbar and a pair of safety goggles. That should do it. She debated getting a bag of that instant concrete to repair the wall, but how the heck was she going to mix concrete in a house where the water was turned off? She'd clean up as best she could, and offer the buyer to send a man in to repair it. With that in mind, she threw in a roll of black trash bags and, noticing a row of knee-high rubber boots, bought a pair in her size. She bet no one had cleared around the house. Her boots were warm but not deep snow proof.

She piled her purchases on the back seat and headed for the house on the outskirts of town.

A problem with snow was leaving clear tracks. After a little thought and careful driving over half-cleared side roads, Annette parked in the lot of the Friendly Market. Amazing how many people were still shopping on Christmas Eve but that worked to her advantage. One car more or less wouldn't get as much as a blink. She packed her purchases in her back-pack, changed her stylish suede boots for the rubber ones and, hefting the pack on her back, set off the hundred yards or so down the road to the corner of her old street. The snow had started again, not like the wild storm earlier, but gentle flakes that settled on her head and shoulders. Good, all the better to cover any tracks she might leave.

The last thing she wanted was a concerned neighbor calling the sheriff.

She walked past the end of the street where she had spent a very lonely childhood, and turned up the alley. Nothing had been cleared here. Even the trash cans were buried under tall hats of white snow and drifts blocked several driveways.

The old carport still remained, neat and spotless after the

efforts of the cleaning crew she'd hired. If they'd cleaned up the hidden key, she really would end up breaking and entering.

It was dusty and rusty but still there. Hanging on a very rusty nail behind a loose board.

She left tracks all the way to the back porch, and hoped the snow continued long enough to hide them. Or at least hide how new they were. She had to cut a few inches of screen to get to the latch, but the door opened fairly easily. Latching the screen and locking the door behind her, Annette crossed the empty kitchen, her footsteps echoing on the tiled floor, and opened the basement door.

The basement had terrified her as a child, dark and full of spiders and odd sounds from the furnace and water heaters. It was lighter than she expected, at least on the north side, where snow hadn't drifted over the windows. The stark cold light was almost enough to work by without her flashlight.

Over on the far wall, just above the workbench, her grandfather's makeshift memorial was undisturbed, the rough inscription just about legible still. Only her father's name, Robert, was scratched in the concrete. Her mother hadn't merited a mention.

The old man had been twisted. Sad, bereft, but twisted, and what strength of will he'd possessed to hold her parents' spirits like this.

And now she was here to undo it all.

Annette unpacked everything, wishing for a moment that she'd stopped to get cocoa or coffee at the Friendly Mart. But no, someone might have recognized her from when she'd worked there on Saturdays. She was cold, would no doubt get colder, but she'd reward herself with hot cocoa with whipped cream when this was all over.

She put on the safety goggles, picked up her chisel and hammer and started to work.

Twenty minutes later, she had a miniscule heap of chips to show for her efforts and had barely made any noticeable difference to the slab of concrete but the physical effort was keeping her warm. Just as well. This was going to take all day.

"You know," Jim Cullen said as he handed Jake his copies, "there's some in this town won't believe it's you behind Warren Corp."

"No doubt the same worthy townspeople who never believed I'd amount to much," Jake replied. "I imagine most people have forgotten me anyway."

"Not all. I bet Pete Bullock hasn't."

That got a laugh, despite Jake's determination not to revisit the bad old days. "I doubt he has." Their fight, which resulted in Pete breaking his arm after Jake threw him down, had earned Jake two weeks' suspension. "Where is he now?" Pete's father had been Christmastown's only lawyer.

"In the state pen." Jim said with a twisted smile. "Embezzlement."

"How?" He shouldn't sit gossiping when Annette was waiting, but this he had to know.

"He took over his father's law practice, and pretty much raided a half dozen trusts. He also used company credit cards to run up vast bills. He's doing twenty years. The town needed a lawyer after that so a buddy of mine from UVA and I came down and set up practice. Three years ago, I bought Carter out. His wife was from Tidewater and didn't like it here."

"Can't say I blame her. There's more here than there used to be but this endless seasonal cheer is getting on my nerves."

"Try it twelve months of the year. We have Christmas in July, Labor Day weekend caroling, May Day wassailing and a special Fourth of July Boar's Head Feast."

"But you stay."

"I've sunk all I have into the firm. It's my home, after all, and, to be honest, much as the endless cheer palls pretty fast, it's been good for the place. You should have seen it six, seven years ago. It had gone way down the tubes from when we were teenagers. Once the canning plant closed down and the paper mill was fined out of existence for polluting the river, there was nothing here. The mines had been worked out when we were kids. An excess of plastic mistletoe is preferable to racing decline."

All very interesting, but nothing he hadn't researched himself, apart from Pete Bullock's felonious enterprises. Jake declined Jim's offer of lunch and was back in his suite—their suite—in fifteen minutes.

Annette wasn't there.

The beds were made, his note placed carefully on the night stand, but no Annette.

Damn! He wanted to eat lunch with her, to tell her in detail about his plans for his new properties and, if the gods and Christmas elves smiled on him, take her back to bed.

What now?

He grabbed a can of soda from the mini bar and unsnapped the top. Might as well wait. Surely she'd be back soon. She'd seen his note re: lunch, hadn't she?

He sat down, propped his feet on the coffee table and sipped. As he went to set the can down, he heard . . .

'Jake, Annette is at the house. She needs you.'

What in the name of tarnation? He looked around. He was completely alone and yet the voice sounded clear and close by. The TV was turned off. So was the clock radio. Had to be a stray comment from someone passing outside in the hallway. In this old building, the hearing vents no doubt carried sound.

Odd though.

He took another sip. Just what he needed: a quick infusion of caffeine. Not that his head needed clearing. He was quite sure what he wanted. All he had to do was figure out how to convince Annette that she needed him in her life. Permanently.

'For heaven's sake! Get moving! You can't hang around here all afternoon. Get yourself over to that house!'

He was not imagining it but . . . had to be hearing his own thoughts. Come to that, why not get out and look around his property? Maybe Annette had gone to have a last look at her old home.

Jake reached for his coat and car keys and went out.

'Thank goodness for that. I thought I'd never move him.'

'Can't stop meddling, can you, Katy?'

'It's not meddling making sure our only daughter gets the man she wants. Besides, she might need help looking for our ashes.'

'More likely she'll be put out at being interrupted. And you don't know he's the one she wants.'

'Pouf! Bob, of course I do. Mothers know these things.'

Chapter Seven

Jake shook his head. Was he utterly losing it? Driving out to the edge of town across half-cleared streets because of a voice in his head? On the other hand, following hunches hadn't served him too badly this far in life. Might as well go with it. If nothing else, he'd take a gander over one of his new properties.

There wasn't any sign of Annette as he pulled his Cayenne to the side of the road, slap bang against the wall of snow and slush thrown up by the snow plow. He was aware of movement in the window of the house opposite and stares from a cluster of kids dragging sleds.

"Merry Christmas!" he said to them as he locked the car door.

One said, "Merry Christmas, sir!"

A tall girl said, "You looking to see the Bookers? They moved out weeks back. The house is empty. No one lives there now."

"It's my house now," Jake replied, glancing towards the Realtor's UNDER CONTRACT sign. "I just bought it."

All five of them stared. Young eyes darting from his car to the old house and back again. Fair enough. He bet no one on this street owned a Porsche.

"Why?" the tall girl asked.

Very good question and no doubt every word he said would be repeated within the next ten minutes to each set of parents. "I used to live here in Christmastown when I was your age. I had a friend who used to live in that house."

"So you just bought it, for that reason?" It was the short freckled boy and Jake had to admit it sounded a pretty lame reason.

"Yes," he replied, reaching into his pocket for the keys. "I just drove over to have a look at it."

"Gave yourself a Christmas gift, sir?" the tall girl asked.

"That's exactly it." Although as far as Jake was concerned, he'd opened his best gift that morning.

The children hung around at the end of the path, watched him unlock and enter the house, then ran off, no doubt to spread the news around the neighborhood.

The chill of the house came right through his cashmere coat. What in the name of tarnation was he doing freezing here, when Annette was no doubt back at the Sleigh Bells Inn waiting for him? Damn, he should have asked for her cell phone number. But he was here now and might as well have a quick look around while he was about it.

Funny really, he'd never been in the house before. Although he'd once ridden his bicycle down the alley late at night, trying to guess which room was hers. Now he owned her room and every inch of the house. Her old grandfather was no doubt turning in his grave.

Jake looked around the wide, high ceilinged rooms and the walls all painted a uniform off white. The kitchen needed renovating and he bet the bathrooms did too but the floors were clean and recently waxed.

And clearly showed footprints.

Interesting.

Footprints led from the back porch all the way across the room to the slightly ajar basement door.

Squatters? Not unless they were desperate. Mind you, anyone homeless in this weather would be truly desperate. Kids playing games in a supposedly haunted house? No, it was just one set of footprints. Whoever it was, Jake figured he could handle one shivering soul.

He opened the basement door and peered down. It was reasonably light. He could see the bare floor and walls. And hear the sound of metal hitting stone in a steady rhythm.

Just in case, he took out his cell phone ready to speed dial 911 if he had to. "Hello! Who's there?" he called.

In reply, there was a cry and then a clear "Damn!" and "Who's there?"

He took the steps at a run. Either his imagination was playing games or that was . . .

Annette, perched on the corner of an old workbench, holding up a bleeding hand.

He took the last few steps at a leap and literally sprinted across the basement to stand at her side.

She stared at him, face ashen, eyes wide inside the plastic goggles. "Jake? What are you doing here?"

"Finding you hurt." His glance took in the the chisel and hammer on the workbench and the pile of chipped cement and dust. "What are you doing?"

Annette looked up at Jake and shuddered. Dear heaven, how could she explain this? What in creation was Jake doing here? Had he followed? Had someone seen her break in? Even if they had . . . "Jake, how did you get here?" Her hand throbbed but she had to know.

"I unlocked the front door and walked in." He pulled a perfectly ironed handkerchief from his pocket.

"How? I just sold it."

He held her wrist and wrapped the handkerchief around her wound. "I know, I bought it. Hold your hand up. If it doesn't stop bleeding, you might need stitches."

The last bit barely registered. "You bought it? Why?" His

touch was wonderful, gentle and soothing but the last thing she wanted, sitting surrounded by rubble with an unfinished job on her injured hands.

He pressed on the wound to stem the bleeding. "Keep your hand above your heart. Looks as though it might stop but you'll probably need a tetanus shot." He paused. "Why did I buy it? Part sentiment, Annette, to remind me of you and part business. There are two old men up near Meadows of Dan who make dulcimers. I want to bring them here and establish a training program, have them pass on their skills and set up a showroom and shop. I thought they could live here and use part of the house as a workshop."

"I hope they don't mind blood in the basement." How was she going to explain this? And why, oh why, did Jake have to be the one to buy the house?

"You know what I'm doing. Now it's your turn."

There was no way she was wriggling out of this. Not with Jake keeping tight hold on her hand. If she told him exactly why she was here in an icy cold house, chipping away at the, no his, wall, he'd think she was nuts. But perhaps part truth might do. "My parents' ashes were sealed up in the wall by my grandfather. I wanted to get them out."

Jake was silent for all of three seconds, then folded her hand up against her chest. "Keep that still," he told her, "and give me the chisel. I'll get them out."

"You'd better have the goggles, too. Chips fly everywhere." Annette reached to pull them off, just as he nodded and stretched out his hand. Brushing fingers, and feeling his touch on her hair brought back a tumble of memories of their rather wild and utterly wonderful bout in bed. Had she been totally nutters? Not if the look in his eyes was anything to go by.

She shifted away, leaning against the wall, away from the corner. Jake climbed up beside her, adjusted the goggles to fit comfortably and set to work. He might not be dressed for it, but he definitely knew how to handle a hammer and chisel. She was in the perfect position to admire the strength of his shoulders and observe the skill of his hands as he carefully placed the chisel near a crack and brought the hammer down hard.

He was making way faster progress than she had with her careful tip tapping. Ten minutes later, her hand had stopped bleeding and Jake, a slight sheen of perspiration on his forehead, eased out the last chunk of concrete to reveal a dark cavity.

He reached in, felt around and pulled out a large canning jar full off dark powder. Her mouth went dry and her throat tight. "It really is there." It was almost a whisper. "Oh, Jake!"

"You weren't sure?" he asked as he reached in and one by one brought out six jars.

"I'd sort of forgotten. I was only nine at the time."

"But you remembered this morning?"

Annette squared her shoulders and took a deep breath. This would no doubt suggest she had a limp hold on reality but . . . She told him about her parents' ghosts and their request. By the time she finished, they were both cold and stiff, but he'd listened without interrupting and with every appearance of believing and accepting her outrageous story. "You don't think I imagined it?" she asked.

God bless him, he shook his head. "Not unless I imagined a voice telling me to come up here."

"What!"

"I went back to the room, hoping you'd be there to have lunch with me. While I was wondering where you'd gone, this disembodied voice told me to come up to the house. So I came. It was a woman's voice. Your mother, I guess."

Annette shivered. "This gets freakier and freakier."

"Maybe, but you have what you came for." He nodded to the six dusty jars. "What next? After you get that hand seen to, of course."

"It's not bad."

"Not now, but get it infected it will be. You need to see a doctor."

"Here in Christmastown? On Christmas Eve? We'd have to go to the hospital in Whytheville or Christiansburg and we're stuck in town."

"There are drug stores. At least we can get something to clean it with." He helped her down. "We'll leave this mess. I'll get someone to come in and repair the wall after the holidays."

He wrapped the jars in the towel she'd brought and packed them in her backpack, before shouldering it himself. "Let's take care of that hand, warm ourselves up, and then you tell me what we do next."

"Jake," she said, "I'm afraid I had to cut the back screen to get in."

He laughed. "Honey, I can have a screen fixed. How did you get in? Kept a key?"

"No. Wish I had. I handed them all over yesterday but I remembered there was one hidden."

He brushed that off as trivial. "We'll take care of all that later. Better get your hand fixed first."

He wanted to drive her, but she insisted they pick up her car. She wasn't leaving it by the Friendly Mart all night, but agreed to take it back to the Sleigh Bells Inn and let him drive from there.

They made it to Barlowe's Drugstore just as it was closing, and left with her hand treated with mercurochrome and the cut held together with butterfly closures. She also noticed the economy size box of condoms Jake added to the purchase. Why not? They looked to be stuck here a couple of days at least.

Chapter Eight

"Nice and festive," Jake remarked, looking at her hand. "Pity we couldn't get green Band-Aids, or better still ones with holly berries on them."

She was tempted to slug him one with her good hand. "I think I've had enough Christmas cheer to last me a long time."

He chuckled in agreement. "It does rather get to you, doesn't it? Still how about lunch? Still want to go to the Dairy Queen?"

"Yes, but . . ." Telling him this would really test his belief in her sanity. "I have to get rid of their ashes." Jake looked but said nothing, so she went on. "That's what was keeping them down here, having their ashes sealed up in the house."

"But they're not walled up any more."

"I don't think it's enough. They need to be released. My grandfather bound them down here. Once the ashes are free, I think my parents' spirits will be." Sounded way off the wall to her but Jake accepted it.

"Where do you want to take them?"

"To the falls. Dad used to talk about going fishing there as a boy and from there, they'll get carried down to the ocean. Mom grew up by the beach."

"Let me drive you up to the falls," Jake suggested. "Want to go straight there, or grab a bite first?"

"Food can wait, Jake." She hugged her backpack to her chest. "I want to get this done while it's still light."

"We will, Annette. I promise. If we have to walk the last stretch and I need to carry you, we'll get it done."

Her hand might be bandaged up, but her legs still worked. The idea of being carried by Jake did rather appeal but she had to do this herself.

They were out in open country now, beyond the town limits. No snow plow had gone this way yet and progress was slow. The road narrowed as they neared the falls. The snow was still bad up here; a smaller, less powerful car wouldn't have made it.

"I wonder if kids still come up here to watch the moon."

"You did that?" Jake glanced her way, an odd look in his eyes. Was he jealous?

"With my grandfather? You have to be kidding! Jake, I never had a date in all of high school. You were the only boy in Christmastown with the guts to approach me." And he'd done a whole lot more than approach.

"Call it the courage of the ignorant. If I'd known what would happen . . ."

"What?"

He shook his head. "Hell if I know. Can't say I regret a minute of what we did but knowing I'd risked getting us evicted scared the bejesus out of me."

"Grandfather had no business to do that but I suppose I should have anticipated that and said, 'No, thank you.'"

"I'm darn glad you didn't. That memory kept me going through many a rough time. I will say, finding you were married, when I had a position and career even your grandfather couldn't object to, was a major downer."

"I think he'd still have objected if you'd been Donald Trump or Howard Hughes but I'd have defied him."

Her last four words had Jake wanting to whoop and shout and sing to the heavens, but considering their mission, he held it in. "We have plenty of time, Annette. We've the rest of our lives together." She went very still and quiet. Had he jumped too fast? But damn, after this morning . . . "Do you want to see me again after this, Annette?"

"Yes!"

That was all right. Hell, it was way beyond 'all right'. He could build a future of hopes and dreams on 'yes'. He'd hold back 'Want to marry me?' until after they took care of this business. She was tense and strung out. Understandable. "Thanks for saying, 'yes.'"

She gave a little chuckle. "Not the first time I said yes to you, is it?"

"Annette, when I'm with you, I feel like one of the gods of creation. I'm just beginning to realize what I'm missing when you're not around."

She was quiet a few moments, hugging her backpack to her chest as he maneuvered the snowy road and thanked heaven for the decision to bring the Cayenne instead of the Boxster he preferred to drive.

"Were do you live?" she asked, at last.

Good question, if they were to see as much of each other as possible. "My company is based in Arlington and I have a house in Olde Towne Alexandria that I use most of the time, but I just bought a farm in Louisa County. That's not too far from Richmond."

She nodded. "You'll know where to come when you want to buy books."

"You bet! What are you calling it?"

"I did consider calling it Prospero's Books, but then decided that people might think it was all classics and literary stuff. Trouble was, all the really clever names like 'Murder One' or 'Bent Pages' were already taken, so I settled for 'Books and More'. Not frightfully original, but it pretty much covers it."

"A good name. Says up front what you sell, easy to

remember and you can use a nice, big font on your business cards and note paper. When are you opening?"

"If all goes well, early April, with a big push for Mother's Day gifts. I close on the shop the second week of January."

"You need anything, call me, okay? I have a good shopfitter and a print shop."

"I will, Jake, if I need anything." He'd bet his last dollar she never would. She wanted to do this herself. He understood. He'd felt the same way.

They reached the falls at last. Beyond the road was an expanse of snow-covered ground and a fringe of trees along the river bank.

Annette gave him a slow, steady look as he pulled the Cayenne to the side and killed the engine. "Thanks, Jake."

"You're welcome, love. Let's find a safe spot to take care of things. I bet the rocks are plain treacherous with all this snow."

It was way easier than they'd expected. In the years since they'd both left town, somebody, or some agency, had built a fishing pier that jutted out toward the falls. A stout railing all around was a nice safety extra.

Jake sized up the changes. All for the better. "Want me to go and leave you to do this?" She was safe enough here.

"Please stay." If her words hadn't caused a big whoop inside, her smile would have. She was for real and serious. He couldn't call it dead serious, given the task in hand. But she wanted him near. Wanted him close. Dare he think, he wondered as walked beside her across the expanse of snow covered ground, that she wanted his support and comfort? Long term?

She set the backpack down on the snow-covered boards, reached in and pulled out the first jar.

This was it! Annette just hoped she had it right and this would release them both. She grasped the rusted screw top and twisted. Wasn't easy with a bandaged hand but the lid gave, but only after she put her whole arm to the job. She sensed Jake was itching to help, the minute she asked. But this was something she had to do. Herself. Just having him nearby was enough.

A little fine gray powder wafted in the air as she jerked the top off. Tension snarled tight inside. What if she'd completely misunderstood what was needed? What if her parents had it all wrong? What if by strewing their ashes, she was tying them down here for eternity?

No! She was not getting blindsided by a bunch of what ifs. Mom clearly asked her to retrieve the ashes. She'd done that. And release them. Which is what she was about to do and she couldn't think of a better place, than up here, high above the town with the air clear and fresh (and darn cold) and looking down toward the frozen spray of the falls.

Holding the open jar in both hands, she reached out over the railing. The ashes soared in a gray misty arc and fell to the water in a powdery film before they disappeared over the edge.

She blinked back a tear and swallowed.

"Okay?" Jake asked.

She nodded. Vaguely disappointed. How silly. What had she expected? A sign? A signal? Bells ringing? An angel choir in the background? There was nothing but the beating of her heart and the roar of the waterfall. She reached for the next jar. That lid was impossible to budge; it had rusted tight over the years.

"Want some help?"

She handed him the jar and he worked at it. After some effort, the lid came loose and he gave the jar back. The contents hit the water in a thicker layer this time, some appeared to land on a twig. That was soon washed away in the fast moving water.

"I wish I knew which was Mom and which was Dad," she said, half to herself. Impossible, she knew, but . . .

"They're together, Annette. Isn't that what matters? And you're setting them free together."

"You don't think I'm crazy?" That was plain lunatic in itself.

"I heard them too, remember." He reached into the backpack and handed her a third jar. "Here. You're doing the right thing."

What it was to be accepted. To have someone understand. How had she managed without Jake all these years? Never mind that, she and him now. She smiled as she took off the lid and the contents of that jar went into the river. The fifth one opened easily. The last took their combined efforts to loosen the top.

Annette had the jar in both hands and was poised to toss the contents after the rest when a voice called.

"Freeze!"

Two sheriff's deputies stood on the shore, guns drawn. Annette jumped in shock and the jar slipped out of her hands and hit the water with a splash.

"Lady, I said 'Freeze'. Raise your hands, both of you, and step this way. Slowly."

Chapter Nine

Jake had his hands up. Annette followed suit. "What on earth . . . ?" she whispered.

"Some Neanderthal overeager deputy with nothing better to do on Christmas Eve," he replied and she actually felt herself smile.

"Stop talking, you two. Get over here. And no fast moves."

Once they were on the river bank, the second deputy walked past them to the pier and returned with her backpack and the empty jars. "Looks like they were getting rid of something, Lewis," he said and held out a jar for the first one to sniff at. Lewis really did look like a big mutt sniffing at a suspicious object in his territory.

"Okay, you two, against the car, hands on the roof."

Jake shrugged, smiled at her and stepped over to the car. She did the same. They didn't have much choice.

"You from up near D.C. then?" Lewis asked Jake after he patted him down and took his wallet.

"Yes, officer, I am."

"This your girlfriend?"

"My fiancée."

Her face must have shown her surprise.

"That true?" he asked her, stepping close.

"Yes," she replied, looking Jake in the eyes. "It is!" Whether that counted as a marriage proposal was an interestingly moot point but might as well play this out. "Just. I'm still not used to hearing 'fiancée'. He asked me because it was Christmas." Sounded good to her anyway.

The two deputies were obviously not of a romantic disposition.

"What were you throwing off the pier?" the second asked, more to Jake than her. "Something you didn't want to be caught with?"

So that was it! Pot growing was no doubt replacing the moonshining that supplemented many family incomes for earlier generations. She'd set the law straight on that and they'd let them go.

"My parents' ashes."

It did not have the result she'd hoped for.

"Yeah! Right!" Lewis said. "Let's cuff 'em and take them both in."

Jake wanted to spit, kick, and lay the pair of them flat but he let them pinion his hands behind his back and shove him into the back of the cruiser. Annette ended up in the other car. They were obviously such desperate and wily criminals they couldn't ride together. As he watched her bundled into the other Crown Vic, Jake vowed if that deputy said as much as an off word to Annette, or dared lay a finger on her, he'd sue with every penny he owned.

Feeling helpless did not sit well on Jake's shoulders. So much for a Christmas Eve seduction dinner. Damn, it would still happen. They couldn't keep them overnight on such a flimsy charge. Come to that what the hell was the charge?

The sheriff's department was now housed in a new building just down the street from the Sleigh Bells Inn. Getting dropped off there would have been really civilized; instead Jake found himself sitting on a hard plastic chair, across the room from Annette. They had taken the cuffs off but that was about it. It had been made patently clear that any attempt at communication between them would be viewed with disapproval.

Sheriff Tate cleared his throat as he leafed through the contents of Jake's wallet. "So, you live in D.C. or Virginia? You seem to have plenty of addresses."

That fact must have made him a desperate criminal. "I live in Alexandria, my home office is in D.C. and I own a farm in Louisa County." None of that impressed.

"Why are you here in Christmastown?"

Better not mention his years of residence if he didn't have to. They probably had a file on him. "I came to buy some property and, by the way, I think I'll claim the privilege of a phone call."

He got that, rather grudgingly after a bit of consultation between the two deputies and the sheriff. "Think you need a lawyer then, Mr. Warren?" the sheriff asked.

"Can't be to my disadvantage," Jake replied, taking his cell phone which the deputy handed over rather grudgingly.

Jake speed-dialed Jim Cullen. No doubt disturbing cookie baking or gift wrapping but hell, he'd charge and Jake would gladly pay.

"Jim. I need your help. Now. Like right now! I'm down at the sheriff's department about to be arrested for I'm not quite sure what and Annette is with me." He spoke loudly hoping she'd hear across the room.

"What the hell have you been doing, Jake? And who's Annette?"

"Annette James." While Jim went silent to digest that, Jake added. "You should congratulate us, we just got engaged but first you need to bail us out."

He gave Jim a few minutes to unravel that little bit. "What the heck were you two doing?" he asked. "Celebrating your engagement under the town Christmas tree?"

"Not precisely. Annette was sprinkling her parents' ashes."

"Okay, Jake! I don't doubt Cheryl will make me pay for this as we have a house full of friends and relations but I'll be over as soon as I can make my apologies here. If only to find out what really is going on. Don't say anything until I get there, and tell Annette the same. I assume you want me to represent her as well?"

"You bet."

That made him feel better. Jake snapped the phone closed and handed it back to the deputy.

"Jim's on his way," Jake called to Annette. "He'll sort things out."

"Must be real nice to have a lawyer on retainer to call whenever you need them," the deputy said.

Jake agreed. It most certainly was. Much nicer than facing the law as a poor teenager from the wrong end of town.

Annette let out a sigh. God bless Jake. Surely Jim would sort this out. If she wasn't so strung out, hungry, and weary, she'd laugh at the ludicrous situation. Trouble was, behind this silly muddle, was the worry that maybe she'd grabbed hold of the wrong end of the stick and completely misunderstood, and her parents' spirits were still trapped down here.

She looked across to where the sheriff and his two deputies stood, heads together, giving her and Jake the occasional dubious glance. This was definitely going to be a Christmas to remember.

"I suppose you want to wait until your boyfriend's lawyer gets here, too." It was the other deputy, Richards, by the name on his chest.

Annette looked him right in the eye. "He's my lawyer, too." The snort was downright rude, but she was quickly distracted from Richards' lack of polish when Lewis told Jake to stand up, snapped cuffs back on him, and took him down the corridor and out of sight. She tried very hard not to dwell on imagined horrors, police brutality and stories of roughing over suspects to encourage them to talk. They wouldn't dare. Not with Jim on the way.

Would they?

"You're looking done in, want a cup of coffee?" It was the sheriff.

Odd, the sudden show concern for her comfort and well-being but she was not about to refuse a much-needed infusion of caffeine. "Please."

He brought it over in a styrene cup with a plastic stirrer and handed her packets of creamer and sugar.

She drank it black.

He took the chair opposite and proceeded to sip his own coffee. "You don't want to be spending Christmas locked up, now do you?"

She agreed wholeheartedly. "You really think it's going to come to that?"

He shrugged. "Look here, you seem a nice enough girl. Why don't you tell us what your boyfriend's game is and make it easy on yourself."

The man was just doing his job after all, but she had to smile. "Jake is my fiancée, Sheriff." Just saying it aloud gave her happy goose bumps. If only it were true but . . . "I'll tell you this much," it was what she'd told the deputies, after all. She'd run with it. "Jake drove me up to the falls because I wanted to strew my parents' ashes there. My father loved that spot. He proposed to my mother up there. Seemed fitting to take them back."

He took a taste of coffee. "You seriously expect me to believe those jars contained nothing but human ashes?"

Other than a few stray particles of burned morgue, yes, but . . . "You think it's something else? Then have them tested."

"We will. That all takes time."

"It takes ten minutes in the lab."

That got his eyes wide open. "And you know this, how?"

"I read it, in a book for Dummies about Crime Detection."
Amazing, really, what one picked up reading behind the
counter on a slow day.

His look implied reading was a federal offense. He shook
his head, stood and walked away. Presumably leaving her to
consider turning state's evidence on Jake. She felt terrible
dragging him into this. What was happening to him now? The
deputy had returned so he wasn't working Jake over but . . .

Her stomach rumbled audibly. Breakfast had been hours
ago. Did they feed you here? On the other hand if food was
on the same standard as the coffee, a crash diet might be a
better idea.

Jim Cullen arrived exactly forty-seven minutes after Jake's
call. She'd been watching the clock on the wall. Given the
weather, the roads, and the day, that was stellar service.

"You all right, Annette?" he asked as he walked in, shaking the snow off his coat.

"Can't truthfully say I'm fine. I'm worried but I am glad to
see you."

"Jake?"

"He's locked up somewhere."

"I'll see what's happening."

He disappeared into an office with the sheriff and Annette
started counting the seconds, not the minutes. Surely a lawyer
could sort out all this nonsense?

Ten minutes later, Jim emerged. "I'd like to talk with my
clients, Sheriff," he said, giving Annette a nod that she hoped
meant 'I've fixed everything.'

Jake was brought back from the cells, minus his tie,
shoelaces and belt but otherwise just as she'd last seen him.
"You okay, Annette?" was the first thing out of his mouth.

"Let's talk," Jim said before she had a chance to reply. Fair
enough, he was the lawyer and presumably knew how these

things were done. As far as she was concerned she didn't want to learn any more about law enforcement practices in Thomas County.

A deputy led them to a sparsely furnished room with only a table and two chairs, and he locked them in while he went off to fetch a third.

"What the hell is happening?" demanded Jake before Annette had a chance to speak.

"Sit down both of you and I'll explain."

Jake pulled his chair over so they were touching knees, reached out and took her hand and draped his free arm over her shoulders. He hadn't exactly branded his name on her forehead but his message was pretty clear.

Annette smiled at him.

Jim seemed highly intrigued. "Off the record here, but are you two engaged?"

"Yes!" It was the closest thing to a simultaneous response. Yes, it was something she and Jake had to talk about but if they could sort this mess out, a mere engagement was a trivial detail. Or rather minor, not trivial.

"Never realized you knew each other."

"I knew Jake in high school." And that was as much as she was telling.

"What about selling and buying the house then? Why not just transfer the deed?"

Good point. "That was my idea," Jake said, before she could fabricate a plausible tale. "I knew she wanted the money and being independent and hard-headed the way she is, she refused a loan. So I bought the house. I could use the property and that way she got a fair price."

Jim shook his head. "There's something you two are not telling and I'm not sure I want to know. Anyway, this is the score as far as the Thomas County Sheriff Department is concerned. They suspect you of being drug dealers from big bad D.C. We're slap in the middle of a 'Wipe drugs out of Thomas

County campaign.' The mayor and sheriff are making good on election promises. Seems you two are prime suspects caught in the act of destroying a cache of illegal drugs." Annette spluttered at that but hushed herself and Jim went on. "I convinced them that it would be unwise to charge a wealthy investor and potential town benefactor without solid proof. They're going to release you both on condition you don't leave the county. Since you can't get out of town right now that's no big hurdle. Once the lab results come in, all charges should be dropped."

"How long is that going to take?" Jake asked.

"Ten minutes." She enjoyed his stunned expression before adding, "Once they get it to the lab, which could take days what with the weather and the holiday."

"You know that?"

She had to grin. "Jake, I know lots!"

"All right, you two love birds!" Jim obviously wanted to get back to home and hearth and she could hardly blame him. "Let's get this straight. You can go, as long as you promise not to leave town until you're both cleared. It was human ashes, wasn't it?" he added.

Annette nodded. "Yes. It really was. They'd been in the house all this while and I decided it was time they were spread to the four winds."

Jim earned his fee. Twenty minutes later, he was driving them back up to the falls to collect Jake's vehicle, waiting just long enough to be sure the car started, before heading off for home. Snow had started again. Light fluffs like goose feathers, spotted the windshield.

"Sorry about dragging you into this," Annette said as they turned toward the town.

"Annette, honey, I wouldn't have missed it for one minute. It'll be quite a tale to tell our grandchildren."

"Grandchildren? Aren't you jumping ahead a bit?" She

could handle making babies with Jake but grandchildren were a bit down the line.

"Not in the least." He took his eyes off the road a second to grin at her. "There's no one to stop us now, Annette."

"There's a drug busting sheriff and a couple of hyper deputies!"

His laugh was like richness poured over hope. "Let them try!" He reached over and squeezed her thigh. "They can't do a thing but apologize when the lab results come in. Will staying in town a few days cause problems for you?"

"I need to call a friend about my cats. Sheba and Bast will be okay for food until tomorrow but they'll need water. How about you?"

"I was planning on staying over the holiday anyway. Now I'll have company. How about room service dinner in our suite?"

"*Our* suite?"

"Yes, Mrs. Warren-to-be, *our* suite. After this nasty little interlude we both need physical companionship. I'm scared and need comforting."

That she almost spluttered at. "You, scared? Come on, Jake!"

"Hell yes. I was scared witless what they'd do to you, with me locked away."

"Actually, they gave me a cup of coffee."

"Sheer favoritism!"

"It was lousy coffee and I think it was a bribe to get me to spill the beans on your nefarious activities." She leaned over and kissed him. "I refused! Rather pissed off the sheriff, I think." She smiled. It was all over and she was going home with the prize. "I love you, Jake. Always have. My grandfather can't keep us apart any more."

Chapter Ten

"My sentiments exactly. Now, about that room service dinner, in *our* suite. I suggest a nice warm shower first, to wash off the jailhouse dust."

Sounded marvelous but . . . "Jake, before anything, I have to make sure my parents . . ." How did one phrase it? Have left? Are gone? Are up in heaven where they should be?

"You bet. I need to thank them for sending me after you."

They fell into a companionable and very contented silence. Until they reached the Sleigh Bells Inn. The sound of carol singing from the bar filled the night air as the attendant, still with antlers and red nose, took Jake's car. Hand in hand, they walked into the warmth of the wide lobby. The log fire in the grate gave a cheerful and seasonal welcome, and cookies and warm cider stood on a table by the tree.

Annette ignored the lot.

Driven by need to find out, and fear she'd misunderstood and failed her parents, she almost barreled through the connecting door and down the hallway to their suite. Outside, she hesitated, only a moment but long enough for Jake to whip out his key and ask, "Okay?"

"I will be."

Inside the room was cold. Real cold as if they'd turned off

the heat and left a window open. The windows looked out onto the dark of the early evening and soft scattering snowflakes but every window was closed.

Annette walked to the middle of the room, very much aware of Jake right behind her.

"Mom? Dad?" she whispered. Scared. Worried. Wanting them to be free. Dreading not hearing them.

The icy room temperature dropped another few of degrees as two shadowy shapes appeared between her and the window.

'Annette, love. Thank you,' her mother's voice said. *'God bless you!'*

'You did good, sweet punkin.' That was her father's voice. *'We knew we could count on you.'*

"I'll miss you," Annette said, her voice tight. "I always have and now . . ."

'We're going,' her mother's voice faded. *'Good-bye.'* The last came like a sigh as the white shapes shimmered.

'You take good care of her, young man,' her father said, flickering in Jake's direction. *'You'd better to see her right!'*

Jake caught the warning right away. "I will, sir. You have my word. I'll protect her and take care of her for the rest of my life."

Annette fancied she heard her father whisper, "good man," or maybe it was "good luck," as the pale shadows dissipated into the air.

She sat down, rather heavily, on the holly-strewn spread and sniffed. She was not going to be sad. She refused to be sad. She'd lost them years ago. Having them for a few hours was an extra gift and she'd done the very best a daughter could do: she'd released them from the snare fashioned (albeit unwittingly, she did concede) by her grandfather.

Jake wasn't sure what to say. So he held his peace. She'd done what she set out to do and now looked bereft. Hardly surprising. If he'd seen his mother's ghost or heard her voice, he'd have been knocked for a loop. He sat beside her and hesitated. When she turned and gave him a weak smile, he put his arm round her shoulders. He knew he'd done the right thing when she leaned into him.

"Oh, Jake!" she whispered.

"Your dad was right, honey. You done good."

She chuckled, reaching out to take his hand. "Right, I'm sure you say that in your high-powered business meetings."

"Of course not! Only to women I plan to marry."

"Yes, well. Maybe we need to talk about this 'fiancée' business."

"Why? You've an objection?"

She shook her head. "Oh, no." That much was good, then. "But I just don't quite see how we'll manage it. With us on opposite sides of the state."

"It's not opposite. Less than two hours' drive unless you pick rush hour. I think you're just trying to make difficulties." He kissed her cheek. "It won't work. Give up. Decide to marry me and then we can order dinner. If you insist, we can talk about it after dinner."

"I can think of better things to do after dinner, even right now, come to that."

So could he.

Annette stood, smiled and pulled off her gloves and sock hat. She threw her coat on the chair, kicked off her boots and reached for the hem of her sweater.

He got the idea. "Need any help?"

"What do you think?"

Once he put his hands on her sweater, he all but tore it off her. Her bra sailed across the room and he had her flat on her back on the bed as he tugged off her jeans and panties in one go and grabbed her socks on the way down. But she wasn't passive by any means; while he stripped her, she went at him. By the time he had her naked, he was the one flat on the bed and she was unbuckling his belt and yanking down his pants.

He couldn't have been happier.

She was better than all his memories and dreams put together. She was love. She was Annette. His.

He'd planned a sweet, slow seduction but she was having none of that. She pulled him close, holding his face in her hands as she kissed. Her mouth owned his, marked him, as their tongues met. He tried to take over, but it was a sweet sensual battle of lips and tongues where neither emerged supreme and they both were winners.

As she broke the kiss to catch her breath, he took over—or at least did his best to. It was a fantastic coupling, fueled by heat and need and desire, by his drive to mark her as his own, and hers to claim him as her partner.

Annette couldn't explain or describe the wild heat that took hold of her, but seize her it had and all that raging heat needed was Jake. It was as if all those years of separation had fueled a woman's need in her lost teenage hopes. Jake was hers. He was naked and in her bed.

She closed her lips over his nipple, feeling the point harden under her tongue. She smiled to herself as her hands strayed over his chest, the tips of her fingers brushing the soft curls that trailed down his chest, over his navel. And lower. She gloried in his beautiful, male body and it was hers for the loving and having and keeping.

And, boy, was she going to make the best of it.

"Should I be worried about that look in your eyes?" Jake asked, looking up with an almost wicked glint in his own.

"Terribly," she replied, not even trying to hold back her grin. "You should be shaking in your shoes. If you had any on, of course."

"And what about you?" he asked. "Getting a bit above yourself aren't you?"

"Not really, since I'm on top of you!" Dear heaven, she was

lovely! Wonderful and . . . She ran her fingers down his belly and through the curls at his groin until her hand closed over his decidedly rampant cock. "I've got you!"

"Indeed, you have," he replied, leaning back. His obvious efforts to look casual and unconcerned were an utter failure. "What do you plan to do about it?"

"Go for a walk!" she replied, hopping off the bed and crossing the room to where they'd tossed his pants. She hoped he had a spare condom handy. She pulled out his wallet and found five. "That was bit overly optimistic, wasn't it?" she asked as she walked back to sit on the edge of the bed.

"Not in the least," he replied. "I'm a good boy scout. I come prepared."

"Five!"

"Why not?" he propped himself up on one elbow and leaned toward her. "I bought a box of three dozen at the drugstore. We're snowed in and forbidden to leave town. What else is there to do? Count the holly berries and the red-nosed reindeers?" As he spoke he tweaked her nipple. "Steal the antlers off the parking attendant?"

"So," she replied, as his hand smoothed up and down her thigh, "you think we should make love like a pair of demented rabbits?"

"Not exactly," he replied, "although that's not a bad idea. How about like a pair of reunited lovers?"

It was a good thought. No, it was the very best. "All right, lover."

Deliberately and very slowly, she ripped open the foil and tipped the rolled up condom into her hand. She grinned at Jake, took his hand off her leg and pushed his chest. He was solid, rock-hard muscle. She hadn't a hope of budging him but most obligingly he laid himself back down on the pillow. Heaven help her! Jake was gorgeous when he grinned like that and, okay, eyes couldn't really smolder but his came damn close.

"Care to share what you have in mind?" he said.

She had planned on seducing him slowly, easing the condom down by slow teasing degrees, licking a line up his stomach and down again, sucking his balls and teasing his cock with her mouth but, darn it!

Next time! She straddled his thighs and rolled the condom down over his erection. She might well be setting a bed speed record and all the better.

He was hard and ready.

She was wet and aching with need.

She shifted forward, kneeling up over him. Leaning forward enough to kiss him, she lowered herself so he was deep inside her.

He kept on kissing, clasping her head with his hands, holding her to him as she rocked back and forth.

It wasn't enough for either of them.

Wrapping his arms around her back, he flipped her over. Now, she was under him, caught in the tight embrace. He eased himself between her legs in one fast move and started pumping, driving his cock into her so she cried out with the intensity of the sensation. Her head sagged back on the pillow as little mewls of pleasure accompanied his loving invasion.

It was wild, crazy, and verging on the insane, but need overrode reason and they needed each other.

As Jake pistoned in and out with an almost desperate ferocity, her climax gathered in a wild rush. She was crying aloud now, calling his name, shouting as she came in a wild frenzy of joy and sheer all-devouring pleasure. Annette lay back, gasping, as the aftershocks of pleasure flooded her mind and body.

As his rhythm continued, she realized, through her own fog of sensation, he hadn't climaxed. She shifted her hips toward his, pressing upward to take him even deeper, tightening and releasing her inner muscles and circling her hips. In moments, he cried, "Oh! My God! Annette!" and came.

She pulled him down on her, wanting to feel the strength of his body against hers.

"I'm squashing you," he said, his voice rough.

"I love you," she replied. "I want to keep you close."

He lay there a little while, then slipped out, nipped into the bathroom and was back carrying two bottles of water. "Don't know for sure, but I think you probably screamed yourself hoarse."

She took the bottle. "Screamed?"

He nodded. "Honey, I bet those overgrown elves and red-nosed-reindeers were listening."

Dear goodness, no! She caught the twinkle in his eyes. "Jake! You deserve a punch for that! They were not!"

"Who cares? Let them listen. You are mine!"

That was a thought to snuggle down on. She nestled in the circle of his arm, rested her head on his broad chest and listened to his heart beat.

"Sleepy?" he asked.

"Not really. Just blissfully content."

That earned her a kiss on her forehead. "Tell you what," Jake said, his lips close so his breath brushed her skin. "How about we take a nice shower, then mosey on down to the restaurant and have dinner and then we come back and practice making love, so by the time we get married, we'll be perfect."

"You're not far off perfect as it is, Jake, but dinner sounds great." Even if it did come with an overdose of Christmas cheer.

Her heart was full enough with joy for twenty Christmases.

Blue Suede Christmas

Karen Kelley

Chapter One

Please God, I need your help. Tony thinks it would screw up everything if we took our relationship beyond friendship and business partners.

Sydney Newman was thoughtful. Could you even think *screw* when you were praying? She took a deep breath, exhaled and tried again.

Please God, I need your help. Tony thinks it would mess up our relationship if we had sex.

Could she think about sex while praying? She covertly glanced across the seat. Tony's attention was on the road in front of him and the snow that had gotten heavier by the hour.

Damn, he looked good enough to eat with his thick sandy brown hair and lazy brown eyes that could heat a woman's blood in record time. Except he'd never really given her *that* look. But then, he didn't have to give her *that* look, she was already horny and it had finally brought out the devil in her.

She was tired of playing it safe. If he wasn't going to take their relationship to the next level, then she would end it altogether. Why should she suffer alone? She'd take him with her on her pity party trip. Now that she thought about it, he should be the one who suffered the most anyway. It was only fair.

But ending their partnership wasn't really what she wanted

so she faced forward again, closing her eyes. She needed to really concentrate—get serious and try to be a little more pious. She took a deep breath and began again.

I need your help, Lord. Could you please send me a fairy godmother or something? Anyone who will help make Tony see the truth. We could be so good together.

"Roadblock."

The voice of God! *Yes, I've run up against every roadblock imaginable but if you could just help me out, I'm sure . . .*

"We'll have to make a detour. Might not be such a bad thing. The road is getting too treacherous and the snow is coming down so hard I can't see more than a few feet in front of the car."

She opened her eyes and frowned. Not God's voice, only Tony's, and she was staring at a big orange sign with an arrow pointing toward the right.

Great. Another roadblock in a life littered with them. She hadn't *really* thought she was only supposed to pray when she wanted something but it was worth a try. She'd hoped God would look into her heart, though. A little help *would've* been nice.

"Thanks for nothing," she muttered.

The car skidded. She drew in a sharp breath and grabbed hold of the door. Tony brought the vehicle back under control and she breathed a sigh of relief, but she couldn't help glancing upward.

Nah. She shook her head as she peered out the windshield. "There's a sign." She squinted. "Christmastown." She couldn't make out how many miles they still had to go to get there.

"Christmastown?" Tony looked at her, then returned his attention to the road.

"I think that's what it said. Odd name for a town."

"Hopefully they'll have a vacancy somewhere because it doesn't look like we'll be going any farther this afternoon."

Disappointment filled her. She was ready to get home, feel her mom and dad's arms wrapped around her . . .

"You're going to have to tell our parents we're ending our business relationship, you know."

She could feel the color drain from her face. Her parents and Tony's mother lived next door to each other and had since Tony was in third grade and she was in kindergarten. Tony's mother was divorced, but she'd remarried a couple of years later. They'd all become the best of friends.

She pictured the expressions on their moms' faces. Her mom would be devastated. Tony's would be so disappointed. She cringed. "You tell them," she blurted.

"I'm not going to tell them. You tell them. This was your idea, not mine. I was perfectly content to continue writing songs together." His knuckles turned white as he gripped the steering wheel.

She sat straighter in the seat. "I wasn't. You know darn well you're attracted to me. Why not at least see if we'd be compatible?"

He shook his head. "It wouldn't work and then where would we be? Look at my parents. They made each other miserable and they'd known each other all through high school. Look at Tammy Wynette and George Jones. . . ."

"They're not us."

"Don't fix it if it isn't broke."

Stubborn, stubborn, stubborn! She glared at him, even though he kept his gaze on the road. "Your father has drilled that in you. In case you haven't noticed, it's broke." She'd never cared that much for his biological father but she'd kept her opinions to herself.

He glanced her way. "No, it isn't broke. And you're biting your nails again. That just goes to show you this isn't what you want."

She looked at her jagged fingernails. If she went through with her plans, she probably wouldn't have any nails by the end of the month. It couldn't be helped. She'd made up her mind and there was no turning back.

"It's a bad habit," she informed him. "It doesn't mean I want our relationship to stay the same."

He automatically reached over and pushed a button on the CD player, skipping past the next song, knowing she hated it. Did he even realize how much he knew about her? You'd think they were already married. Except neither one of them was getting laid.

At least she hoped he wasn't. He might as well suffer right alongside her. She knew he dated, as did she, but she wasn't even going to think about Tony having sex.

And that's exactly why she had to end their relationship. She was dying a slow, painful death.

"Damn it, Sydney, we've worked hard to get to this point in our career and you want to throw it all away. Having sex would ruin everything."

She raised an eyebrow. "I've been told I'm not that bad in bed."

He grimaced. "That's not what I meant. I'd rather not talk about sex any more."

"Why? Do you think I'm still a virgin?" She watched his changing expressions but couldn't figure out what he was thinking. "I filled out a quiz once, you know."

"A quiz?"

"Yeah. In *Cosmo*. It was when I was in college. 'How to find your best sex partner.' It turned out to be a guy in my biology class—I think." She frowned.

"What do you mean—you think? What'd you do? Go to bed with the first man who correctly answered multiple-choice questions? Eight correct answers and he gets to jump your bones?"

"I meant, I think I had the right guy."

He raised his eyebrows so she continued.

"I was depressed."

"What's that have to do with anything?"

Men. They just didn't understand PMS. In that department, Tony was just like all the rest. "I was eating chocolate." He still looked confused. "It was hot outside." Still no light coming on upstairs. "The chocolate was melting and I dropped some on the page."

"And that's how you lost your virginity?" His frown deepened into furrows across his forehead.

She shook her head. "No, that was in college, during my analytical period. I thought I could find the right man by process of elimination. I actually lost my virginity my junior year in high school. Bobby Adams." She sighed. Now he'd been a wild child.

"Bobby Adams! Were you insane or what?"

She straightened in her seat. "Just because he didn't play football doesn't mean he was a bad person."

"He had a motorcycle. The guy was strange."

Her smile was secretive. She'd loved his motorcycle and his black leather jacket and the way he'd wrapped his arms around her and pulled her tight against him. But then she'd wised up and realized he wasn't the brightest bulb in the string.

"Just how many guys have you been with?"

"I'll show you my list if you'll show me yours."

Silence.

She knew he'd been with girls—women—but it was an unwritten law they didn't speak about that part of their lives as they searched for their soul mates.

Somewhere during her search, she realized it was Tony who made her heart beat faster, made her body go from cold to hot with just a casual touch. She'd fallen in love with him.

Tony hadn't seen the wisdom of her enlightenment. At least, not yet. There was a good chance he might never see it. If that was the case, they were going to end up very lonely people. She turned her gaze out the window and stared at the mountains of snow.

Cold and lonely.

Tony cast a quick glance in Sydney's direction. She looked forlorn as she stared out the window. Damn it, he couldn't take away her pain this time. It just wasn't possible.

He gripped the steering wheel a little tighter. Not only because of the icy conditions but because he wanted to throttle her.

She'd dropped her bomb a couple of weeks ago when she told him she was ending their songwriting partnership. Since then he hadn't written a thing. All the words that had been there just dried up. What the hell was she thinking?

That was the problem, she wasn't thinking. It wasn't the first time. She'd have to put *harebrained ideas* on her résumé. In love with him? Sydney was only going through another one of her phases. He cared for her, sure, but loving her would be a disaster.

For just a moment he envisioned Sydney coming toward him in a flimsy negligée. Her waist-length auburn hair curling around a breast . . .

His pulse skipped a beat. His palms began to sweat.

No, it wouldn't work. Look what marrying your best friend had done to his parents. They couldn't stand the sight of each other. Get them in the same room and it was an all-out war.

He drew in a deep breath. If he were smart, he'd say good riddance and be done with Syd. She'd been a pest since he'd moved in next door to her. He'd never met a bossier female. She was the one who had to win, to be first.

But there was more to her than that. He liked that she didn't take bull from anyone. She was feisty. And she really hated bullies.

He began to relax, smiling as he remembered back. When she was in third grade, Sydney punched the schoolyard bully right in the nose because he was picking on a new kid. That was his Syd, always jumping in with both feet.

He grimaced. Just like she was doing now. Sometimes it paid to reason things through. To think before she leaped. If the schoolyard bully hadn't been so shocked, he would've decked her. Then where would she have been?

That's why they made a good team. He was the reasonable one and she was . . . well, she was just Syd. His friend. *Not* his lover. He just had to convince her it wouldn't work. Yeah, she was sexy and funny and sometimes she did make his pulse speed up but it was only because she was his friend—nothing more.

"There's a gas station," he said, glad he had something else to think about.

He pulled under an awning strung with red and green Christmas lights. A red model car with a waving Santa sat on top of each gas pump. More lights draped from gas pump to gas pump.

Before he could get out of the car, a man came hurrying out the door wearing a red and green hat, red and green coat, green pants, and boots that curled up at the toes and had a bell on each end.

"Is that an elf?" she whispered even though the elf couldn't hear her.

"Too tall." He pushed the button that brought the window down.

"Merry Christmas," the elf said with a beaming smile.

"Merry Christmas," they replied at the same time.

"We were detoured," Tony told the big green elf. "Is there someplace where we could stay the night?"

"The Night Before Christmas Motel is all full. Same goes for Away In The Manger Bed and Breakfast. You might try the Sleigh Bells Inn, though."

"Does the whole town do this?" He looked pointedly at the man's clothes.

His forehead wrinkled. "Do what?"

"Never mind." Tony got the directions, filled the tank and

hurried inside to pay. Once inside, he handed the elf his credit card.

"You're lucky. They've had motorists stuck all day. Even had the helicopter out earlier. More snow expected tonight, too, so you were smart to stop." The elf removed his coat and Tony saw he had a name—Joshua. How appropriate.

"I guess we had someone watching out for us."

Joshua frowned. "Funny thing about Christmastime."

"What's that?" he asked as he returned his credit card to his wallet.

Joshua scratched his head, then straightened his elf hat. "Well, 'bout this time every year strange events start happening. Especially at the Sleigh Bells Inn. You and your lady best be watching out for . . . unusual things."

Tony kept his smile in check. The tourist trap. Of course people would want to know more. Maybe spend money. Stay a few days longer.

"You mean it's haunted?"

"I best not be saying anything more seeing as how you'll be staying there." He looked around as if a ghost might jump out and grab him.

"Thanks for the weather info." Tony pushed the door open and stepped out. Ghosts. Sydney had tried to convince him that her dead Aunt Ina had visited her once. Just another one of Syd's harebrained ideas. He didn't believe in ghosts and never would.

Chapter Two

"We're not in Kansas anymore," Sydney murmured as they drove slowly through the town. Christmas lights were strung on just about everything that wasn't moving. She wondered if they could see Christmastown from outer space. A beacon of light in a sea of white.

Speaking of which. "It's almost stopped snowing."

"When I went inside to pay, the elf said there was more expected. We'll be better off staying the night."

That was fine with her. As much as she'd like to get home, she was tired. They'd been fighting the icy conditions for the last couple of hours. Besides, there was something about the town. It seemed magical and . . . abnormal all at the same time. She wanted to look around a bit.

There were still quite a few people on the sidewalks carrying packages, apparently doing last-minute Christmas shopping. Some were obvious tourists snapping pictures. But some wore coats with hems that brushed the snow and big hats from a period long ago when things weren't quite so complicated. Combined with the millions of Christmas lights, it reminded her of a Norman Rockwell painting . . . on drugs.

"Oh, look." She pointed to a five-foot, hip-shaking Santa in a drugstore window.

Tony raised an eyebrow. "His batteries are a little too juiced up."

He was right. Santa looked bawdy the way he was thrusting his hips. "They certainly have the Christmas spirit," she said.

He turned a corner. "Yeah, I'd say they've hit the spirits a little too often."

She laughed. Some of the tension of the last few weeks left when he joined in. This was her best friend, the man she'd slowly fallen in love with.

"I like when you laugh," he told her. "You haven't laughed in a while."

She glowed on the inside. Maybe he was loosening up.

"It's nice having my *best bud* back."

She smacked him on the arm.

"What?"

"In case you haven't noticed, I'm not your *best bud*. I'm a woman."

"A temperamental one, if you ask me."

"Well, I didn't." She returned her gaze to the street. "That must be it." She pointed toward a large mansion. She was so ready for a soak in a tub filled with soothing bubbles.

A sign out front proclaimed it as the Sleigh Bells Inn. He pulled under the awning. A parking attendant wearing a red nose and antlers hurried out, slipped on a slick spot and danced around until he got his footing, then hurried to their car.

"Welcome and Merry Christmas," Rudolph beamed as brightly as his red nose. His smile turned into a frown. "And watch your step. With the wind we had earlier there are some slick spots even under here."

"Is there a vacancy?"

"Computer has everything scrambled. Afraid Mizz Charlaine had it in a bit of a mess earlier. I'm sure they'll be able to find you something, though."

Rudolph got their bags out when Tony raised the trunk.

"Maybe we'd better hold on to each other," he said as she got out of the car.

She eyed him with suspicion. "You just want to make sure if you go down someone goes with you."

He grinned. "You're right."

She'd known he couldn't stay upset with her for long, but having Tony pull her close and hold on to her was pure torture, even worse when she looked into his laughing eyes. Why couldn't he fall in love with her?

As soon as they stepped inside the hotel and were on safe ground, Tony let go. Coldness seeped through her worse than the bite of the north wind.

She tugged her coat closer and looked around. The interior was as decorated as the rest of the town but she rather liked it. She bet they could write a song . . . no, there was no more *they*.

She slipped her cell phone out of her pocket and made a quick call to her parents, telling them about their delay, then handed the phone to Tony.

"You're smirking."

"Your battery is probably dead. You always forget to charge your phone."

Tony took the cell phone and punched four on speed dial. Smart aleck. After talking to his mom, he gave Sydney back her phone. "Mom sounded relieved we wouldn't be driving any farther tonight."

"So did mine."

Rudolph brought the luggage in and they walked toward the front desk. As they approached, a woman behind the desk looked up.

"Merry Christmas! I'm Melanie, can I help you?" She had a twinkling wreath on her head. Sydney wondered if it had fallen off a wall and just landed there or if it was actually intentional.

"Do you have a couple of rooms?" Tony asked.

The woman bit her lip. "Darn computer has been giving us fits. One minute we do and the next we don't. I've been trying all day to get it working properly and I think I've just about got it fixed."

While she searched for rooms, Sydney inhaled the strong aroma from the seven-foot cedar tree that stood in one corner. The limbs on the tree twinkled with colorful lights and cascading silver tinsel. A bright silver star sat on top. Pumpkin spice scented candles filled the room with a warm glow and a fireplace popped and crackled, enveloping the room with welcome heat. It reminded her of home and she didn't feel quite so cold any more.

"The tree is spectacular," she breathed.

"A fire hazard if you ask me," a man grumbled as he came around a corner and kept going.

The woman behind the desk lost some of the color in her face. "My husband." She worried her bottom lip, then looked at them. "It's not really, you know—a fire hazard, that is. We're very careful about things like that since . . ." her words trailed off as if she'd said too much but now Sydney was curious to know the whole story.

"Since . . . ?" she prodded.

"Well, it happened so long ago. They had a bad fire in the back of the buildings—before we took over and turned the place into the Inn."

"Buildings?"

"This used to be a mansion, then it housed the town hall, the library and the police department and we also bought the building behind—that was the old . . ." She coughed. "The morgue," she mumbled.

Sydney's eyebrows shot up. "The morgue?"

"Um . . . yes, but it's been completely renovated since the fire."

"How did the fire start?" Sydney found it unusual that a fire would start in a morgue.

"Accidentally, I suppose. No one knows, but there were bodies waiting to be buried," Melanie whispered as if she were afraid a pissed-off ghost would jump out and grab her.

"No dead bodies lying around any more?" Tony asked.

"Oh, no, only . . ."

Sydney noticed Melanie's words had a way of trailing off.

"Only what?" Tony laughed. "Ghosts?"

Melanie didn't answer for a moment. Apparently, the Sleigh Bells Inn had added their own tourist attraction.

"There were bodies in the morgue when the fire started. Some of them had been cremated." She quickly glanced around as if a spirit might appear any second.

"Double whammy." A shiver ran down Sydney's spine.

"Don't worry, we don't believe in ghosts," Tony assured the woman. Sydney wanted to tell him to speak for himself. Not that he'd believed her when she told him about her visit from Aunt Ina right after the elderly woman passed on to the next realm. He'd had the gall to laugh. She hoped he did see a ghost. It would serve him right.

A bellman wearing a snowman costume took their keys and luggage. He led them past a wide door at the end of the hall.

"Exactly where was the morgue located?" she asked the snowman.

"You'll be staying in it," Snowman beamed. "You're lucky, most people pay more for those rooms because they say they're haunted."

"Are they?" She really didn't like the idea of staying in a haunted hotel. Of course, the alternative was sleeping in the cold car and she liked that idea even less.

"I haven't really seen a ghost." He frowned. "I'm sure they're there . . . if you want them to be."

The loyal employee.

"Why is the whole town so . . . decorated?" Tony asked.

She had to admit, she was up for a change in conversation.

Talking about morgues, fires, dead bodies, and ghosts creeped her out.

"The whole town almost went under so they put together a committee to revitalize the community. Nobody wanted Christmastown to die." He grimaced. "That would be like having no Santa."

She didn't want to be the bearer of bad news so she refrained from mentioning that there really wasn't a Santa.

"Anyway," Snowman continued, "the town decided to capitalize on the name and we started going all out on the Christmas theme. Every day is Christmas."

Sounded like too much of a good thing if you asked her.

"Here we are." He unlocked the door and set her luggage inside before Snowman and Tony continued to the next room.

She closed her door and walked to the middle of the room. "You've got to be kidding."

There were birds everywhere—in threes. Three on a desk in the corner, three tiny ones looped on each of the four corners of the bed like tassels. Three more in the center swag of the curtains and three propped in a corner.

"Don't tell me. Three French Hens." She shook her head and retrieved a feather off the floor. One of the birds was molting.

Still bent over, she paused. Was there music piped in? A nice thought . . . but "Blue Suede Shoes?" Elvis was one of the greats, in her opinion, but she would've thought a Christmas song more in accord with the theme.

She straightened, her feet freezing to the spot when her gaze swung to the far corner. A heavy mist seemed to form from out of thin air.

This wasn't really happening. She chuckled but it came out sounding more like a hacking cough. All that talk about ghosts had spooked her.

"When warm air meets cold, it causes a sort of vapor

and . . . and there's probably a draft somewhere, after all the Inn is old and . . ."

She closed her eyes and took a deep breath. This wasn't real. She was only tired from the long drive. Calm washed over her. She opened her eyes.

Slowly, the vapor began to take shape. White pants, white shirt, white cape.

No, no, no!

". . . and the vapor could form white clouds . . . maybe," she quickly told herself, words trembling.

But she'd never seen a cloud, vapor, or fog with coal-black hair and wearing a pair of sunglasses. No matter how long she'd lain on her back and looked up at the sky, the most she'd ever been able to see were puffy white marshmallows.

Her heart pounded inside her chest. Oh God, she was going to faint.

"You're . . . you're . . . Elvis," she finally managed to get out between dry lips. So, it was true. Elvis was dead.

Chapter Three

Sydney clung to the bedpost for support and like a broken record repeated, "You're Elvis."

"Thank you, thank you very much." One side of his mouth curled. He swung his hip to the right, his white jewel-encrusted cape swirling around him.

The curtained French doors swung open.

Sydney screamed.

"You okay?" Tony rushed to her side and pulled her into his arms. "You're shaking like a leaf."

Maybe she should scream more often. She buried her head against his chest, breathing in the scent of the woods and spice, hearing the beat of his heart . . . and feeling so very safe. Before she had a chance to get comfortable, he took a step back.

"What happened?" His worried frown told her how much he did care as his gaze immediately scanned the room in case there might be an intruder hiding behind something. Except the only intruder was a ghost and he'd disappeared as soon as Tony stepped into the room.

"Elvis." That was the only word that would come out of her mouth. She pointed toward the vacant corner. Oh,

Lord, she hoped her hair hadn't turned gray. She was too young for gray hair.

Tony squinted, then walked over and picked up a trio of glued-together hens. "No, they're just birds with Santa hats and white beards." He held them up to show her. A feather floated to the floor. "And they're molting. Apparently, you're in the Three French Hens room. I have four turtledoves everywhere, except mine aren't losing feathers."

She took a deep breath. Her pulse had finally slowed to a more normal rhythm. "That's not what I was talking about. Elvis's ghost was in the corner." She pointed her finger at him. "Right where you're now standing."

"Elvis. The ghost of Elvis was here. Right here." He pointed toward the floor.

She could feel herself trembling on the inside. "Yes, Elvis. He was dressed all in white and he had black hair and long sideburns and he wore sunglasses and . . ."

"The older Elvis."

"Yes!" She bobbed her head up and down.

"You missed taking your medication, didn't you?"

She crossed her arms and tapped one foot on the hardwood floor. "They're allergy pills."

"Oh, I just knew you were taking something. I wasn't sure what they were."

"You thought I was on Prozac or something?"

He shrugged. "I didn't know."

Why wouldn't he think she was crazy? She had to work with him every day. He would make a sane person loopy. Especially if the sane person was in love with him.

Darn it, she'd seen what she'd seen, and heard what she'd heard. Elvis had been in a corner of her room. Hadn't he?

"Snow blindness," he offered.

She tilted her head and glared at him. "In case you haven't noticed, it's not snowing in my room."

"You know what I mean—from the long drive. You were looking out the window pissed-off most of the time."

"I was not pissed-off." He was the one who'd acted as if his lips were glued shut for the first couple of hours. "Do the French doors have a lock?"

"Yeah, but they weren't locked."

She strode to the open doors and waved her arm for him to exit. His frown deepened as he marched past her.

"You were the one who screamed. I came to your rescue. Isn't that what you want—a knight on a white horse? Someone to sweep you into his arms then dump you into his bed?"

"I saw Elvis, and I don't need rescuing. Besides, I screamed when you opened the door and startled me." Which reminded her. "What did you want?"

"I was going to ask if you wanted to get a drink at the bar but that might not be a very good idea." He eyed her suspiciously.

She shut the doors behind him, clicked the lock in place, and jerked the curtains shut. "I'm not tipsy, either."

"Could've fooled me," was his muffled reply.

When she turned around, Elvis was sitting on her bed. She drew in a sharp breath and reached for the doorknob, willing to let Tony do all the rescuing he wanted but stopped at the last second. She had a feeling the ghost would disappear again and she didn't want to hear any more sarcasm from Tony.

She chewed her nails instead.

It might be a trick. A dying town? Show a few sightings of Elvis and fans would flock to the Sleigh Bells Inn.

She was being duped—big-time! Did they think she was that gullible? They'd better think again.

She planted her hands on her hips. "You're not real." She stared at the . . . the vision in front of her. "You don't look that much like Elvis, either."

"I'm not Elvis."

"Ah ha! Then whoever you are you can turn off whatever projector you have on and vacate my room. I knew you weren't a ghost." Damn, and she'd made a fool of herself—again.

"I didn't say I wasn't dead. I said I wasn't Elvis. I'm an Elvis impersonator."

She leaned against the doors. "A dead Elvis impersonator. Now I've heard everything."

"It's true."

She looked at the image a little closer. An Elvis impersonator would explain the bad wig. But a ghost? Uh-uh, she didn't think so.

There was one way to find out. She eased closer until she could wave her arm through him, except when she did, it felt like running an ice cube over her skin. Ah, jeez! She jumped back, rubbing her arm.

"Hey, that tickled. Not to mention the fact we hardly know each other."

Oh, Lord, she was going to be sick.

The night after Great-Aunt Ina had been buried, she'd stood at the end of Sydney's bed and smiled. It had been colder in her room then, too. She'd shivered beneath her blanket and snuggled her Teddy closer. But she hadn't been scared. Aunt Ina had been nice and baked good cookies.

Her mother told her seeing Aunt Ina was a gift and that sometimes spirits made a room colder. Okay, she could believe ghosts existed and all that. But an Elvis impersonator?

"You don't look at all like him," she told the spirit.

"Watch this."

One second he was on the bed and the next he was off and standing beside it. For a rotund man, he moved fast.

Duh—ghost.

He stood still for a moment then thrust one arm and leg out in front of him. "Hyaahh!" He quickly brought them back in again, nearly losing his balance and toppling onto the bed.

She laughed. How could she be afraid? "You're not very good, are you?"

He jutted his chin out. "I played Vegas."

"And now you're dead," she said.

He flinched as if she'd just told him he had bad breath. Pity washed over her.

"What happened?" she asked softly.

"Car accident about twenty years ago. I was on my way to New York and the big time. Had a gig up there." He grimaced. "Now I'm stuck in Christmastown."

"Can't you walk toward the light or something?"

"Not until my ashes are buried. I'm kind of stuck here."

"I thought you were in a car wreck?"

"I was but then the morgue burned down." He sighed. At least it sounded like a sigh. "My life wasn't much better than my death. It seems I'm destined to play the wrong gig all the way around."

His life was a lot like hers. She knew exactly how he felt. She and Tony were meant to be together but she couldn't convince him of that fact. The poor dead Elvis impersonator was in the same boat as she was. But that still didn't mean she wanted a ghost hanging out in her room.

"Tell you what, Tony is staying in the next room over and I bet if you asked really nice, he'd help you find your ash." She cleared her throat. "Ashes, I mean."

"Sorry, it's just you and me. It's not good to let a lot of people see you when you're dead."

Great. Why did she always get trapped with the wrong men?

"You like him a lot, don't you?"

"Who?"

"That Tony fellow."

Did everyone know she liked him? She'd just as soon keep her problems to herself. She certainly didn't want anyone's pity. Ugh, that would be too much.

"Pfft, like Tony? We're practically brother and . . . and . . ." She choked on sister. Couldn't get it to come out. It was stuck right there on the roof of her mouth and wouldn't budge. "It doesn't matter."

"I think it does. I can help you get him."

"You? A dead Elvis impersonator?" But she couldn't stop the little spark of hope that flared inside her. She hadn't had a bit of luck, but if . . .

"Okay, if you don't want my help. If you'd rather live in Heartbreak Hotel than have a hunka hunka burnin' love . . ." He began to fade.

"Wait!"

He faded back in.

He had the Elvis curled lip down pat. A sarcastic ghost. Just what she needed.

She eyed him with more than a touch of apprehension. "What exactly can you do? I mean, what would *you* know about catching a man?" She couldn't believe she was even discussing this.

Silence.

He straightened his cape and lightly fanned his fingers over the jewels on the front.

It only took her a few seconds to figure it out. Great. A *gay* dead Elvis impersonator.

She'd asked for a fairy godmother and she'd gotten a fairy Elvis impersonator. Maybe when she'd prayed for a fairy godmother she shouldn't have added *or something* because she had definitely gotten the *or something*!

"Whatever you have in mind, it won't work," she said, knowing exactly what he was going to tell her to do—throw herself at Tony. She'd already been about as straightforward as she could. How much more blunt could she get than by saying she wanted to have sex with him?

"What do you mean, it won't work when you haven't heard my plan?"

She walked to the window and stared out, not answering.

"You have something against Elvis impersonators?"

She glanced over her shoulder, then back out the window. "No." The snow was beautiful. So pure, so white. She could see the festive lights of town. It was Christmas Eve, she should be happy. She only felt lonely. As if Tony was already out of her life.

"Is there . . . something else you might have a problem with?" he asked in a highly affronted tone.

"I don't care if you're gay, if that's what you mean." She turned around, propping herself against the window edge.

He sniffed. "Then, darlin', don't have a blue Christmas. I can help."

She nibbled on her bottom lip. What did she have to lose, really? She was already breaking up the partnership. Nothing could be worse. She'd never again stumble down to Tony's apartment in her ratty blue bathrobe and orange house shoes that had lost their fluff a long time ago.

"Whatever your plan is, it'll never work. He only sees me as his *best bud*." Her stomach turned even saying his nickname for her.

"Promise to help find my ashes and I'll make it work."

He looked sincere.

A little angel, who looked just like her, seemed to appear on her right shoulder. She was dressed all in white with a little golden halo.

'Oh, Sydney, haven't we been down this road before? Why do you always tempt fate and get yourself in trouble? You should let everything happen in its own time.'

'Don't listen to her,' a raspy voice spoke from the opposite shoulder.

Sydney's eyes widened when she turned her head. On her other shoulder she could almost see a miniature of herself dressed in a shiny red leather vest and hot pants, stiletto heels on her thigh-high boots, and carrying a whip.

Damn, she looked pretty hot.

'Fight dirty,' her devilish side said. *'You want him, then go after him.'*

'Don't do it,' Angel warned again.

She ran her teeth over her bottom lip. There was some truth in what Angel said. It wouldn't be the first time she'd jumped in with both feet. Tony wouldn't save her this time. Not when he was her victim.

She thought about it for a few seconds, then before she could change her mind, blurted out, "Okay, you've got a deal."

Her sigh was long and deep. The devil always seemed to win.

Chapter Four

Tony stripped off his clothes and opened the shower curtain, testing the water temperature before he got under it. For just a moment, he leaned forward, palms on the red and green tiles and closed his eyes, letting the water sluice over him.

He didn't want to think. He didn't want to feel.

It was hopeless. When he closed his eyes, he saw Sydney. Sydney smiling, Sydney teasing, Sydney laughing.

He was scared shitless. Losing her wasn't an option. He had his future mapped out. They would work together for the rest of their lives. Someday they'd probably even marry— but not each other.

The perfect scenario.

Well, except that he'd never really thought about Sydney with another man. The image never formed. He rather liked the idea of her staying single even though he knew that was selfish of him.

He finished his shower and got out, reaching for the towel as he did.

She said they wouldn't be like his parents but he couldn't help comparing them. His dad once said that Tony's mother and he were best friends but marriage had changed everything. Little things they used to love about the other suddenly became irritating. Arguments turned into wars. They'd go days without speaking to each other.

Cold chills ran over him. He couldn't do it. He refused to take the chance of losing her forever. He'd make her come to her senses before it went so far that she left. He had to. Anything less was not an option.

He tossed the towel to the floor and walked to the other side of the room, but stopped halfway. He could hear muffled words coming from the other side of the curtained French doors. Was there someone with her in her room? He frowned as he stepped closer.

So he was eavesdropping. Whatever ammunition it took to make her see her idea of breaking up the team was not okay by him. Fighting dirty didn't bother him one iota.

He eased back the curtain. She hadn't closed hers all the way. Now he was a peeping Tom. Not that it helped. As hard as he tried, he couldn't see who she was talking to but she paced furiously back and forth across his line of vision. The curtains muffled her words but, from her tone, she was pissed about something.

Elvis? Had she just said Elvis? Was she talking to her ghost? It was worse than he'd thought. She was losing her mind. Maybe those pills weren't allergy pills after all. What if she *were* crazy?

No, not his Syd.

But she was acting awfully strange.

He drew in a deep breath and let the curtain on his side fall back into place. First, she said she was in love with him and they should sleep together. Now she was talking to the ghost of Elvis.

She was losing her mind. The stress of writing songs day in and day out had been too much for her and she'd finally snapped. *But she loved writing songs,* he told himself.

He'd have to watch her. Maybe he could make her confront

her delusions and prove to her that's all they were. Somehow, someway, he'd make it right—just like he always did.

This wasn't going to work. What in the world could a gay dead Elvis impersonator tell her to do that she hadn't already tried?

She was almost afraid to find out. But then again, what did she have to lose—besides any smidgen of self-respect that she might have left.

She sighed, ready to give anything a shot. "What do I do?"

"Flirt!" He clapped his hands.

"Flirt with Tony?" She raised her eyebrows. For one inexplicably wild moment, she'd actually thought he might have the answer to her dilemma. "That's your big plan, Elvis?"

He slapped his hands on his hips and glared at her. He definitely didn't look like Elvis right now. He was going to give her nightmares if he wasn't careful.

"Yes, flirt, and you can call me El."

El Flame maybe? Okay, clear the mind. "Flirting won't work."

"Have you even tried it?" he asked.

She sat on the bed and leaned back against the mound of pillows. Had she actually flirted with Tony—ever?

"I told him I wanted to go to bed with him," she said.

"Now that was subtle."

"Don't be sarcastic."

"What'd he do?"

"He choked on his burger."

"You told him while the man was eating? That could've been lethal."

She grimaced. "Yeah, I know that now. When he was able to take a deep breath he ranted and raved for at least ten minutes."

"Do you blame him?"

"No, but he could've waited. I really liked that burger joint but they asked us not to come back again."

"You shouldn't have just blurted it out. It's a wonder you didn't cause the poor man to have a coronary."

"So what was I supposed to do? I've known Tony most of my life. I thought he'd appreciate it more if I told him exactly how I felt." She sat up in the bed. "Honesty should be the best policy."

"Darlin', not when love is involved."

He might have a point. So far, her honesty had only scared the hell out of Tony. If she didn't make him see they would be good together then she'd be taking a bus home after the holidays.

Couldn't he tell her heart was breaking? Dammit, she refused to live without him.

"What are you thinking?"

"That smacking him might be a better idea."

"No, you can't hit him."

It had sounded good to her. It might knock some sense into him. But flirt? He was her friend before she'd realized she loved him. "I'm not sure I would know how to flirt with him."

"It's the same with each man. A touch of your hand on his, long deep soulful looks." He glanced at her. "You can do that, can't you?"

When he kept staring at her, she caved. Sometimes she was such a pushover. "Okay, I'll try."

"Good. That's settled then." He glanced toward the mirror, and frowned. He turned one way then the other. "I do wish I had a reflection. Does this suit make me look fat?"

"Give me a break," she mumbled as she went to the French doors and unlocked them before tapping lightly on the glass.

A few seconds passed before the knob turned and the door opened.

He didn't have a shirt on. His delicious skin was exposed all the way down to his low-riding jeans. Oh, honey, she wanted to run her hands over his six-pack abs, rip her top off, and press naked skin against naked skin.

Would that count as flirting? Hmm, she didn't think so but it sounded damn good to her.

"Did you want something? Like to apologize or tell me you've changed your mind about ending our partnership?"

He was watching her awfully close. Had she grown a wart or something? She cleared her mind. It didn't matter. She was supposed to be flirting.

"No towels. I wanted to take a long . . . hot . . . bath." She ran her tongue across her lips very slowly. This was good. How could he resist her? For added measure, she reached out and laid her hand on his. "Do you have an extra one?" She said on a breathy whisper and opened her eyes wide, staring up at him.

He leaned slightly toward her, his gaze fixed on her lips. She held her breath. It was working. He was going to pull her into his arms and plant a wet one right smack on her . . .

". . . lips."

"Huh, what?" she asked.

"Your lips look chapped. Hang on." He turned and went to the bathroom. A few seconds later he came out with a towel, and then went to his suitcase, digging around inside. "Here it is." He came back and handed her the towel and a tube of ChapStick.

She took the towel and ChapStick from him, then looked down. "What?"

"For your lips. They look dry. Was that all you needed?"

She nodded. He shut the door.

Where was the kiss? The passion? The sex? She'd flirted, and had done a damn good job, too.

"Very well done!" El clapped his hands as he reappeared on her bed.

Her mouth twisted into a frown. "Yeah, if I'd tried any harder he might've given me some lotion for my dry hands, too." She threw the towel and ChapStick on the bed. "Great advice. Flirt with him? Oh, yeah, fantastic idea. I flirted and he didn't seem to notice. It's hopeless." She plopped down on the chair.

"It can't be hopeless. I don't want to be stuck in Christmastown for the rest of my . . . my . . . death."

"I didn't say I wouldn't try to find your ashes." Sheesh, he was worse than a hormonal female. She certainly didn't need him to go off on a crying jag. If ghosts could even cry.

"You will look for them?"

"I said I would, didn't I?"

"Good 'cause I'm not rockin' in my jailhouse."

She grimaced. "That was really bad."

He raised an eyebrow. "What do you expect after twenty or so years being dead? I'm getting stale."

"So how am I supposed to find your ashes? With all the renovations added to the inn did you ever think they might be lost forever?" She worried her bottom lip. El was starting to grow on her. Now that was a creepy thought.

"I was cremated before the fire so I never got a proper burial. I'm in some jar in the basement." He shuddered. "Can you even imagine how it would feel to know you're stuck in some smelly old basement for the rest of eternity?"

"But you're not. Your body is only a shell that you sort of shed after you die. The soul lives on."

"But I don't want to be stuck in some old basement. I want my ashes scattered to the four winds." He raised one arm dramatically and waved his cape.

"What if the wind isn't blowing?"

He glared at her. "Don't be obtuse."

"Why didn't you get someone else to find your remains and scatter them? I mean, you've been a ghost for a while now."

He sat in the other chair. The only problem was, his bottom

protruded through the seat. Very unnerving. She shook her head and concentrated on his face.

"I scared them. The ones I didn't scare got pissed. They said I was an embarrassment to the real Elvis."

Ahhh. He looked so dejected. "I think you make a pretty good Elvis. A lot better than some impersonators," she lied.

He looked up. "Really?"

She nodded then wondered if a person could go to hell for lying if it was a good lie. Was there even such a thing as a good lie?

She looked at El. "Okay, where exactly is the basement?"

Chapter Five

What the hell was she up to now?

Tony grabbed a shirt out of his suitcase and jerked it on. Hell, he wasn't born yesterday. He knew exactly what her game was. Flirting.

And it had damn near worked. He stopped buttoning his shirt as he'd remembered the way she'd looked at him: soft, sultry. Like a woman who had sex on her mind.

Damn it, Sydney wasn't supposed to act like that. Not around him. Hell, not around any man for that matter. It made her too . . . too . . . Ah, man, he knew exactly what it made her—too damn tempting.

He finished buttoning his shirt. Syd was off-limits. Period.

A door closed. His eyes narrowed. It sounded suspiciously like hers. She'd told him she was going to take a bath. Now what was she up to? He strode to his door and eased it open a crack. She was just locking hers when he glanced out. He moved back so she wouldn't see him. What the hell was she doing?

She'd lied about taking a bath.

Never trust a woman. Damn. He eased the door open a crack as she walked past. She was carrying on a conversation, waving her arms like a lunatic. Trouble was, she was completely alone. Sure, he knew lots of people talked to themselves. This was different.

And she wasn't going toward the lobby, that was obvious. She was up to something and he intended to find out what. When she went around the corner, he slipped out of his room and covertly followed her.

But when he got to the corner, she wasn't there. What the hell? There were two closed doors. Surely she hadn't trespassed. But he didn't think she'd disappeared into thin air like her imaginary ghost, either.

He tried the first door—locked.

The second one wasn't.

Taking a deep breath, he opened it. There were stairs going downward with only a dim light to keep anyone from tripping and plunging to their death or at the very least, breaking a leg.

He quickly closed the door behind him and stood there for a moment listening. It was faint, but he could hear her voice and, apparently, she was still talking to herself.

The light was dim as he descended the stairs into the bowels of what he suspected was the old morgue. How many people had been brought here to be embalmed as they lay on a cold slab of stainless steel, every last drop of blood drained from their lifeless bodies?

It was a good thing he didn't believe in ghosts and things that went bump in the night or Sydney would be on her own right now.

He slowed as her voice grew stronger, stopping before he got to the last step, then glancing around. A long hallway stretched into the shadows with doors on either side. One was open, faint light spilling out.

"Good Lord, there have to be at least a hundred bottles down here," Sydney said.

Tony sat on one of the steps and rested his arms across his knees. What the hell was she doing? The bar was upstairs.

Maybe this was the wine cellar rather than the old morgue. It was worse than he thought.

His Syd, his best bud, was stealing booze.

Withdrawal? It would explain her seeing ghosts. Ghosts pretty much ranked up there with pink elephants. Damn, he hadn't noticed she drank. Sure, a glass of wine now and then. Sometimes a beer—usually his even though she proclaimed not to like the stuff. Denial.

"Which one are you in?" she asked.

Huh?

"I'm supposed to look in every bottle? That's going to take forever."

Voices were telling her to drink. Probably her imaginary ghost. That way she could blame the ghost rather than herself for her drinking. Maybe they were telling her to have sex, too.

It was time she confronted her voices. He stood, walked over and slipped inside the room, easing the door closed behind him. The last thing he wanted was someone to come upon them. He didn't relish spending Christmas in jail for trespassing.

He glanced around. Man, the room was a shambles—dimly lit, dank, and covered in at least two layers of thick dust.

"Where'd you go?" she asked.

She hadn't spotted him yet as she planted her hands on her hips and faced row upon row of jars. "Yeah, right, go away then. I can work faster without you around."

She turned and came face to face with him.

And screamed.

He flinched. "Be quiet or you'll get us both thrown in jail for trespassing."

How had Tony gotten down here? No wonder El had vanished. "You followed me," she hissed, ignoring his jail comment. She'd already thought about the consequences but helping a friend meant that sometimes you have to take a risk.

"I'm trying to keep you out of jail for being somewhere

you're not supposed to be. What the hell are you doing down here anyway?"

Now what to tell him? "I was . . . looking for something," she said, evading his question as much as possible.

"The bar is upstairs."

"Funny. I wasn't looking for something to drink." What? Now he thought she was an alcoholic. Of course, she saw ghosts so she must be drinking on the side. She should tell him she rode a pink elephant down the stairs just so she could see his reaction.

"Then what exactly are you looking for?" he prodded.

She'd known he wouldn't give up. "If you insist on knowing, I was looking for a jar."

"Why? And you're chewing your nails again."

She was. She immediately stopped. He was the reason she scared the hell out of her manicurist. She crossed her arms in front of her. Nasty habit. But then, he'd terrified the bejeebies out of her.

"I was looking for Elvis's ashes. He can't leave Christmastown until his ashes are set free upon the wind." Did that just sound utterly ridiculous? From Tony's expression, she was afraid it had.

"Let me help you upstairs and we'll talk about it there."

"Why? Do my legs look as if they won't carry me?"

"You're sick."

"No, I'm not."

"Yes, you are."

"No, I'm . . . Look, we can go back and forth for hours but I really need to find Elvis's ashes."

"Please, Syd."

She sighed. What was she going to do with him? She loved him so much and the only thing he felt for her was pity. She didn't want sympathy. She wanted him: heart, body, and soul.

"Okay, I'll go back up with you." Then she would sneak down later and look for ashes. Whoopee. Just what she wanted to do on Christmas Eve, traipse up and down stairs. She wasn't at all fond of the StairMaster at the gym.

She followed him to the door, but he didn't open it.

"Change your mind?" she asked.

"It's stuck." He got a better grip, grunting as he attempted to open it again. "It's not budging. Crap, see what you've gotten us into now?"

"Ha! I didn't tell you to follow me. And I left the door cracked. You're the one who closed it. I believe that makes you the one who's gotten us in this predicament."

He turned around, hands planted on his hips as he glared at her.

"You're not stopping, are you? I mean, you *can* get us out, can't you?"

"Not unless I can find a crowbar or something that I can use to pop the door open."

"I really didn't want to spend that much time down here, Tony. In case you haven't noticed, it smells horrid. I'd much rather spend my evening in the bar . . ." Her words trailed off when he raised an eyebrow. "What? I meant a soda and maybe a burger."

That reminded her. She was hungry. As if to confirm her thoughts, her stomach growled.

"Hurry and find something to pop it open. Being down here is starting to creep me out."

"Heaven forbid you should get creeped out since you were the one who came down here in the first place."

"You don't have to get sarcastic about it." She turned on her heel and went back to the jars.

"I doubt seriously you'll find a crowbar on the shelves."

"I wasn't looking for a crowbar." She tugged on the stopper of one jar. It came loose with a pop and a small cloud of dust. She sneezed, then rubbed her nose. "I figured while you're trying to open the door I could at least be looking for El's ashes."

"El?"

She peered inside the jar. There was something swimming around in liquid and the odor wasn't very pleasant. It didn't look like a pickle, either. She pushed the stopper back in and replaced the jar not even wanting to imagine what had been inside.

"He told me to call him El. When you think about it, it makes sense. He's not really Elvis, after all. He's just an . . ."

"Elvis impersonator," he finished.

She paused in tugging out the next stopper. "You believe me," she said with more than a little astonishment.

"No." He moved aside some boxes and looked behind them. "I just remembered you saying your ghost was an impersonator."

"I guess you think I'm crazy."

Silence.

"I'm not, you know. El isn't the first spirit I've seen. Aunt Ina came back right after she died . . ."

"And stood at the end of your bed. Yeah, I remember you telling me that story, too."

The next jar was empty. "I don't lie."

"No, but you can sure bend the truth until it almost breaks."

"Not funny."

"It wasn't meant to be."

"Now you're being ugly."

"What are you going to do, tell my mother?"

She looked over her shoulder, arching an eyebrow. "Maybe."

He smiled, but just as suddenly as it appeared, it disappeared. "Aw, Syd, what's going on? First, you get some wild notion in your head that we should sleep together, then you quit the team, and now you're seeing ghosts and talking to something that isn't there. Has the stress been that bad?"

"Only in trying to convince you that we're meant to be together." Sometimes she wondered if he was really worth all this trouble.

But as she watched him look behind boxes for a crowbar, she knew why she'd fallen in love with him. Maybe not exactly when, but she knew the why. He'd always been there for her, encouraging her when she didn't think she could do something. He would always tell her no mountain was too high for her to climb.

And when he touched her, it was more like a lover's caress and it made her heart beat faster. She ached all the way to her toes because she wanted him so badly. And she thought he wanted her, too. She'd seen the confusion in his eyes. The way he'd stare at her when he thought she wasn't paying attention.

She closed her eyes. *Please God, I love him so. Just make him see it, too. I really do need your help.*

She tugged the stopper out of another jar. Fumes rose at the same time she inhaled. She wrinkled her nose as the noxious odor hit her square in the face. The room blurred. She blinked several times but her vision didn't clear as she put the jar haphazardly back on the counter. She tried to hang on to the edge so she wouldn't fall over.

"Tony." Man, praying was not working out for her. Damn, she should've paid a lot more attention in church.

She bet she wasn't supposed to think *damn* and *prayer* in practically the same breath, either.

"Sydney!"

His voice came from a long way off. In what seemed like slow motion, she began to fall, but before she could hit the cold hard ground, he caught her.

"What happened? Did you get stung by something?"

"Fumes. Jar." She looked at him. "Will you kiss me before I die?"

"You're not going to die."

"Please"

He hesitated, then brushed his lips across hers. Before he could raise his head, she forced her arm up and behind him, bringing his lips back down to hers even though the movement was an effort.

He deepened the kiss. She sighed with pleasure. This was what she'd been wanting. Too bad she was going to pass out. Sometimes she had the worst damn . . . darn luck.

Chapter Six

Tony lost himself in the kiss. Sydney didn't exist. In his arms was a vibrant seductive woman. She tasted sweet, she tasted hot, and—oh man—she set his blood on fire.

Just as suddenly, she faded away, going limp in his arms and he came back to his senses.

"Syd, don't you dare pass out on me." Son of a bitch this wasn't happening. He laid her gently on the floor and rushed to the door.

He yanked on the knob while bracing one foot against the wall. "Open, damn it!"

Nothing. It didn't budge an inch. He raised his fist and pounded. Again, nothing.

He hurried back to Sydney. What the hell was he supposed to do? He wasn't a doctor. He patted her hand then realized how lame that was. *What should he do?* God, he couldn't think.

CPR, that was it!

He didn't know CPR! His respirations increased. He was light-headed and felt dizzy. Okay, he was hyperventilating. *Calm down.* How many episodes of ER had he watched where they'd done CPR? Too damn many to count. He leaned over her and opened her mouth, made a tight seal, then blew.

Wait. That wasn't right. He was supposed to check to see if she wasn't breathing first. He focused on her chest and watched the gentle rise and fall.

She had a nice chest. All curves and . . .

What was he doing? This was Syd, his best bud. She wasn't a . . . a woman. At least not one he should be lusting over.

She coughed. He breathed a sigh of relief. Her eyes slowly opened.

"What happened?"

"You inhaled some fumes." He helped her to sit up. "How do you feel?"

"Woozy." She looked at him. "Did you kiss me?"

She didn't remember their kiss. Good. He didn't plan to tell her, either. "I did mouth-to-mouth."

"Oh." Her forehead wrinkled. "Did I stop breathing?"

He could feel the warmth crawl up his face. "Not exactly." He shrugged. "I sort of panicked." His stomach churned. For a second there he'd thought he was losing her permanently.

"I guess I'd better watch the jars I open from now on."

"I don't think you should open any more at all."

"I have to find El's ashes."

He ran a hand through his hair. "Damn it, Sydney, you need to face the facts. There are no such things as ghosts."

She pushed out of his arms and stood, grabbing the counter when she weaved.

"If you don't want to stay down here, then leave. I don't need your help," she said.

"And how do you propose I do that?"

She waved an arm toward the door. "I would suggest you use the door since it's standing wide open."

He frowned. "It must've loosened when I banged on it."

"Well, go, I don't need your help."

"Fine, I will." He marched to the door and started out, stopped at the last minute and dragged a box over to keep it from accidentally shutting again.

Ungrateful, that's what she was. He walked halfway up the stairs, turned around, and sat down. Just what he wanted to do on Christmas Eve, sit on rickety stairs so he could make sure Sydney didn't get hurt while she looked around a dusty basement for a dead Elvis impersonator's ashes. If he was feeling creative, he could probably get a song out of this. Trouble was, he didn't feel at all like writing.

"Now you show up," she said. "You don't think materializing in front of Tony would've helped my cause?"

Apparently, Elvis was back.

"Yeah, but Tony thinks I'm crazy," she said.

"You've got that right," Tony mumbled under his breath. He shifted on the cold hard step. There might be a doctor in town willing to make house calls. But on Christmas Eve? Not likely.

"I know, I know," she continued talking to her imaginary ghost. "You've already told me that it's not good if very many people see you. Sheesh, you don't have to repeat it."

Sydney glared at El. It would help her cause a heck of a lot if he let Tony see him. Ungrateful ghost. The sooner she found El's ashes the better. It was really spooky being in a room with a dead person's ashes, not to mention his ghost.

"Sorry," El apologized.

"I don't want to stay down here any longer than I need to. It's creepy. Can't you at least describe the jar?"

He shook his head. "I've never really looked for it."

When she raised her eyebrows, he continued.

"The dust." He produced a white handkerchief from thin air and waved it in front of his face. "It's so . . . so gloomy down here."

"But you'll let someone else do your dirty work."

"It's not like I could do anything if I did find the jar. It has to be a living breathing human being who scatters my ashes."

"Aren't I the lucky one," she muttered.

There was a tall white jar at the back but she couldn't quite reach it. Bracing her foot on the lower shelf, she boosted herself up and leaned forward as far as she could. She could almost reach it. . . .

"I don't know why Tony wouldn't fall all over himself to sleep with you. I would give anything for an ass as tight as yours. Jane Fonda workout?"

"Do you mind not staring at my ass? I *am* the one trying to help you cross over."

"It's boring down here."

"Are you sure someone didn't knock you off because you talk too much?" Got it! She scooted backwards until her feet were on the concrete floor again.

"Are you being sarcastic? After all the help I've given you with Tony?"

As she turned around, he brought the white handkerchief to his nose and sniffed. Great. A dramatic sarcastic dead gay Elvis impersonator.

"Is this it?" she asked, so ready to get the hell out of Dodge.

The handkerchief was gone in a flash. He leaned forward. "I'm not sure."

It looked less like a jar and more like an urn. She blew on it. A cloud of dust rose and she sneezed.

"Bless you."

Was there an echo down here? She could've sworn she heard more than one "bless you". She shook her head and read the fancy engraved lettering. Disappointment filled her.

"What?" El asked.

"I don't think these are your ashes."

He seemed to fade before her eyes.

"Don't worry, El, we'll find them. I'll just put Truman Alfonso Helgensen back on the shelf and . . ."

"That's me!" El materialized stronger than ever. "You found my ashes!"

"You've got to be kidding. You're Truman Alfonso Helgensen?"

El planted his hands on his hips. "I didn't have a choice. I was named after my grandfathers. Why do you think I go by El?"

"Good reason." Moisture suddenly formed in her eyes. "I'm going to miss you."

He caught his breath on a sob. "Now let's not get sentimental. We knew you'd probably find my ashes and set my soul free." He waved his arm in front of him then brought his fist to his mouth. "But I'll miss you, too."

"At least you're getting what you wanted."

"Oh, contraire, I haven't given up on you snagging Tony."

"If I set you free, you'll never know. But that's okay. You need to find peace."

He shook his head. "Not until midnight. You can't set me free until then. That's the rules."

She had a feeling El made the rules up as he went. She rather liked the idea that he would be around a little longer, though.

"Then let's get out of here." As she went to the door, she thought she heard footsteps ascending the stairs. Had Tony stuck around to make sure she would be okay? Probably. It made her feel good to think that he hadn't left her down here all alone.

But as she hurried to her room, she didn't see a sign that he'd been hanging around. Maybe she just wanted to think he'd always be there watching over her. She wouldn't blame him if he had left her. She hadn't been very nice, and after he'd done mouth-to-mouth.

She stumbled on a step and juggled the urn before she had a tight grasp on it once more. She breathed a deep sigh of relief. That was a close call. She needed to think less about Tony and more about keeping El's ashes safe.

As if she could stop thinking about Tony.

Speaking of which, Tony had said he'd done mouth-to-mouth after she'd passed out, but her memory was returning.

She distinctly remembered asking him to kiss her before she died. And she *had* thought she was dying at the time—sort of.

His lips had brushed across hers but she'd pulled his head down and he'd deepened the kiss. Chills of excitement washed over her. And he'd kissed her back. It wasn't all her. Hope flared. Maybe she had a better chance than she'd first thought.

She fairly waltzed into her room, then set the urn on the dresser.

"You seem happy," El said as he materialized next to his ashes.

She jumped. "Warn me when you're going to pop in like that."

"Boo."

"Not funny."

"So what are you happy about?"

"He kissed me." She hugged her arms around her middle.

"I saw."

She frowned. "You don't think that was worth sharing?" She thought he was supposed to help her get Tony. He could at least tell her when something was working. A little encouragement would be nice occasionally.

An idea popped into her head. Maybe she could entice Tony to do more than kiss. Delicious sexy thoughts tripped across her mind. She closed her eyes and visualized him slowly pulling his black T-shirt over his head, tanned muscles rippling . . .

"Do you often go into a trance?" El asked.

"Only when I'm thinking about Tony stripping off his clothes."

"Why think about it?"

El had a point. It never hurt to try. She strode to the French doors and pulled the curtain back on her side. His curtains were closed. She tapped on the door. A few minutes later she heard the lock turn.

He'd locked his side?

What? Did he think she'd jump his bones? Okay, so maybe he knew her better than she thought.

He opened the door and just stood there. "You wanted something?" he finally asked.

"I'm sorry."

"Apology accepted." He started to shut the door but she pushed against it.

"You didn't ask me what I'm sorry for. I was ungrateful after you tried to save me by doing mouth-to-mouth."

His face turned a little red. What exactly was he remembering? The taste of her? The heat? Had she fired his blood?

"No problem, but the next time you plan to pass out don't eat garlic." He shut the door.

She just stood there. Was he telling her she had bad breath? Her forehead wrinkled. Her breath didn't smell icky. She brought her hand up and breathed in her palm. Minty fresh.

"My breath doesn't stink!"

Silence.

She knew he'd heard her. But a few minutes later, she heard his door open and close. He was leaving . . . without her. She flung the curtain closed and plopped down in the chair.

"You do love me, darn it. Why won't you admit it?"

"Because he's afraid."

She jumped, having forgotten that El was still hanging around.

"There's nothing to be afraid of. That's crazy."

"Is it?"

He floated through the canopy and down to the bed. Very unnerving.

"He's afraid he'll lose his best friend."

"But he won't."

"He doesn't want to take that chance. You've got to show him how wrong he is."

"I've tried. Nothing works."

"Maybe it's time you show him exactly what he'll be giving up."

She wasn't sure about the gleam in his eyes. She was starting to feel like the proverbial sacrificial lamb.

Not good. Not good at all. But hell, what did she have to lose?

Chapter Seven

Tony sat at the bar staring into his glass of beer. He'd taken one swallow and realized he didn't want it, but he didn't want to go back to his room, either.

Not that the bar was much better. It was crowded and noisy. A group of carolers had stopped by and sung a few songs, then moved to the Christmas tree and the bar quieted to a dull roar.

Ho-ho-ho. This was the worst Christmas he could ever remember.

His Sydney was losing her mind. How many people saw the ghost of Elvis? Correction: dead Elvis impersonator. And he'd heard her talking to herself again before he left his room.

He probably shouldn't have told her that she had garlic breath. She didn't. She'd tasted like mint, mixed with way too much heat. Damn it, she wasn't supposed to make him feel like that.

He'd hoped she wouldn't remember the kiss, either.

Luck was not on his side.

He rubbed his forehead. What the hell was happening? She was starting to make him imagine all sorts of things—like she might actually be right. That taking their relationship one step further might not be so bad.

No, she was wrong.

Sure, he had feelings for her that went beyond normal friendship. He liked the way she smiled, the way she jumped in with both feet, he liked coming to her rescue. He drew in a deep breath.

If it's not broke—don't fix it.

And they weren't broke. She just needed a little time to see that for herself and maybe take a vacation from the stress they'd been under lately. Prozac . . . Zoloft. Yeah, that's all she needed.

He took a drink of his beer. He might as well since he'd ordered the damn thing. Maybe he'd get so plastered he'd forget Sydney was leaving him.

"You look like you have the weight of the world on your shoulders," the bartender said as he wiped the counter with a white towel. "My name's Chris."

The last thing Tony wanted was conversation. He ignored him.

"I'm a pretty good listener. Sometimes talking helps."

"Nothing will help."

"Try me."

Still, he hesitated.

Ah, hell, what difference did it make? Talking might make him see what needed to be done. He glanced around. There probably weren't more than eight people left in the bar. It seemed nearly everyone had left while he was feeling sorry for himself—and he had every right.

Hell, talking would pass the time.

"My business partner decided to call it quits."

"How long you been together?" Chris asked.

He thought back to the day he and his mother had moved to Abbyville. Sydney was the icky girl next door until she proudly showed him she could thread a worm onto a fish-hook. They'd been best buds ever since.

Damn, it seemed like forever, like yesterday.

He studied Chris who didn't look as if he were old enough

to tend bar. Tony raised the glass to his lips, took a long drink, then lowered it.

"We've been together a long time," he finally said.

"Sounds like he means a lot to you."

"Yeah, *she* does." But he guessed that didn't mean squat anymore.

"Female, huh? Well, from my experience . . ."

Tony looked at him over his raised beer.

Chris laughed. "I'm older than I look, and I've heard a lot of stories about all kinds of break-ups. Experience usually says she's found another partner."

"Not the case this time."

"Then it's got to be a man."

He was thoughtful as he let the bartender's words sink in. "Yeah, but the man is me."

Now what did he do? Sydney wanted a lover and a business partner all rolled up into one, but he couldn't do it. Surely, she would come to her senses.

"That does make it a little more difficult."

Someone ordered a drink and Chris went to the other end of the bar, leaving Tony to nurse the rest of his beer. Damn, what the hell was he going to do?

"Is this stool taken?" A sultry voice asked.

Tony turned in his seat, and looked right at the deep vee of the woman's dress. Ah, crap, he didn't need this, either, but his gaze was drawn down to the incredible legs that showed beneath the very short hem of her clingy black dress as she slid onto the seat.

He groaned.

Slowly his gaze worked upward. What was it about sexy women this week? Had it been that long since he'd gotten laid? He'd wanted time alone. When the hell had he become a chick magnet?

"Listen lady, I'd just as soon not have any company if . . ."

His words came to a grinding halt when he realized he was talking to Sydney.

"I wanted a drink." Sydney motioned to the bartender who was walking back their way. "A frozen margarita, please. With a swirl of sangria," she added.

"What the hell do you think you're doing?" Tony quickly looked around, glad the bar was dimly lit. Damn, the dress barely covered her.

"I just told you. I decided to come down for a drink."

She put her fingers to her lips and he noticed her nails were still short but she'd applied polish. A deep red, but they weren't working as a stop sign.

"Oh, did I interrupt something? Are you trolling the bar for a date?"

His eyes narrowed. "What game are you playing now?" Something was going on.

"Game?" Her eyes widened. "No game."

She took her drink from the bartender and dropped a ten on the counter, then raised the glass to her lips.

"Umm, this is so good."

When she licked the ice off the straw, he almost lost it. *She's my friend, nothing more,* he repeated over and over in his head.

"I just wanted to check out the action," she told him.

It took him a couple of seconds to remember where he was and who he was with. When he did, he frowned. He didn't like the thought of her checking out anything. He didn't believe her, either.

"If this is another ploy on your part to try to make me see you as something other than my friend, then it won't work."

She shook her head. Her hair fell around her shoulders in soft waves. The light from the flickering candles sent shimmering highlights through her deep auburn tresses. For a second he wondered what it would be like to twine the silken strands around his fingers, bring them close to his face. Inhale the herbal essence. He swallowed past the lump in his throat.

She laughed. Deep and throaty. Where the hell had she learned to laugh like that? And what had she done to her eyes? The lids were a smoky brown and she'd put liner on them. They weren't just green. They were a fathomless jade and right now her gaze was sliding over him in a way that made him want to pull her into his arms and lower his mouth to those luscious lips and see if she tasted as hot as she had earlier.

"Is that what you're thinking? That I'm trying to seduce you?"

He cleared his throat, looking at her from narrowed eyes. "Aren't you?"

She smiled. "Would you like for me to? Do you think you'd be able to resist?" She ran her finger down the side of his face, across his lips, scorching him with her touch. "A jukebox," she said as she looked behind him, sliding off the stool.

"It won't work." He smiled as she walked away and the invisible chains she'd bound him with fell away.

She looked over her shoulder. "Are you sure?"

The chains hadn't fallen away, just loosened so he would feel confident, but one look from her and they tightened until he could barely breathe.

She sauntered to the jukebox, her hips swinging seductively from side to side. Where the hell had she learned to walk like that? His eyes narrowed on some guy who approached her. When he touched her shoulder, Tony figured Sydney would belt him. She didn't. No, she laughed up at him. Damn, couldn't she see the guy was a loser? When she moved on, he breathed a sigh of relief.

He motioned for Chris to fill his mug.

His breath caught in his throat when she leaned over to look at the song selection. He breathed easier when she didn't spill out of her top.

"Fill it up?" Chris asked.

"Yeah."

"That the partner you were talking about?"

He nodded, not able to take his gaze off Sydney. Who would have thought she'd look this damn good? This damn hot? Hell, all she ever wore around him were loose-fitting sweats. It wasn't right that she would look like this. A best bud was not supposed to be this hot. It wasn't decent.

"You're a fool if you let her get away."

Chris didn't understand. Making love to Sydney would ruin everything. He took a drink, gripping the mug's glass handle and wondering why it didn't shatter.

When a slow, sultry beat began to play, he looked toward the jukebox. Bad move. But he couldn't look away. She faced him, ran her hands through her hair bringing the long tresses up, then letting them tumble back around her shoulders. She closed her eyes and swayed to the music.

"Dance with me," she mouthed and reached out her hand.

Did she think he would crumble like the walls of Jericho? Not a chance. He swiveled around in his seat. Nope, he was made of stronger stuff.

But he hadn't noticed pretty boy come in until the guy walked past him and made a beeline for Sydney. Not cool.

He frowned, raised his glass to his lips, and took a long swallow. Who the hell did this guy think he was?

The stranger began to move with her. Not touching, damn close, though, as they swayed together.

She'd tell him to go to hell. Sydney was trying to seduce *him*, not this . . . lothario. He grinned, waiting for the axe to fall.

It didn't fall. Hell, it didn't even chip at the guy's ego.

He took another swallow of beer and set his glass none too gently on the counter.

Romeo put his hand on her hip. She laughed up into his face, raised her arms, snapping her fingers to the music. He slid his arm around her waist and dropped her back, then brought her up again.

Her laughter filled the room.

Tony ground his teeth together.

If she was trying to seduce him, then why the hell was she flirting with this jerk . . .

That was it. She was trying to make him jealous. He chuckled. He wasn't playing her game.

Just as he thought. She walked toward him, the man at her side. Tony wasn't about to say a word. Nope, she was going to have to tell Romeo that she was only using him.

She puckered her lips and blew Tony a kiss . . . good-bye? What the hell? He watched as she left with the other man, hips swinging seductively.

Great. Just great. Maybe she hadn't been trying to seduce him. She hadn't actually said she was but she'd damned sure implied it. He downed the rest of his beer and ordered another. Getting stinking drunk looked pretty damn good right now.

"I think you're making a mistake by not going after her, dude," Chris told him.

The look he gave Chris had the bartender clamping his lips together and not saying another word. Good. Tony didn't want conversation.

He took the refilled mug and downed a third of the contents and all the time he imagined the young punk's hands on her, caressing each delicious curve, his lips brushing across hers.

"Merry Christmas!" a group of three men said as they entered the bar.

He turned and glared at them. Their smiles disappeared as they hurried to the back of the bar.

Merry frigging Christmas.

Chapter Eight

Sydney handed Jerry the ten she'd promised him, but he pushed it back toward her with a shake of his head.

"Are you kidding? That was the most fun I've had since college."

But she didn't want it to be fun. Jerry had been her trump card, but Tony hadn't gotten jealous. He'd sat there as she walked out of the bar on the arm of another man.

Maybe deep down inside Tony only thought of her as his best bud—just like he'd been trying to tell her. And maybe she just wanted him to love her so badly that she'd created her own little fantasy world. And maybe it was time to come back down to Earth.

"Thanks," she told him and started to turn away.

"Hey, if it's worth anything, the man's a fool."

Her smile was a little wobbly. "You don't have to try to make me feel better."

His gaze lazily roamed over her. "Take my word for it, baby. He's a fool."

It didn't really matter what Jerry thought. Apparently, Tony didn't care. She headed toward her room. Jerry had only soothed her bruised ego. Her heart was still broken.

She made her way to the room, her footsteps heavy. She barely glanced at the decorated Christmas tree.

Tony was never going to see her as anything other than his best bud. She might as well give up. They could've had such a wonderful life together. And kids. She wanted to have at least two.

He'd shattered her dreams.

Would it be possible for her to enter a nunnery? Would it matter that she wasn't Catholic? A nunnery was probably out of the question. It wasn't really in her nature to be pious, either.

Then again, there was that little problem she had of thinking about sex with Tony—a lot. Thinking might be just as bad as doing it.

This was all Tony's fault. All because he had some crazy notion they would end up enemies. Tammy and George her foot! And his parents' bad marriage! She'd met his father and could see who the problem was in that union. Good thing Tony took after his mother.

Humph! Maybe she was tired of pursuing the unattainable. In fact, maybe she didn't want Tony after all. Maybe he wasn't good enough for her.

She stopped in front of her door, unlocked it, then went inside giving the door a healthy slam.

"How'd it go?"

"It didn't."

She glared at El. It was his fault, too, for encouraging her to flirt. Like she needed to flirt with a man to get his attention.

She glanced at her reflection in the mirror. She looked hot—damned hot. She could have almost any man. What the hell did she need with Tony?

"We'll just have to think of something else."

"I'm tired of thinking. He has no feelings for me other than friendship. Scram and let me be pissed-off in peace." El wasn't the only one who could cause objects to fly across the room and she had a feeling that's exactly what was about to happen.

"Did you try to make him jealous?"

"Yes. What part of 'go away' do you not understand?" The only thing she could find to throw was a pillow. She threw it against the door. It didn't matter that no harm was done. No tears, no rips, and feathers didn't fly everywhere. But it felt good.

"You're angry."

"Ya think? What gave you the first clue?"

"Don't be ugly. Tell me what happened."

He wasn't going away. She'd created a monster by encouraging his matchmaking.

"Help me out here," he prodded.

She glared at him. "You're not going to leave me alone until I spill all the sordid details. All the embarrassing details of my attempt at seduction, are you?"

"You looked hot. No man would've been able to resist you. Tony is no exception. So tell."

"I flirted, I lightly touched, and I paid a frigging employee to come on to me. No reaction whatsoever." She plopped down in the middle of the bed, drawing her feet beneath her. "Tony didn't seem to care at all. He refuses to take our relationship to the next step. When we leave the inn, our partnership will be over." She took a deep breath. "And our friendship as well. There's too much damage to be fixed."

"You can't rush it. Seduction is like a dance; you get close and then pull away."

"Someone needs to explain the steps to Tony because he keeps stomping on my toes." And my heart, she could've added.

There was a pounding on the French doors separating her room and Tony's. She uncurled her legs from beneath her. Her gaze met El's.

He smiled. "I believe that's jealousy knocking upon your door."

She wasn't so sure she wanted to let jealousy in. But when

the pounding started up again, she hurried to the door. She didn't want to get thrown out of the inn, either.

The man on the other side didn't look at all like Tony even though she knew it was. His eyebrows were two slashes that formed a vee. He didn't look at all happy. She took a step back, then another until she was a safer distance away from the dark cloud filling her room.

"Where is he?"

"Who?"

"The guy you left the bar with."

The devil on her shoulder nudged.

Sydney shrugged. "We had a quickie and I sent him on his way."

"You're lying." His hands fisted and unfisted.

She raised her chin. "Why should you care who I sleep with?"

"I'm still your friend."

She opened her mouth. . . .

"*'Now, Sydney,'*" Angel spoke softly.

Okay, okay. "We parted ways before we got to my room."

He looked around as if he didn't believe her. When he didn't see anyone, his expression relaxed. "Good. You didn't even know the guy."

She studied him—really studied him. El said Tony was jealous. The signs were there: unreasonable anger, wanting to know exactly what she had been up to with the other man. . . .

El was right. Why else would Tony storm into her room? This went way beyond friendship.

"You're attracted to me," she said with a touch of wonder. All was not lost.

He flinched. "No, I'm not."

"Yes, you are."

"You're my best bud," he stuttered. "Of course I wouldn't be attracted to you. That's crazy."

She sauntered over, stopping only inches away. "No, you're

definitely attracted to me." She ran her hand down the side of his face, her fingers across his lips. "Do I make you tremble?"

"You need medical help, Syd. I mean, you said you talked to a ghost and . . ."

She shook her head. "We're not discussing the ghost. We're discussing whether you're attracted to me or not."

His lips formed a grim line. "Okay, so I'm attracted to you. It doesn't matter. I'm not going to act on what I feel. It would ruin our friendship and I won't let that happen."

"Even if it means denying yourself?"

"Yes," he stated emphatically.

"Are you sure?"

"I'm . . ."

She reached behind her and slid the zipper on her dress downward.

He grabbed her hands. "What the hell do you think you're doing?"

She wiggled away from him and slipped out of her dress. He sucked in a deep breath but made no move toward her.

"Why, Tony, don't you have a clue? I'm seducing you."

She opened her arms wide, knowing exactly what she was doing to him as she stood in front of him wearing a thong, thigh high black silk stockings, stilettos and just a wisp of black lacy fabric that couldn't really be called a bra—not legally, anyway. Not that there was a damn thing legal about anything she had on. If Tony walked away from her now, he'd have first-hand knowledge of what pissed-off really meant.

He moaned. "You're killing me, Syd."

"Good, it's about time you got a taste of what you've been doing to me." She reached behind her again knowing there would be no going back after this, but she was willing to risk it.

"No, no. Don't do it," he said.

He held up his hands but it was too late as she unhooked her bra and let it fall to the floor.

"Make love to me."

"Ah, damn, Sydney, it didn't have to come to this. We could've stayed friends."

"Who said it was an ending? Baby, this is only the beginning." She walked toward him. She would be forever humiliated if he turned and walked out of her room.

But he didn't. He pulled her into his arms and lowered his mouth and she breathed again. His tongue searched and found hers. He tasted like beer. So he was a little drunk. Was that the reason he'd given in so easily? Right now, she didn't care, didn't want to think. She only wanted to feel.

But she couldn't with clothes between them. She stepped back long enough to tug his shirt over his head. She drew in a deep breath. Magnificent. She couldn't resist and ran the palm of her hand over all that naked skin. She felt the shudder that swept over him. Nice.

She reached for the snap on his jeans. He stayed her hands. "Ah, please don't stop me now." She'd die, absolutely friggin' die if he did.

"Stop? I couldn't even if I wanted, and right now—I don't want." He massaged her breasts, tweaking her nipples. It was all she could do to keep her knees from buckling. She reached for him again. This time, he didn't stop her. By the time she got his zipper down, she was panting.

He moved her fumbling fingers and shoved his jeans and briefs downward, then kicked out of them.

"Ah, damn, Tony." She reached out and touched him. He quivered. "You make me burn just looking at you."

Something close to a growl came from him as he pulled her close and lowered his mouth. His tongue sparred with hers at the same time he cupped her butt and pulled her tighter against his erection. She rubbed against him, wanting more, needing more.

She stepped away, kicking off her shoes and quickly stripping out of her thong and hose. Then she was pressing against him, pushing until his back was against the wall—just where she wanted him. They were way past running away from the inevitable.

But he took her unawares when he reversed their positions and took control. In this instance, she could care less about relinquishing power. Especially when he moved his mouth down her neck, nipping at her ear. Heat flooded her body when he moved to one breast, tugging gently on the nipple with his teeth, then licking across the hard nub with his tongue.

"Yes," she cried.

"You like that?"

"God, yes. Please don't stop."

"Oh no, I haven't even gotten started. You've tormented me every day for weeks. Twisting that tight little ass in front of me—teasing me until I couldn't think, I couldn't work. I haven't written a song all month."

"Good."

He paused, raising his head and looking at her. "Good?"

"You tortured me a lot longer."

"I don't want to think about it. Later," he mumbled and went down on his knees. "Beautiful," he breathed, the warmth of his breath caressing the fleshy part of her sex.

She arched toward him, her hands splayed on the wall as she braced herself for what she knew was about to happen. Still, she jerked when he licked her. She whimpered when he spread her lips and kissed her. And when he sucked her inside his mouth, she cried out.

He massaged her butt, pulling her closer to his mouth. His tongue worked magic as he sucked and licked her sex, tugging on the sensitive area. But when he slipped a wet finger inside her and began to slowly move it up and down, she lost it.

"Tony . . . I . . ." But she couldn't say any more as wave after wave of her orgasm washed over her. She began to sink to the floor, barely aware when Tony picked her up and carried her to his bed in the other room.

The bed moved and he was lying next to her. Maybe it was

about time she discovered everything there was to know about him. Already the fires were beginning to burn inside her again.

She rolled to her side facing him, then moved on top. He grunted when she rested her sex against his erection.

"Are you hurting?" she asked innocently.

"I could drive a nail into concrete with my dick—what do you think?"

She chuckled. "Want me to kiss it and make it better?"

He sucked air. "You're really trying to kill me. Go ahead, you can admit it."

She shook her head. "Nope, I'm taking you alive." She opened his bedside drawer and rummaged inside it. Nothing. "Protection?"

"Pants. I can't move. You'll have to get it."

She scrambled off the bed but slowed as she sauntered to the door, knowing he watched her every move. Torture? Oh, yeah. Served him right, too.

He groaned. She smiled.

It felt so good to have control again. But it wasn't in her to torture him for long. She grabbed the condom out of his pants and hurried back to the other room. She already had it open by the time she straddled him again. But she slowed as she slid it down his length.

Very nice.

He sucked in a breath. The expression of need on his face told her everything. He wanted her . . . *her!* She wasn't his best bud. She was a woman he could love. At least she hoped he would love her come morning.

He reversed their positions before she had a chance to protest. "You take too damn long. I want you now."

"Then take me." She wrapped her legs around his waist and nudged his erection with her sex.

That was all the encouragement Tony needed. Not that he

needed any at all at this stage of the game. He slid inside her moist heat. She was still slick from the orgasm she'd had earlier.

Her body closed in around him. For a moment, he didn't move. He wanted to stay like this for a few seconds and just feel himself inside her. But the effort it took was almost too much. He slid farther inside the tightness of her body, sinking all the way, watching her face, the way she bit her bottom lip.

There was just something about watching a woman's face when she was in the throes of passion. There was nothing more exquisite, nothing more erotic, nothing more of a turn-on.

He stroked her, gently at first, sliding deep inside her and moving almost all the way out, before dipping back inside. Her heat wrapped around as she clenched her inner muscles. His dick quivered, ready to explode but he kept himself in check.

"Now, Tony, now," she whimpered.

He gritted his teeth and drove inside her faster and faster.

"Harder," she pleaded.

She met his thrusts, their heavy breathing the only sound in the room. Her flesh stroked him like a fiery hand until he could hold back no longer.

He cried out as his world exploded around him and he collapsed on top of her. His body trembled from head to foot. It was all he could do to ease off her and roll to his side.

As his breathing returned to normal, so did the realization of what he'd done. Damn, how could he be so weak? Why had he drunk that last beer?

But then, he knew why. He'd been jealous as hell thinking of Sydney with another man. And when she began stripping, he hadn't been able to do a damn thing but watch.

"What are you thinking?" she asked softly.

What was he thinking? That he'd trespassed. He'd never wanted to cause her pain. He was supposed to protect her, take care of her and, instead, he'd crossed the line.

Chapter Nine

Aw, damn, he'd just had the best sex ever and it was with Sydney. Life wasn't fair sometimes. Tony mumbled something to her, rolled out of bed, and made a dash for the bathroom.

Running away? Oh, yeah. As fast as he could.

He took a quick shower, but it didn't wash away his guilt. As he was drying off, he happened to glance at his reflection in the mirror and felt disgusted.

He'd been weak. Given in to temptation. Done exactly what he'd told himself he wouldn't do. Man, how low could he go? Sydney had looked at him as if he was a damned hero or something. Okay, he admitted that had felt nice, but he couldn't tell her that.

They'd been weak. They could survive this complication in their relationship. He ran a hand through his hair. Who the hell was he kidding? Getting intimate had ruined everything. Hell, even now he wanted to crawl back under the covers and pull her against him.

He closed his eyes. Damn, she was sexy as hell and soft and curvy in all the right places. When he opened his eyes, he was hard again. He glared at his dick.

"It's all your fault. You became the brains of this operation and literally screwed everything up."

Sydney had probably already realized the mistake they'd made. It always took women less time to grasp stuff like that. He grabbed his pj bottoms that were hanging from a hook on the door and pulled them on. He might as well face her and get whatever good-byes she wanted to say out of the way. He'd known it would come to this.

But when he opened the bathroom door, Sydney wasn't in his bed. Damn, it was worse than he'd thought. She was probably in tears, huddled beneath the blanket on her bed.

He tapped lightly on the French doors. "Syd, sweetheart," he spoke softly. Hurting her was the last thing he'd ever wanted to do.

Silence.

He pushed on the door, moving the curtain out of his way as he stepped inside her room and stopped dead in his tracks. She wasn't huddled under anything. She was rushing around half-dressed, hopping on one foot as she pulled on a pair of jeans.

Aw, hell. "Running away isn't the answer, Sydney."

She jumped, lost her balance and fell across the bed. "I wish people would stop scaring the daylights out of me." She stood again and tugged the zipper up. "What were you saying?"

"I said running away isn't the answer. We'll do something to work this out."

She smiled. A slow, seductive, and damned sexy smile as she sauntered toward him wearing a pair of low-riding jeans and the bra she'd had on earlier. She didn't stop until she stood in front of him.

"Is that what you think I'm doing? Running away?"

"Aren't you?"

She shook her head. "You won't get rid of me that easily." She brought her arms around his neck and pulled his mouth down to hers. She tasted like mint toothpaste as her tongue caressed his. He pulled her closer, cupped her butt. There was no doubt that she knew exactly what she did to him.

When the kiss ended, the only thing he was thinking about

was carrying her back to his bed and making delicious love for the rest of the night.

"I want you, too," she said as she accurately read his thoughts. "But I have an errand to run."

He glanced at the clock on her nightstand. "It's almost midnight. What kind of errand would you be running this late?" Surely she was pulling his leg. Except she looked serious as hell. He had a strong suspicion he wasn't going to like what she was about to tell him.

"I have to scatter El's ashes." She grabbed a red turtleneck sweater and pulled it over her head.

"Huh?"

She stopped long enough to look at him. "El. You know, the dead Elvis impersonator."

"Of course. And exactly where are you going to get his ashes, Syd?" He asked as if he were speaking to a confused child.

"Don't humor me, Tony."

"Why don't you come back to bed? It's cold outside and you don't know the area. You'll get lost out there all alone."

"I promised."

"But you don't have his ashes." This was a lot worse than he'd first imagined. Making love had triggered something that must've made her condition worse.

She nodded to a dirty white urn on the dresser. "They were in the basement."

Oh, crap, this was so bad. Now she was stealing. He eased over to the jar and picked it up as she sat on the side of the bed and pulled on her boots.

"Careful," she warned.

Possessiveness. That was a sign of a mental disorder. He wasn't sure which one but he was sure it wasn't a good one.

He read the words on the urn.

REST IN ETERNAL PEACE
TRUMAN ALFONSO HELGENSEN

Oh, God, Sydney had stolen some poor guy's ashes and planned on dumping them outside somewhere. He was pretty sure that was illegal. He had to try to reason with her.

"Hon, this is some guy named Truman."

"That's El's real name." She chuckled. "Now you know why he doesn't use it. Parents really need to think before they name their kids. He had to carry the stigma of that name all his life and even into death. There it is—emblazoned on an urn for all of eternity—at least until it corrodes or something."

"You can't go dumping his ashes. . . ."

"I have to. I made a promise."

He ran a hand through his hair. What should he do? He took a deep breath. What would it hurt if she scattered some guy's ashes in the snow. It would still be a gesture of love in her eyes, even if it were illegal.

And if he refilled the urn and snuck it back down to the basement, no one would be the wiser—he hoped. It was either that or take the chance of doing jail time. They'd be right up there with Waylon and Willie, Johnny Cash and Johnny Paycheck. They could title their next song: "I'm Thinkin' About You In Your Cold Cell, But Are You Thinkin' About Me In Mine?" Or "Prison Stompin' Boogie."

Now he was losing his mind. He had to get a grip. Maybe Sydney's mental illness was catching. When she grabbed her coat, he made up his mind.

"Wait."

She raised an eyebrow. Damn, she looked really cute. No, no, no he couldn't think about that. Maybe a doctor could give her something so she would forget the last few hours—maybe even weeks—and everything would go back to normal.

But right now, he had to keep her safe. "I'm going with you."

She glanced at the clock. "Okay, but hurry. This has to be done at midnight."

"Why?"

She shrugged. "Beats me."

She could've suffered some kind of trauma at midnight when she was a child. On Halloween maybe. If someone had scared the hell out of her, it might have manifested a psychosis that had lain dormant until a few weeks ago when it reared its ugly head.

Come to think of it, he'd scared the hell out of her on Halloween when she was twelve. Had it been midnight, though? He'd jumped out of the bushes dressed like Death; she'd clobbered him with her bag of candy and run home.

Oh, man, major guilt complex.

He grabbed his clothes and quickly pulled them on. In Sydney's state of mind, he wouldn't put it past her to leave without him.

"Ready?" she asked from the doorway.

He nodded and grabbed his coat.

"By the way, in case I forget, you have a really nice butt."

Not only was she stealing some pour soul's ashes, but she'd become a peeping Tom, too. He'd think twice before he scared anyone again.

The inn was eerily quiet as they crept down the hall. The lights on the tall Christmas tree shimmered in the dark. He jumped when a log in the fireplace popped, sending a shower of glowing embers up the chimney.

She opened the front door and slipped out, holding the urn close to her chest. He was right behind her. It was a good thing there was a full moon lighting their way.

Now he knew it was true the loonies came out during a full moon. He definitely had first-hand knowledge.

"There's a flowerbed you can dump the ashes in," he told her.

She glared at him. "I'm not *dumping* them anywhere."

"It's cold out here."

"You're the one who wanted to come with me."

Only because you stripped in front of me. Mind out of the gutter! *Don't even go there*, he silently told himself.

"It has to be perfect," she continued. "El wants his ashes scattered to the four winds."

"I hate to tell you but there's not a bit of wind tonight."

"Then we'll just have to pray it picks up."

They made their way around to the back of the inn, tromping through the snow. They went past the gazebo, past the pine trees, and stopped at a clearing.

"Here," she said as she turned, looking in every direction.

"Good, if you haven't noticed, it's freezing out here." He blew on his hands and rubbed them. "Dump . . . I mean, scatter them to the four winds and let's get back inside."

"We need to say something. We can't just fling them without saying something."

"Bye?"

"You are so not funny, Tony."

He hadn't been trying for funny. It really was cold and he wanted to get back inside. The guy was dead, had been dead for a while. He decided not saying anything was a better idea.

She ceremoniously raised the urn above her head. "Dear Lord, we offer up the ashes of Truman Alfonso Helgensen." She bit her bottom lip. Then as if an idea had just come to her, she continued, "He brought many a tear to women's eyes with his Elvis impersonation."

He snorted, but when she cast a glare in his direction, he quickly changed it to a cough.

"Please, take him into your care. Help him toward the light."

She lowered the urn and pulled on the stopper . . . and pulled . . . and pulled . . . and pulled, then removed her gloves and pulled once more.

If it weren't all so pathetic, he'd laugh. Sydney's state of mind was no laughing matter, though.

"Here, let me." The sooner they finished this, the sooner they could go back inside where it was warm.

He took the urn and tugged. Nothing. He would not let a

bottle get the best of him. He placed it between his feet, got a good grip and jerked. The stopper came out amazingly easy with a loud pop. His arms windmilled as he tried to regain his balance. It didn't work. He fell back into the snow. The contents of the urn landed in a pile on him.

"Don't move! El is on top of you."

He stretched his neck until he could see the pile of ashes in his lap. This was really gross. He had some dead guy's ashes on his lap.

"Scoop them up and just . . . just toss them into the air—away from me, though," he said.

"Hold still. This should be done ceremoniously. These ashes used to be someone. We need to be respectful."

He looked at the ashes again and grimaced. "It's kind of difficult when the guy is sitting on my lap."

"If you'll be still, I'll move El."

She grabbed the urn and began raking Truman into it. Thinking of the ashes as Sydney's imaginary Elvis ghost seemed disrespectful.

And that wasn't the only thing that seemed disrespectful.

"Sydney!" He grabbed her hand. "You can't keep dragging your hand across the front of my jeans."

Her gaze was innocent when she looked up. "But how else . . ." She glanced back down. "Oh."

"Oh" was right.

"Here, let me do it." He swallowed back his distaste of raking some dead guy's ashes back into an urn.

And after a few minutes he knew there was no way he would get them all. Sydney looked expectantly at him as if he should be able to get every little ash. It wasn't going to happen. No way. No how. It was time for desperate measures.

"Look, a deer." He pointed behind her.

Sydney automatically turned around. He came to his feet dusting the rest of poor Truman off his jeans.

She quickly turned back, a suspicious frown turning down her mouth. "Did you get him back inside the urn?"

"Could I do anything less? Like you said, this is a solemn moment."

She still didn't look as if she believed him but apparently decided to let it go as she straightened, taking the urn from him.

Again, she held it up. "Dear Lord, take our friend . . ."

"Our?"

Her sigh was long and deep. "Dear Lord, take *my* friend upward so that he might know peace for all eternity."

As she tilted the urn, a brisk wind sent cold shivers down his spine. Damned convenient of the wind to pick up at that particular moment. And was that "It's Now Or Never" playing? Coming from the inn? Now *he* was losing his freakin' mind.

"Good-bye, El." Sydney sniffed.

He put his arm around her. "He's gone to a much better place."

"I know, but I'll miss him. He was sweet."

"I'm freezing. Can we go back inside now?"

"A moment of silence would be nice."

Another moment and she wouldn't have to worry about it. He'd be frozen stiff. He frowned. And that wasn't the only stiff thing. What the hell was wrong with him? He'd had sex one time with Sydney and now he had a perpetual hard-on. This wasn't supposed to happen.

"We can go inside now." She abruptly turned on her heel, leaving him to follow or not.

He hurried after her. She was his friend, his best bud, but all he could think about was crawling between the sheets with her. How in the hell had she managed to change the equation to something more?

Chapter Ten

Sydney slowed the nearer she got to the inn. El was gone. She'd hoped he would at least have said good-bye. For a moment, she'd thought she'd heard an Elvis song but just as quickly, it was gone. Her shoulders slumped but she hastily pulled herself together. This hadn't been about her. El was in a much better place.

She sniffed again as she reached the inn. Good-bye, friend. Darn, how could she get so attached in such a short span of time?

"You okay?"

She nodded, feeling a little better that Tony cared enough to ask. They eased the door closed after they were inside and walked as quietly as possible past the front desk.

"You two must be chilled," Melanie said. "I have hot chocolate if you'd like some."

They jumped.

She poked her head over the top of the desk, the lighted wreath perched haphazardly on top of her head. In the dim light, she looked like she had no body.

Sydney slapped a hand to her chest. "You scared the hell out of us!" It took a few seconds for her heart rate to slow to a more normal pace.

Then she realized what she'd done.

Great, she'd just yelled at the owner. They'd be lucky if Melanie didn't get in a huff and toss them out on their ears.

"You're right, of course," Melanie said. "I'll be more careful in the future. What were you doing out in the cold at this time of the night, anyway?"

"Uh . . . uh . . ." Sydney looked at Tony for help.

"We couldn't sleep," Tony came to the rescue. "We thought taking a walk would help."

Melanie looked pointedly at the urn. "Did you take El with you for company?"

Sydney could feel the color drain from her face. "You know about the dead Elvis impersonator?"

But El hadn't said a word about anyone else knowing he existed. They were friends. Friends would share something that important.

Tony laughed. "We know about the need to draw in tourists but we're not taken in by the rumor there's a ghost." He glanced her way. "At least I'm not," he amended.

It took an extreme effort for her not to stick her tongue out at him.

"Oh, El is most certainly real—for a ghost," Melanie said. "He's been haunting the inn since we remodeled the morgue. He's quite harmless."

"My friend has a . . . mental condition," Tony said with more than a touch of exasperation. "I don't know if she told you about the ghost or what but I'd just as soon the problem wasn't aggravated."

"Duh, I'm standing right here and I don't have a mental condition."

"Now, Syd . . ."

She shook her head. "No, you're wrong this time." She held up her hands. "I know, that's hard for you to accept, but in this case you are *so* wrong. There is a ghost."

"Yes. She's right." Melanie bobbed her head. "El. He was an Elvis impersonator." She lowered her voice. "And he's gay."

Tony rolled his eyes. "A *gay* dead Elvis impersonator?" She ignored him. "How do you know about El?" Not that she really minded sharing him, but it would've been nice to talk to someone about him. Melanie could've come to his . . . uh . . . funeral.

Melanie chuckled. "I've known about El for some time now. He's such a joker. Every year he talks someone into disposing of his ashes at midnight. Usually there's something going on in their lives and he tries to fix them." She glanced at the urn, then at them.

Sydney bristled. "I don't need fixing." She turned on her heel but thought of something else and whirled back around. "If someone disposes of his ashes every year, then whose ashes were these?"

"They were from the fireplace," Melanie explained.

The fireplace! She'd frozen her ass off and made a fool out of herself over ashes from the stupid fireplace? She'd kill him.

She marched down the hall ready to do just that, but stopped in her tracks.

Damn, she couldn't. He was already dead. It was a nice thought, though. She took off again. She could at least tell him how pissed she was.

"Sydney," Tony called as he hurried to catch up. "Please tell me you're not buying into all this. It's a tourist trap. There are no such things as ghosts."

She opened her door and stomped inside her room. "Okay El, show yourself!"

"Yes. Please show yourself," Tony said with dry sarcasm.

"If you insist," El said and then appeared.

Tony took a step back, grabbing the bedpost. "Wow, they're good. He almost looks real."

"He's not real. He's a ghost."

Tony frowned. "There has to be something projecting the

image." He walked over and ran his hand through El, then jerked his hand back.

"Are you flirting with me?" El asked. "If you're not careful Sydney will get jealous."

"You are so not funny," she told him, then looked at Tony. "It's cold because he's dead, a ghost," Sydney explained. "It was the same when Aunt Ina came to visit after she'd crossed over. Now do you believe me?"

"There is no such . . ."

Sydney held her breath as El swooped through Tony. Right through him. Her stomach churned. Tony visibly shivered and grabbed for the nearest chair, sitting down with a thud.

"What . . . what . . ." he stuttered.

"You didn't hurt him, did you?"

"Of course not," El said.

A shot glass filled with an amber liquid appeared in front of Tony. He automatically took it, downing the contents. Realization dawned on his face.

"You're a ghost, and you look like Elvis."

He curled his lip. "Thank you, thank you very much."

Poor Tony, he looked as if he was going to . . . she caught him as he pitched forward, taking them both to the floor. She grunted when he landed on top of her. She could barely breathe. With a supreme effort, she finally managed to roll him off.

"Tony?" She patted his face.

"It's always a shock to non-believers to realize they've been totally wrong," El said.

"Especially if you're never wrong. Which Tony rarely is. I can count on one hand the times Tony missed something."

"Does that include being wrong about your relationship?" She nodded.

"But we fixed that?"

"We?"

He sat on a corner of the bed. "Who do you think locked you in the basement?"

"It was cold down there." She glared at him.

"But he kissed you."

"I vaguely remember it so it doesn't really count."

"Not my fault." His white handkerchief appeared. He coughed and brought it to his lips, patting softly. "And you did have a wild time in bed."

Heat crawled up her face. "You watched?"

He slapped his hands on his hips. "Don't be crude," he huffed. "I left before it got interesting."

She breathed a sigh of relief. Just as suddenly, her heart fell. "That's all we did . . . make love. There were no commitments."

He settled next to her. "Then you'll have to show him what you feel for each other is real love and not just friendship."

The warmth of his spirit surrounded her, but knowing he cared didn't change the way Tony felt about her. She was still his best bud . . . except they'd had sex.

"I'm not so sure he loves me the way I love him."

"Fate brought you two together. It was no accident that the house next to yours came up for sale at the very same moment Tony and his mother were looking for a place. You're soul mates. That's why you kept coming back to each other through the years. You're meant to be together. Now convince him."

Tony groaned and opened his eyes. "What happened?" He struggled to sit, she helped him, sitting beside him on the floor.

"You saw El. I think it was a little too much to take in all at once."

"Ghosts are real," he said with wonder.

"And I'm not crazy."

His gaze locked on hers. "No, I guess you aren't."

"I love you." Before he could say anything, she hurried on.

"I loved you as a friend for a long time, but my feelings slowly changed. I wasn't even aware when they did. All I know is that they did change, and I fell in love with the man you had become. And what's more, I know you care for me, too, and not just as your best bud."

Tony struggled to his feet, then walked to the window, staring down at the snow, the shadows the light from the moon cast, and he knew Sydney was right. He'd been fighting taking their relationship to the next level for a long time because of his parents' broken relationship. If it isn't broke— don't fix it.

Were they broke?

He turned and looked at her, saw her worried expression as she stood waiting for him to say something . . . anything.

What was the alternative? Letting her go? It felt as if a knife stabbed him in the chest. It had been stabbing him since she told him she was quitting the team.

Somewhere down the line, he'd fallen in love with her, too but he'd been afraid of his feelings.

"Will you still be my best bud?" he asked.

She ran to him, throwing her arms around his neck. "I love you so much," she said.

"I love you, too." He lowered his mouth, tasting her again and he knew this was right where he belonged—in her arms.

Was that "Can't Help Falling in Love" playing? Well, the ghost had certainly gotten this one right because Tony hadn't stood a chance. He couldn't help falling in love with his Sydney.

Holly in His Heart

Dianne Castell

Chapter One

Holly Green stood in front of her office window, framed with flashing snowmen, and stared at the Christmas Eve moonlight glistening off gently falling snow. "What a bunch of white crap," she muttered as the front door opened behind her. "That's what snow is, little pieces of white crap dropping from the sky determined to screw up our town."

"Thought you liked snow," came a voice behind her. One of those blasts from her past, making her spin around to tall and studly in flyboy jacket and white scarf . . . sort of like the Red Baron with even more attitude . . . standing right there in her office!

"Thought it was your thing?" He dropped his duffle to the floor and folded his arms while taking her in from head to toe. "That Holly Green was the queen of snow and Christmas, and that being mayor of Christmastown was the best darn thing in the whole world."

"Case?" She could barely breathe and blinked a few times to make sure she wasn't imagining him. "You're really here! Finally! It's about time!"

"The snow had a little something to do with it."

"It reminded you of Christmastown and me, didn't it? Holy reindeer!" Her heart hammered and she felt giddy with excitement over his five o'clock shadow that looked more like a forty-eight hour shadow and his mussed black hair with snowflakes that didn't look like crap at all. Case . . . her lover, her man, her ex-fiancé . . . was back for her on the day she loved more than any other, Christmas Eve!

Tearing across the office she jumped into his arms, forcing him to catch her as they slammed against the wall, knocking her autographed picture of Santa Claus to the floor with a solid thud.

She kissed Case's Virginia-winter-cold cheeks. She nibbled the warm, seductive lips she missed so much and inhaled his scent of pine and wind and flyboy essence. Except she hated flyboy essence since flying was the thing that took him away from her. But now he was here! "It really is you?" she muttered as her mouth skimmed his neck and ears. "You returned just like I knew you would, though I thought it'd be a little sooner."

"I sort of—"

"Who cares." Her mouth took his again while tugging his jacket back over his shoulders.

"What are you doing?"

"Sex," she muttered into his mouth. "Right now. Oh, Lord, yes. I can't wait another minute. Take me . . . or I'll take you as long as someone takes someone right now."

"Huh?"

"S-E-X . . . Sex! Put A into B . . . me being B." She kissed his chin, his stubble against her lips so male, so pure heaven, so missed. "It's been over two years and that's some dry spell." She tossed her green elf hat into the air then skipped behind him and pulled his jacket completely off.

"But . . . Maybe we should—"

Her tongue caught his, making the rest of the words mumbled but she knew what he was going to say. They couldn't *do it* out in the main office giving all the town square—complete with twenty-foot tree, blinking lights, holiday visitors and ten dancing reindeer—a front row seat to the hottest sex on earth. With Case it was always that way and would be double that tonight considering how long she'd been without satisfaction. She backed him around the corner to the file room while undoing his belt.

"Holly?"

"Yes?" she panted as she unzipped his fly, her insides melting as she scooped his erection . . . oh my God, it really was an erection! Heated shaft! Fabulous love machine! . . . in her palm this minute. "Oh, yes, yes, yes! Meeeerry Christmas to me." She grinned up at Case and winked. "And you, too."

"Oh, babe." His eyes weren't focusing. "I must be dreaming."

"This is no dream. I've had 'em and this is one heck of a lot better." His erection pulsed against her fingers, getting bigger, harder, more delicious than she remembered. She was so tired of remembering. She needed the real deal and here it was ready for action. Action was such a great word! She kicked off her boots.

"I need to tell you—"

"I can wait to hear it because I've been waiting for you and *this* a lot longer." Hating to let go, she pulled her red velvet top over her head. "In fact, I've waited two years, two months and fifteen days. But I knew you'd be back and here you are on Christmas Eve, a little present all for me. And you are some present." She slid out of her red velvet slacks and stood in red lacy bra, panties and matching white fur-trimmed garter belt with fishnets. "And here I am, a little something all for you."

"How'd you know I'd be here and to dress like every man's Christmas fantasy? I didn't even know I'd be here tonight and—or, do you always dress like this?"

"Honey, this is just for you, except during the summer I ditched the garter belt and fishnets, too darn hot, and do black lace, not Santa attire. I knew you'd come sometime and I wanted to be ready. Then here you are right on time for a private Christmas viewing."

He gulped and she loved that she had that effect on him. "That is some view."

"Low carbs and twenty minutes on the treadmill every day." She twitched her hips, licked her lips and pulled a condom from her bra, waving it in the air. "I'm ready, more than ready. So come and get me, big boy, it's Christmastime in Christmastown!"

His eyes darkened and he raked his fingers through his hair mussing it and now looking as if he'd already made her Christmas wish a reality. "You're more than I can resist." He scooped her into his arms and she yelped and giggled. His strong back muscles rippled under his blue wool sweater, reminding her just how physically powerful he was and not just in the sack. His chest was still broad and firm. Thank heavens he didn't let himself go to pot! He sat her on a file cabinet. H to S property assessments would never be quite the same again. Forget Hurley to Stevenson, from now on she'd always think Horny to Satisfied . . . very, very satisfied. She couldn't wait!

Her bare legs parted letting Case step between, the roughness of his jeans rubbing the inside of her bare thighs— another reminder of his maleness. Then the tip of his erection touched her strip of red panties and a jolt of familiar white heat sliced right through her in anticipation. She tore open the blue foil package. "You're mine, Case, all mine. Finally," she said, her voice shaky. Then she slid on the protection, reveling in his strained condition.

"You are incredible," he growled as he cupped her derriere with one hand, the intimate touch making her stomach flip. He pushed the panties aside and entered her in one long stroke that drove the air right out of her lungs. The air sizzled and that the office circuit breaker didn't explode was a miracle.

"I missed you, Case. I missed you so darn much."

And then he was in her, completely, assuring her that waiting for Case McGill and only him was worth every second as she climaxed in a blinding long, long, long overdue orgasm. "Case! Case, oh. Holy crap! Case!" He pumped into her again and again reaching his own release, heat radiating from his body, beads of sweat popping over his upper lip.

"Dang!" he gasped, holding her tight, his cheek to hers. "Oh, sweetheart, you give a whole new meaning to holiday cheer."

"And oh what fun it is to ride! That works pretty good, too." Her forehead sagged onto his shoulder, her breathing erratic, her bones like rubber bands. "I wanted to enjoy us together a little longer than ten minutes but once I saw you standing in the doorway it knew I'd never make ten whole minutes—"

"Hello," came a voice from the front office. Chills danced up her spine killing anything that resembled *enjoy* deader than a Christmas goose. "Holly? Where the dickens are you, girl? You'll never guess who's here, blast his no-good, rotten hide? Case! Saw his plane on the landing strip we lit up for Santa's arrival. Can't believe that varmint has the nerve to show himself back here."

Case's eyes widened against hers and he whispered, "Buck?"

"You're not one of Dad's favorite people . . . still. He thought you loved this town and me and then you left both of us."

Case took himself from her, and the shock of having him being an intimate part of her then not was one miserable feeling and she hated it more now than ever.

"Hey, Holly," her dad yelled again. "Whose jacket and duffle is this on . . . Is Case already here? And did you lose your elf hat? What the hell's going on?"

Case discarded the condom in the trash, zipped in record

time and sauntered into the front office saying, "Hey, Buck! Long time no see."

"Well, hell, it is you," Buck grumbled. "Where's Holly? Does she know you're here?"

"She's sort of busy with mayor stuff and all and—"

"And Case needed a map of the town," Holly offered as she breezed into the room waving a brochure and hoping everything was fastened and tucked. "Case hasn't been here since Diehard didn't die so hard and got a makeover into Christmastown. I had new maps in the storage room that I wanted to show him."

Buck frowned at Holly. "Something's different about you. Is your sweater on backwards?"

She swallowed, willing her eyes not to bulge right out of her head with telltale guilt. "Newest fashion. Saw it in *Cosmo*. Sweaters on backwards, shoes on wrong feet. Thought I'd give it a try."

The door opened as Willa Watkins stormed in. The place was more Grand Central Station than office and that was a good thing since it took Dad's attention off Case and her sweater. It wasn't so good in that she couldn't have Case to herself. She glanced at him, trying not to salivate. Shouldn't she be all salivated-out right now? That was some sex!

"It is you," Willa huffed and pointed at Case. "'Bout damn time you got yourself here. So, hot-shot, where are the toys, the presents, the boys' choir club from Richmond? We all looked in that plane of yours out on the runway and there's nothing but a wood crate with Jimmy Ray Anderson stenciled on it."

"Uh, why would I be bringing presents and a boys' choir here?"

Willa gave him a *duh* look as she pushed back her fur-lined Laplander hat complete with bill and ear flaps. "Because you landed on the lit runway we set up, so I'm guessing you're the Christmas Express we hired, though why Holly ever hired you after you left her and this town is the big mystery of the year."

"Holly didn't hire me. I'm flying Big Jimmy Ray from Huntington to Savannah for Christmas and was forced to land."

Forced? A bad feeling sat in Holly's gut. "Who's Jimmy Ray?"

Buck said, "And where the devil is he? Out in the snow to freeze? Just like you to leave someone stranded."

"He's in the box, a coffin in the back of the plane. His family wanted him home for Christmas to be with his loved ones and that's what I'm doing."

Willa's eyes got beady. "You mean to tell me you're not the Santa Express?"

"I am for Jimmy Ray."

"I should have known!" Willa screeched. "Dang it all, Case McGill. You're never around when you should be and then when we don't need you, here you are big as you please, stirring up trouble—"

And stirring up me, Holly added to herself. "This is not Savannah. Did you miss a little turn at the second cloud on the right?"

He nodded at the window. "You know that white crap you were talking about earlier, you should see it at a thousand feet in the dead of night. I was following this familiar route and saw your runway lights. There aren't many places to land in these mountains. And as for your Santa Express, I hate to tell you but nothing's flying in this soup except more snow. Didn't your Santa-for-hire call?"

Holly said, "Phones are out because of the storm."

"We are so screwed," Willa yowled, whipping the brochure from his hand and pointing to the front. "Right here it says we have the Santa Express flying in on Christmas Eve. This is Christmas Eve and we have no presents, no Santa, no plane, zip, nada, nothing. It's the big attraction and it's not here."

She tossed her gloves in the air and Holly wanted to toss Case through the front window. He was here because of rotten weather not because of her.

Willa continued, "All our hard work to make Christmastown successful up in smoke. No one will ever come here again after this."

"Too bad we didn't go with Hauntedtown," Buck added. "We got ourselves a flying coffin."

Willa said, "And you just wait till that holiday critic guy staying at the Sleigh Bells Inn finds out we flew in a dead guy for Christmas. We'll wind up with a minus four suitcase rating and be a laughing stock."

Holly looked at her watch. "Get the council together for a meeting at Barlowe's. Christmas morning is in nine hours; we need an idea. We can say Santa's been delayed but he's got to show up sometime." Willa and Buck left and she glared at Case. "You took advantage of me."

He gave her a devil grin. "With your special Santa suit, I think it's the other way around, not that I'm not complaining."

She looked deep into his incredible, deceiving, two-timing blue eyes. "You broke our engagement, left me here, flew off into the wild blue yonder to open your own plane business and why I thought you'd someday change your mind and come back is complete insanity on my part."

"I wanted you to come with me when I left, remember? There was nothing here for either of us. Diehard had died. Fly off with me now when the snow clears."

She swiped her hand around the room. "Hello? I'm the mayor of this town. In fact, the year-round Christmas theme was my idea and it's just starting to pay off. Christmastown needs me now more than ever."

"I'm the owner of my own business and it really needs me."

"So nothing's changed, has it? Least now I know enough

not to live in some fantasyland of us together living happily ever after. And I can buy more comfortable underwear."

"I'd like to say I'm sorry about all this but I'm not. You are one terrific—"

"Piece of ass?"

"I was thinking Santa."

"You're nothing but a horny, lily-livered, low-down booty calling—"

"Hey, I wasn't the one dressed in Santa-baby skivvies."

She snatched Balthazar or maybe it was Gaspar, never could figure out which wise man was which, and flung the statue across the room, missing Case by inches. "Go!"

"All right, all right. I can take a hint." He grabbed his duffle and jacket.

"Hint? This is explicit instructions that you better leave now before there are two dead people in that coffin because right now I'm so pissed I could make it happen."

Case stepped into a snowdrift and slammed the door behind him as another wise man crashed against the other side. All he'd wanted was a place to land in a snowstorm and suddenly it's Santa undies, flying statues and a mind-blowing quickie in the back room on the file cabinet.

Except the quickie was way more than that. No matter how many times he'd tried to shove Holly out of his brain these last two years, two months and fifteen days it never really happened and it wasn't just about her sweet curves and having terrific sex. He'd missed her sass, the fire in her eyes when she was mad, like now, her laughter and quick jokes and every other inch of her that made him smile.

She opened the door and Case held up his hands in surrender. "There are three wise men, meaning one more to go and your aim's getting better."

"I've decided you're not worth the trouble." She tramped off down Jingle Bell Lane. Zipping his jacket against the swirling snow, he asked, "Headed for Barlowe's?"

She stopped. "You know, Case McGill, some women get flowers and candy and jewelry and slippers for Christmas. I get a dead guy? I got a right to be upset."

"This wasn't a planned event."

"And that's the whole point. You weren't thinking of me, you just showed up when it suited you. I pined after you for years and what do I get? A coffin!"

Snow collected in her long auburn hair, a million shades from gold to chestnut. "Hey, I pined, too. But you have a life, I have a life and they sure as hell aren't the same."

"Stupid me. I always thought you'd find a way to make them the same."

He followed her across the square bright with lights twinkling. "Go away," she called over her shoulder.

"I need a room. Think the Sleigh Bells Inn will have one for me?"

"Think pigs can fly? You're not Melanie's favorite person, either."

From the sounds of things he wasn't anyone's favorite person around here. Following dreams had consequences. He caught up to Holly as they passed tourists listening to glowing reindeer doing a hip-hop version of "Santa's Coming To Town." "Don't take this the wrong way but the place looks like Christmas threw up."

"Yeah, well, that's the whole point. It's escape. People live in the real world of work and worry twenty-four seven. This is glitz and crazy and pure fun and no problems except how much chocolate can you really eat in one day and if the Santa in Barlowe's Drugstore gyrates his hips hard enough, will his pants actually fall off?"

Case laughed and it felt good with all the tension between them and battling a blizzard for hours. "Hard to believe twenty years ago tonight, the police station, town hall, and morgue burned to the rafters. We stood right over there"—he pointed to the corner—"and watched the flames shoot to the sky. The Sleigh Bells Inn is a great improvement."

She looked up at him, her green eyes driving him nuts. Not that he could actually see the green but he remembered . . . often. "Don't you dare try and sweet-talk me with a trip down memory lane."

"Wouldn't dream of it." But he knew he would dream of her tonight. Having Holly all soft and sexy and sitting on that file cabinet ready for him and wanting him was burned into his brain forever.

She opened the door of the Victorian house that was the inn, the little bell affixed to the jamb tinkling their arrival. Case shivered as a sudden chill swept past him in a puff, making him look around, thinking the door still open but it was shut tight as a lid on a pickle jar. Well, dang. He could still talk Virgina-ese like a pro. Some things he'd never forget, like buckwheat cakes, country sage sausage, and Holly, especially Holly.

Fire crackled in the hearth, candles flickered on the mantel, and a Christmas tree complete with star on top brightened the corner. Scents of cinnamon, cedar, and holly filled the place . . . except that Holly beside him had a great smell all her own.

"Well if it isn't the Savannah Stud himself," Melanie said from behind the registration desk, a blinking red and green wreath perched on her head. Looked like she was about to get beamed up to the mother ship. She said, "Heard you landed on Santa's field out back. Heard you had a dead body in that there plane of yours and I heard you and Holly here already exchanged presents of a personal nature."

Holly's eyes rounded. "How'd you know I . . . we . . ."

"Didn't know 'til now. But I should have. When it comes to Case your brain is Jell-O."

"Well, that's all over with. You can forget about Jell-O and Case, that's what I'm doing. Pretend he isn't here, like nobody's standing beside me, just a big empty space. I came to get you for the meeting at Barlowe's to figure out what to do about our MIA Santa situation and we need two more dancing elves over at the toy shop. The little darlings keep shorting out."

Case reached for a fresh gingerbread cookie by the cash register and Melanie smacked his hand. "Those are for the guests."

"Count me in." Case felt his stomach growl in cookie deprivation. "I need a place to sleep and food since we all know my parents moved to Arizona last year and that makes me currently homeless around here."

Suddenly smiling hugely, Melanie tilted her head looking pleasant, or as close to pleasant as Melanie ever got. Okay, what brought that on? Gas? She gave a little finger-wave to an older man with a graying goatee and red and green plaid jacket as he strolled down the hall looking as if he owned the place. Melanie sing-songed, "Merry Christmas, Mr. Brinch."

Holly added, "Be sure not to miss taking a sleigh ride in this wonderful snow we're having tonight."

The man smiled back. "And Santa is on his way as we speak, correct?"

"Just delayed," Holly said in a happy lilt that probably belied the rock of worry sitting in her chest. How was she going to solve this problem?

Melanie cooed to Case, "Here you go, Mr. McGill." She handed over a key with a cow attached. "Wonderful having you with us on Christmas Eve. Such a special time in Christmastown. True magic. You'll just love our Eight Maids A-Milking room. So quaint, so pastoral, so unique, just like all the other wonderful things happening here."

The man continued on and Melanie leaned over the counter and grumbled to Case in a low voice. "That was the vacation critic from *Holiday Havens*. If he sees you shivering on a park bench it won't be good for the town and right now we have enough bad stuff going on. So it looks like I'm stuck with you here for the night. We're using the Eight Maids A-Milking room for storage because it needs redecorating. There's a bed and the room's over the old morgue. Just be glad I'm not putting you in the basement. Follow me. The spare elves are up there and I can get them while I'm showing you."

Holly took the key. "I'll fetch the elves, you keep an eye on Brinch. Booze up his eggnog and feed him some of your rum balls, that'll put him in a happy state and, with our Santa situation, we're going to need as much happy as we can get around here."

Melanie nodded at Case. "You sure you want to be alone with him?"

"Him who? I don't see anyone. Do you see anyone? I'm just going to get plastic elves and be on my way to the meeting. Nothing to worry about."

Case followed her up the stairs, enjoying the gentle sway of her slender hips even if they were under a coat. Torture, that's what it was, pure torture to be with Holly and want her and know he didn't have a snowball's chance in Savannah of getting her. He wanted her right now, dammit, in this hallway decked out with blinking snowflakes and he didn't give a Christmas fig if Brinch or anyone else tripped over their prone, fornicating bodies.

Chapter Two

Dammit all! Case thought as he continued on down the hall, shoving the image of him and Holly together from his mind. Why couldn't he have landed in another town? Because no other town in the mountains had a landing strip, that's why and it was only a fluke Santa Express got him to this one.

"Here we are," Holly said by the door with a cow silhouette. She unlocked it to . . .

"Jeeze Louise!" Case said followed by a low whistle. He trailed Holly inside to boxes and stacked furniture and cow everything. "Don't think I ever saw cow lamps topped with white shades and black spots. Guernsey? My cow-ology isn't too great. Even a cow bedspread? If the pillows are udders I'm out of here." But suddenly he wasn't thinking about the spread or pillows as much as the bed part and how much he wanted Holly in it.

She tossed him the key, snapping his thoughts back to the moment, where he and Holly and bed were nothing but his Christmas fantasy.

"Home sweet home, flyboy, or should I say, moo sweet moo." She picked up two red elf boxes and started for the door, then turned back, her eyes dark and sad. He felt like crap because he was the one who put that sadness there, he was sure of it. "You and I are finished for good this time. You stay away from me, far, far away and I stay away from you. As soon as the snow stops you hit the road . . . make that the runway." She held out her hand for a shake. "Do this for both our sakes. Okay?"

He didn't want just her hand he wanted every inch of her next to him and he wanted to talk with her and have fun and joke and . . . Except none of those things should happen. "Okay."

They shook, the thought of this being the last time he'd touch Holly depressing the hell out of him. She closed the door behind her, his heart like a lump of lead. "Well damn. This night just keeps getting better and better."

Another breeze made him shiver all over, like stepping into a shower with cold water instead of hot.

"Well now, I think you just might be right as rain about that, least ways for me it's getting better and better, especially since I heard you landed here."

He glanced around. "Uh, where are you?"

He searched under the bed to dust bunnies, in the closet and around the pile of piled boxes and stored furniture. "Melanie? Is that you? Dammit all! Are you trying to convince me I'm as nutty as one of your ten-pound fruit cakes? Well, it's not going to work."

"For pity sakes, boy, I'm not Melanie and I'm up here on top of the dresser pretty as you please and I do mean the pretty part."

Case spun around to see a woman in a red sequined dress, feather boa, silver stilettos—one dangling off the tip of her toe—and a long silver cigarette holder poised between her fingers. A thin ribbon of smoke circled toward the ceiling.

"Who . . . What . . . How the hell did you get in here?"

"Just floated in like a gentle Southern breeze. The name's Sweet Savannah Sue." She took a drag of cigarette, red tip glowing. "I sort of drift about from place to place as it suits me. I got a right sweet drift, don't you think, sugar?" She tossed the end of her feather boa over her shoulder and offered him a sexy pose.

He rubbed his eyes and plopped down on the end of the bed. "I must be one hell of a lot more tired than I thought. I'm losing my freaking mind. I didn't even see you come in."

"You're getting yourself all upset and you don't want to be doing that on my account. You see, I heard about you and where you're heading for and I'm needing you to do me a little itsy-bitsy favor."

"And I'm needing a drink."

"I can't endure one more Christmas in this here environment. Don't know about you, but I've never seen anything quite like it." She fluffed her blond hair done up in a perfect big-do. "I'm wanting to get myself back to Savannah, back to my beloved Percival."

Case's eyes widened. "Percival?"

She batted her lashes, looked skyward and put her hand to her heart. "My Percy, my love, my hunka-hunka man is waiting for me on Lily Mae Dawson's mantel, that's my niece. She promised to keep Percy and me together. So you see, you've got to help me get out of Christmastown and back where I belong. Not to mention I've had enough snow and Santa crap to last me a lifetime." She laughed. "Not my best analogy, is it, sugar?"

He couldn't breathe. His heart raced. He rubbed his eyes again. "Holy shit, you're a . . ."

"Ghost, honey. The word's ghost. Sweet Savannah Sue is part of the hereafter. But I'm in the wrong place. All you have to do is wheedle your way into Holly's house and you can make all things right. Well, at least they'll be right for me. But just between us, I think your situation with Holly is downright hopeless."

Case stammered as he peered at the hazy figure. "What the hell . . . ?"

"I'm miserable too, but change is in the air. After that fire happened twenty years ago they put things back together and the plaque on my urn got switched with Duke Green's, Holly's uncle. You see, I'd been in Diehard doing the annual Christmas party for the Squirrel Lodge boys like I always do. Had stripped down to my elf bra and panties then I went and had a big old heart attack right there on stage. Merciful heaven!" Sue fanned herself with her boa. "The men were so darn grateful for me putting on such a fine show for so many years they went and had me cremated and did a ceremony right nicely. Then the fire happened, the urns switched and Duke got shipped off to Savannah and here I am sitting on Holly's mantel."

Case massaged his temples. "I don't believe in ghosts. I don't believe in ghosts."

"And that's fine and dandy by me, sugar, just so long as you get my urn and fly me out of this Christmas hell and get me back to grits and pralines and my precious Percival where I belong."

Case searched his duffle hoping to find one of those little bottles of booze he might have picked up at some hotel. "Just float yourself on down to Savannah. The snow probably won't even get in your way. Dear God, I'm talking to a ghost!"

"It's just not that easy." She crossed her legs the other way and re-fluffed her hair. "I go where my ashes go, it's the ghostly way. I can only float so far from them. Just like the only folks who hear me are the ones that need to and you need to or I'm never getting home. Percy's been waiting for me and I know I've been waiting for him. I'm here to tell you, twenty years is a long time to wait, especially for some things. A woman like me has mighty powerful needs."

Case's head snapped up. "What needs? You're a ghost."

"Ever hear of out-of-this-world sex? Well, honey, where do you think that term came from?" She laughed and his head felt as if he'd double-dosed on cold medication.

"You couldn't possibly wave that cigarette thing of yours and conjure me up a beer? Maybe a six-pack?"

"Ghosts don't do magic."

He refrained from an eye roll. "Of course they don't. They just live in urns and have sex. Look, I'm sorry for what happened, I really am, but I cannot get ashes out of Holly's house. I can't go anywhere near her. We shook on it, made a deal to steer clear. Can't you find another Percy around here? It has been twenty years. Time to move on?"

She scowled. "Why that's just out-and-out blasphemy. You can't replace one love of your life with another. It's just not done."

"I need to put as much distance between me and Holly as possible. I've messed up her life enough, so I'm flying out of here early tomorrow and that's it and there's no way for me to get your urn."

"Oh, sugar. Without a fuel pump you aren't flying anywhere." She tossed her hair. "So, it's either you get my ashes or you'll get to stay here until the roads clear and someone can find you a fuel pump for a Cessna 172. That should take a good week or so in these parts. And, to spur you on your way, I'll serenade you about my Percy, my one true love." She tipped her head back and warbled, "On the first day of Christmas my true love sent to me—"

"Holy shit, you're terrible!" He cringed and put his hands over his ears.

"Think of me as the ghost of Christmas future, and my future is not to spend another blasted day in this loony bin."

"I think that's the pot calling the kettle—"

"On the second day of Christmas my true love sent to me—"

Case ran out the door, slammed it shut and closed his eyes. Here he was standing in a hallway chased out of a cow-crazed room by a . . . He put his ear to the door. Yep, a singing stripper ghost. And Ebenezer Scrooge thought he had it bad with all his ghosts! What now? Get the urn? Wait for a fuel pump? Walk to Savannah? He'd go nuts being around Holly for a week and not having her. He'd go really nuts listening to Savannah Sue! So . . . damn, shit, hell . . . just how big was an urn and what would it take to get it out of Holly's house without being noticed? And how did a ghost know what a fuel pump even looked like?

Pulling on her gloves as she left Barlowe's Drugstore, Holly looked up. "More white crap. Enough already! We get it, it's a white Christmas. Done!"

She turned the corner to her house and spotted Case tangled in strands of lights and sprawled across the Santa sleigh perched in front of her porch between the dancing snowmen. Case struggled to sit, getting more tangled up. His gaze connected with hers. "I'm looking forward to Easter. In fact, Easter has never sounded so good."

"Good grief." She brushed the snow off him, concentrating on that and not how much she liked having her hands on Case even with gloves and jackets in the way.

"I think I snapped every bone in my body."

"What are you doing in the sleigh? Why are you here? What happened to you and the cow room and our handshake?"

"I developed a cow phobia." Rubbing his head, he stood and held up the lights. "They were out." He pointed to the roof. "Up there. And I knew you wouldn't want faulty Christmas lights on your house with you being the mayor and all. Gives a bad impression."

"You were on my roof in who knows how many feet of snow for lights? Are you nuts?"

"Look, maybe I can fix the lights from inside."

"Go back to your room, leave me alone."

"Inside would be good. And would you happen to have a sandwich lying around? I could really use a sandwich. Or I can cook. Actually I'm more of a great microwaver." He climbed from the sleigh, took her hand and led her up the porch steps. "But right now I'm mostly starved."

"You have a bump on your head." She touched a goose egg forming over his left eye and he flinched.

"A sandwich for old times' sake?" He nudged the door.

"We aren't all that old. But I can't have you looking like you do wandering the streets with Brinch on the prowl." She puffed out a deep breath. "All right, all right. I'll run your clothes through the dryer so you don't catch pneumonia and feed you. Then you go back to your cow room and stay there. I don't care how bad it is."

"It's getting worse and remember the last time I was in this doorway? I think you threw something at me."

"You were leaving to go start McGill Transport in Savannah. That day, the weapon of choice was banana cream pie. The spot's still on the floor, a little something to remember you by."

He captured her chin in his palm his eyes twinkling. He was happy and, unfortunately, he made her feel that way, too. "Not exactly a good reminder." Then his eyes got serious. "I'm sorry about that, I really am. I wanted a new beginning and I wanted you with me. I thought you'd come eventually but then you never did."

Think about something beside Case being sincere and hand-some! Wisecracking Case was so much easier to shrug off. "Santa," she said, stepping out of his reach. Too close to Case was too much temptation to kiss him again. She needed distraction fast or there'd be more things gyrating on her lawn than snowmen. Like the two of them right there in the sleigh. "We don't know what to do about our no-show Santa." She unlocked the door and led the way inside. "The stores are staying open till one AM but that's not a substitute for presents. Everyone coming to Christmastown filled out a wish list of what they wanted Santa to bring and now—nothing." She pulled off her boots, dropping them on the rug by the front door. Case did the same. "Except lots of snow."

Okay, this was better. Discussing business, doing routine things, nothing personal, not looking at Case. "Get a fire going, wood's already set in the hearth. That will warm you up." Something she didn't need at all with him around. "I have fried chicken left over from last night." She turned and held out her hand. "Now strip and give me your clothes."

Oh crap! She did a mental head bang against the wall. Just when things were going non-personal she had to say that! "I mean . . ."

He gave her one of his easy half-smiles. "I'll build that fire in the living room and it'll be enough to dry me out. We can keep this simple."

"Wait." She put on her adult hat. "Okay, this is stupid. We can do better than act like fourteen-year-olds playing spin the bottle in the closet. We just had sex in a file room, for Pete's sake, I think we're beyond worrying about shedding garments. After tonight you're out of here, anyway. Bathroom's still upstairs. Dad keeps his robe behind the door. I'll put your clothes in the dryer."

"Me in Buck's robe?"

"Or my pink chenille. Take your pick." She folded her arms. "Climbing around on roofs does have consequences."

Case headed for the stairs and in a few minutes she heard the fire crackling. She loaded a tray and headed for the living room wondering what Case would look like in pink fluff, except . . . except Case wasn't wearing fluff. Instead he had a towel around his waist and studying something on the mantel while she studied him. One little flick of that towel and . . . and—She dropped the tray and Case spun around, the towel slipping but he grabbed it just in time. Rats!

"Damn you, Case McGill. Here I am two years in celibacy hell and you show up in a towel and I'm supposed to resist." She snapped the towel from his hand. "And you're wearing briefs? Take me out and shoot me. Nothing ever goes right."

"You were expecting—"

"Satisfaction. The good, old-fashioned, take-me-now kind that's guaranteed to put a smile on my face. I need a smile, Case."

"You already smiled. We both did."

"I need another." She tackled him, landing them both onto the sofa, sinking them down into the pillows. He nibbled her neck, making her shiver head to toe, her pulse racing like the slot cars over at the toy shop. "And you're leaving, so it's not like this counts for anything except—Oh, lordy, Case what are you doing to me?"

"Making sure your breasts are as soft and sweet as I remember. Missed them last time, don't want to make the same mistake twice. Where's Buck?"

He unhooked her bra. If she died now she'd do it as a happy woman, though in about ten minutes she'd be even happier. "Buck who?"

"Pissed-off dad if he finds me with you."

"Not going to happen. He's a singing Christmas tree over at the theater."

"Then we don't have much time." He pushed up her red lacy bra, freeing another condom. "When you said you were prepared, you weren't kidding." He kissed the tip of her nose while his fingers claimed her hardening nubs, making her insides liquefy and her head spin. She couldn't imagine making love with anyone but Case. He knew just how to please her, what she wanted most. He smoothed back her hair, his tongue doing magical things to hers. She said, "I love you naked."

"I'm not."

"That's encouragement."

But instead of taking off his briefs he bent his head and sucked her nipple deep into his mouth and she nearly slid off the couch. "Case," she hissed, letting the familiar heat of lovemaking wash over her.

"You started this," he breathed against her hot skin. "And

I'm damn grateful." His tongue tantalized her other nipple. "You taste Christmasy. Cinnamon."

"It's ginger." She tangled her fingers in his chestnut hair, remembering the silky texture. "I was filling in at the bakery and if you don't stop . . ."

His gaze met hers. "I have no intention of stopping."

"Oh, thank God!"

He unzipped her jeans, then stood and slid them down her hips like he had so often before, the inferno in his eyes making her sizzle. It was a ritual, an intimate promise of what was to come. Except . . . except what was coming could be Buck. "Hurry. I hear singing something coming our way. Could be the trees."

"You are more beautiful than ever."

She held out her arms. "Lose the sweater and briefs and flattery, flyboy. Time's a-wastin'"

He paused, his eyes dark. "We never catch a break, do we? We're always on a mission, have a plan, something going on in our lives besides us."

"But we do have now. Let's take it and figure out the rest later."

He yanked off his sweater then took the condom and covered himself. Much too slowly he climbed on top of her until she grabbed his shoulders and pulled him down, his chest on hers, his mouth squashing hers. Before he could say anything she kissed him hard and wrapped her legs around his back, her sex completely open to him, her body craving his. This was so not the way to get over Case!

He braced himself over her and for a second she remembered the simple, uncomplicated way it was between them years ago. Just wild love and insane sex. Once upon a time they would have done whatever it took to be with each other but now . . . not so much. That realization filled her with sadness as he slowly slid into her, her wet heat welcoming him, opening for him . . . only him. What happened to them, to the good times? The loving times. Reality! Curse reality!

"Oh, babe," he whispered as if holding onto a dream that wouldn't last. "I missed you so much. I love you, Holly." And she loved him, too, but it wasn't enough, no matter how wonderful the sex, how terrific the man, because they were missing something.

He climaxed, taking her with him in a blinding storm of sensation and wonder that completely consumed her for the moment but then the moment passed in a heartbeat just the way it always did and she hated it.

"You are amazing," he whispered.

She kissed his cheek. "It's you, all you. That's why I waited, Case. I knew there'd never be anyone like you, in and out of bed." She framed his cheeks with her palms and looked deep into his smoldering blue eyes. "You are the best, but . . ."

"But?" His eyes cleared. "I hate that word."

"I have to move on. I can't pine for you forever. It hurts too much and I'm not getting any younger."

He pushed himself up but his eyes were still on her. "Think I like hearing about the pining part better."

She shrugged, trying to make light of the situation because it would be easier than acknowledging how sad she felt. "I need to find a nice guy between twenty-five and sixty."

"You're going to look for someone else? Another guy? Like hell."

"Jud Wheeler at Santa Sleigh Rides, Mac O'Donnell at Barlowe's Drugstore? You're not here anymore, I have to get over it." *I have to get over you!*

"We're making love and you're making plans to ditch me."

"You ditched me and I can't wait another two years for you to crash land in my backyard."

"I didn't crash."

He pulled himself from her and she missed him but that was too bad. She had to get over him . . . somehow . . . maybe.

"And you have to move on, too." Did she really just say that?

He studied her for a moment. "You really mean this, don't you?"

"Yes," she lied through her recently whitened teeth. "You'll have to find someone in Savannah. A nice southern gal with big hair and just a few teeth missing and a good family with only one moonshine still in the backyard and who uses no-trans fats for her chicken frying and fritter baking. I want you to be happy and healthy."

Except the only person she wanted Case to be happy with was her but there was no way or they would have thought of it by now.

The doorbell rang and Case groused, "You have no privacy in this town. It's like being in one of those damn snow globe things that's always getting shaken up and you can forget about Jud and Mac and anyone else you're planning on hooking up with. There's no time for romance with you being mayor. Hell, you're lucky you can squeeze in a kiss and, just for the record, I don't want you kissing anyone else, dammit. No one. Period."

The bell rang again and Holly said, "Dad must have forgotten his key. What do you want from me, Case? That I should be a monk?"

He stopped dead and gazed at her. "That's all guys and you'd cause havoc."

"Havoc sounds pretty good coming off a two-year dry spell. I can do havoc."

He stomped his way to the kitchen. "I'll get my jeans, you get the door."

"Fine!"

"Fine!" And for the second time tonight she re-dressed. She hadn't done this much dressing and undressing in one day since . . . since Case left! Blast the man for messing up her life and for making her care about him. Well, she was done! The caring would always be there but the *in her life* part was over!

Chapter Three

Holly went to the door and yanked it open to, "Mr. Brinch? Dorothy?" The singing trees must have caroled their way on by. Holly looked from the stuffy reviewer in his pointed green wool hat to the woman who'd edited the town newspaper for as long as Holly could remember.

Dorothy said, "I know you're busy, Holly, but I told Mr. Brinch—"

"Eugene," Brinch corrected with a smile as he took her hand.

"Right, Eugene," Dorothy beamed before her expression returned to anxious and she bit at her bottom lip. "He needs to ask you again about the Santa Express, make sure all his facts are straight before he files his review with his magazine."

Brinch puffed himself up. "Is it really true about there being no Santa Express? That is the rumor and that's false advertising because your brochure clearly guarantees a flying Santa. If he doesn't show, it makes Christmastown look like a scam and you certainly don't want that."

Holly seethed, then managed to speak in a pleasant voice. "But the town didn't plan on the blizzard. It's not our fault that it snowed and planes couldn't land or take off and—"

"Sounds like an excuse, if you ask me," Eugene pontificated.

"And maybe the Santa Express will come tomorrow," Dorothy offered. "It can't snow forever."

"Wanna bet?" Holly said as Brinch said, "You know this does not bode well for a good review for my column. You advertise one thing and do another." He scribbled. "Seems I have all I need right now."

"What do you need?" Case asked as he drew up behind Holly. She could feel the heat from his body soak into hers, making her warm all over. He held up a strand of lights to Brinch. "Electrical difficulties. I'm checking for a short circuit in here."

The short circuit was Holly's brain for thinking Case would come back, and then doing the horizontal hula twice . . . not once but two times, for heaven's sake . . . when she knew he wouldn't stay.

Brinch studied Case. "Aren't you the man who brought a casket instead of presents?"

"Didn't know about the presents but the casket part's true."

Brinch made more notes while shaking his head. "This is all very confusing, indeed. I'll have my review ready by tonight but Dorothy informed me the phone lines are down so I can't fax it to my magazine."

Dorothy said, "Later maybe, much later. Lots can happen by tomorrow." She gave Holly a hopeful look and Brinch added, "I need to get my review submitted by noon."

Holly said, "Christmas Day?"

"A review about Christmastown done on Christmas Day does ring true, does it not? Something you should think about as mayor of this town and given your propensity for giving out false advertising."

He took Dorothy's hand. "Well, my dear, there's no reason for us to stay and chat further. Your mayor seems to have electrical problems. But you, on the other hand, have been so helpful. So please let me buy you a hot chocolate at Sugar Plum

Treats. I trust the phone services will be restored soon. I like to keep on top of things."

Eugene and Dorothy shuffled down the sidewalk and Holly grabbed a handful of packed snow and aimed the ball at Eugene's big, fat, ego-inflated head until Case grabbed her arm and whispered, "He's not worth risking more bad press."

"That man's going to trash our town in his stupid magazine. We've worked too hard for this to happen. We've got to do something."

"So stop him," Case heard Savannah Sue say from the porch swing.

He cut his gaze to her. "What are you doing here?"

Obviously Holly couldn't see or hear Sue because Holly dropped the snowball and looked at him as if he had three heads. "Uh . . . I live here."

Sue gave herself a little push in the swing, her feather boa swaying with the motion. "My ashes are in that urn on the mantel, remember? The urn you need unless you intend to stay here all week lamenting your fuel pump." She pointed her cigarette holder to Brinch. "And are you really going to let that heartless, no-'count, Yankee pen-pusher insult this here town? Mind you, I'm not a fan of the red and green circus going on but that pompous ass has no right to ruin it and these fine people because it suits him."

"What do you expect me to do?" Case asked

Holly said, "I didn't ask you to do anything."

Sue tsked. "Holly's just so precious. I got to know her right well all these years sitting on that there urn. You find some way to help her out, now, you hear or more will go missing than just a fuel pump."

"How can I help? I don't have a clue."

Holly touched his cheek. "What are you talking about, Case?" For a second he wasn't sure. Her warm fingers on his face scrambled his brain cells until Sue said, "Think of the things that make you like this place at Christmas. You lived here for twenty-seven years, something kept you around that long."

Case gave a sly smile. "Holly."

"What?" Holly said, now looking at him as if the guys in the white coats should be coming for him any minute.

Sue groused, "Besides Holly, you over-hormoned orangutan. What did you do as a kid here that makes for a real country Christmas and remember this is a family gig."

Case nodded. "You know, I think you're onto something."

"Where? Onto what?" Holly looked around. "You really did whack your head. I'll get ice . . . or snow. We got more than our share of that."

"Mr. Brinch," Case yelled to Brinch crossing the street. Case motioned him on back to the porch and Holly stage-whispered, "What are you doing? Haven't we seen enough of this guy?"

Case shoved his hands in his pockets going for the good-old-boy look to set the stage. He said to Brinch coming up the walk, "You should know that around here it's not all about the presents." And that part was true enough. "Years ago this was a coal mining town. Not much money for Christmas gifts then but Christmas was always special and the folks who live here are what made it that way."

Case looked at Sue and she gave him the thumbs-up sign as Brinch's brow narrowed. "What are you talking about?"

"There's more to Christmas than stuff under the tree. We go beyond the promise of Santa." Though he'd love to get Holly as a little present under his tree anytime. "We have Christmas Eve traditions. Things like night sledding where the four-wheel-drive cars line on Craig's Hill and light the way for the sleds all the way down. And there's the Christmas taffy pull over at Sugar Plum Treats where the families make their own candy and wrap it and put it in special tins."

"With their names on them," Holly tossed in, understanding where he was going with this since they spent so many

Christmases together making taffy and sledding and sipping spiced cider by the fire. "And song charades at the Christmas Carol Theater and a scavenger hunt. The family who completes the list can win an all-expenses-paid return trip to Christmastown next year."

Brinch stroked his chin, the green hat perched on his head listing slightly to left. "Kind of like an old-fashioned Christmas, I suppose. But you billed the Santa Express as your main attraction."

"But there are things that families can do together, bonding things they don't get to do in the city, Hallmark-greeting-card kinds of things," Holly said. "And, since the weather has delayed Santa's arrival, we can concentrate on these other aspects of this great time of year that are more meaningful."

"Sounds boring." Brinch tucked his notepad in his coat pocket his lips in a pout. "But I suppose in all fairness I should wait 'til after this night is over to write a review. That will give me the real flavor of the place and make the story more interesting, for good or bad."

Dorothy slipped her arm through Brinch's and gazed adoringly up at him. "That is very nice of you, Eugene. I knew you would be a fair man." He patted her hand and Sue piped up with, "Well, I'll be a monkey's uncle. Eugene's got a case of hot-pants for our Dorothy and she's all atwitter, too. We got an advantage here, Case. Go with it."

"How?" Case said, the others staring at him, since they couldn't hear Sue, and he made no sense at all. "I mean . . . How wonderful of Eugene not to prejudge the town and give it a chance to show another side of Christmastown. You and Dorothy would make a wonderful team for the scavenger hunt. What do you say?"

Brinch's eyes brightened. "I suppose that could be a bit of fun." He tipped his chin looking smug. "I won the prep school scavenger hunt when I was just eleven. I have a knack for that sort of thing."

He and Dorothy moseyed off and Holly whispered to Case, "Now you really got us into something. Can we make this all happen? We don't have a lot of time."

"We did it when we were young and, besides, Dorothy's our secret weapon. I think she and Eugene have fallen for each other. But what she sees in the man is one hell of a big mystery."

Sue said, "Seems to me Buck suggested that very thing to Holly a time or two when you two were dating." She stood. "I'm going inside and start packing."

Pack? How did a ghost pack? He looked around at the snow falling and Holly standing beside him. A sense of peace he hadn't felt since he left Diehard settled over him. McGill transport was thriving but was he? 'Course he was. Stupid question. He had money in the bank, customers, three planes except . . . "This place is perfect. A little cheesy, make that a lot cheesy, but pretty close to perfect in its own way." He kissed Holly on the top of her head, her silky hair against his lips pure heaven. "Or maybe it's the company."

"But we still don't have Santa."

Case kissed her on the forehead this time. "Screw Santa."

She slowly stepped back, gave him a hard look . . . hard looks were never a good thing . . . then cut her hand through the air. "Wait a minute."

Wait a minute was never a good thing either.

"Wait just a darn minute. You're doing it again, wheedling your way into my life. You're supposed to be going back to your room and staying there. How are we going to move on if we work together on this?"

"This is just one night. Besides, my bringing a coffin instead of presents disappointed a lot of people and made your situation worse. Let me help make things right then I'll fly out of here. And it's your idea to move on, not mine so I don't mind a little wheedling."

"This is so not fair. You get me used to having you around

and then *bam* you leave." She puffed out a lungful of air into the chill making a moisture cloud. "You gave me the idea for the old-fashioned Christmas so you've paid your coffin debt. Go back to your cow room and leave me alone. This is my town and my problem. I can handle it. What I can't handle is you being here."

He rocked back on his heels. "Really?"

"But I'm getting over it. And the next time you need a landing strip, for heaven's sake find someplace else."

"Deck the Halls" hummed from the jukebox in the corner as more snow fell outside the frosted windows of Sugar Plum Treats. Holly studied the pans of red and green taffy cooling on the tables as Mr. Dobbs in reindeer apron and matching blinking antlers gave instructions on the art of pulling taffy. A perfect Christmas setting like when she and Case were growing up and especially that first Christmas after they were engaged. Magic, pure magic. Forget Case! Think perfect Christmas now. Norman Rockwell, eat your heart out.

A little boy in an elf hat yelled. "This isn't candy."

"Of course it is," Holly soothed using all her strength to push Case McGill out of her brain and concentrate on the fact that the town was her life now and what mattered was a good review for Christmastown.

"It's gross," said a boy across the table. He folded his arms and pouted. "I want a Snickers, I want bubblegum."

"This is much better than any of that," she said. "Just wait." The mother and father beside her nodded and smiled. All was right with the world. Where was Brinch to see just how wonderful things could be without the Santa Express? Maybe he was at the theater watching charades and family times together there.

"Isn't there an Xbox game for this making candy stuff? That's more fun," a girl squawked as another girl said, "Xbox is so lame. Nintendo's better. I hate green candy." She grabbed the still-warm pan. "Ow!" It flipped in the air and landed on the floor with a loud clatter and someone shouted, "Yeah! Food fight!"

"What? No!" Holly's stomach flipped just like the pan. "Wait. Norman would not approve. No taffy flinging." She waved her hands as a wad of red taffy sailed through the air. "Stop! It's Christmas, for heaven's sake!"

A green glop flew the other direction landing on a snowman's nose and the two little angels beside her pulled at a tray yelling, "I want red. No, I want red." Parents looked horrified; kids didn't care.

Case bolted through the front door, his eyes instantly wide. She saw him mouth *What the heck?* He snaked his way through sticky hands, flying candy and frustrated parents and jumped up on a stool yelling, "All right, you guys, that's it. No throwing candy—"

A blob of red smacked him in the side of the head as another salvo went airborne looking like red and green confetti except a lot stickier. "Someone could get hurt." Another splotch landed on his jacket. He jumped down. "Crap. They're not listening to anything I say."

"Crap's a bad word," said a girl, who then grinned and flung a chunk of green across the shop at a boy on the other side. He laughed and returned a glop of his own. Mr. Dobbs waved his hands frantically from behind the counter doing no good at all and Holly said, "I'm calling Sheriff—"

"He's at the theater," Case yelled over the racket. "That's why I'm here, came to get you to help out. There was an argument about the names of the eight reindeer that got ugly. Some insist there are nine. Is Rudolph in or out?" Pieces of candy decorated his hair. "How can people argue over reindeer?"

Buck pushed open the door and stumbled his way to Holly. "Great Caesar's ghost, girl, this place is a war zone and it's not the only one. There's a blooming sled fight over at Craig's Hill, do you believe that? And four families are having a snowball confrontation at the town square about who made the best snowman. And is a snowwoman eligible for the contest? Something about being politically correct. What the heck's politics got to do with snowmen . . . women?" Buck spread his arms. "What's wrong with these people?" A green chunk of candy landed on his head and he rolled his eyes up to try and see as it dripped on to his nose. "All they do is fight."

Case said, "With Santa on the lam the natives are restless. They need to let off steam." He grabbed Holly's hand and said to Buck, "We'll run snowman interference, you get Willa and take on the sledders. If Brinch sees the town like this, we're finished."

Holly watched another torrent of candy zing through the air. How could all this happen? Handling the situation herself went out the window. More like it went out with candy, sleds, and reindeer. "Eugene's on the scavenger hunt. Dorothy promised to keep him busy, but they'll be back soon enough and we have to get the town under control."

Buck hustled back to the door, dodging three kids bombarding three others. Parents congregated along the perimeters, content to let the food fight run its course. Dobbs sat cross-legged on the counter beside his cash register, glassy-eyed, shaking his head, eating the chocolate chips out of the cookies and throwing the rest on the floor. The true sign of a baker pushed to his limit. Holly said, "Think he's going to be okay?"

"No one's getting hurt, nothing's broken. Messy, but not terminal." Holly snagged her coat and they darted their way through the chaos then stepped outside to the blessed quiet of winter. The town square twinkled with lights and snowballs. At least they weren't sticky. She pointed. "Turned over picnic tables as barricades to hide behind. I'll use the divide-and-conquer strategy to straighten this out."

"I?"

"As in me. It's one thing I can handle alone right now.

There's a picnic table in the middle. I'll stand on it and tell them to stop."

Case grinned, crinkling the scar at the corner of his left eye from when he'd slid into home plate in the high school playoffs. What a day. The town hero. There were other lines now, little ones from peering at the landscape while flying into so many sunsets and rises. An aviator's appearance and handsome as any flyboy cliché.

"Sweet cakes," he said. "They're gong to annihilate you. Let me go in and—"

"Hey, they've got to respect Christmas . . . goodwill toward all, peace on earth, merry gentlemen. I'm the mayor, dammit! An elected official and you have cows waiting, though I really appreciate you trying to help at the candy shop." And if she kept being with him like this she'd die a slow death when he left all over again.

He put up the hood on her jacket and tucked a strand of hair behind her ear, making her feel cared for and cherished. "You take my breath away, Holly Green."

He kissed her, his lips warm and sweet, his fingers on her face filling her with a happiness she didn't want to feel but it settled in anyway and wasn't keen on budging. "Why do you have this effect on me?"

"Because we're in sync . . . usually."

"Why couldn't I be in sync with Harry from the market or Jim from the post office?"

He kissed her again. "Stay right here. I don't want you hurt." Still under the influence of Case McGill's touch, she didn't get what he intended to do until he ran toward the snowballs, jumped up on the picnic table and waved his arms. "Stop. This is crazy and—"

A snowball smashed against his forehead, then more on his head and back and legs, covering him in white polka dots. She ran and climbed up on the table beside him, waving her arms. "I'm the mayor of Chistmastown and I forbid you all from having a war here over snowmen and—" A snowball hit her chin, then her knee, then her butt. "Ouch!"

Pulling Holly with him, Case jumped off the table and dove underneath, snowballs flying around them. She panted, "They're maniacs! All of them. Certifiably insane."

"I thought they'd listen this time since there are more adults than children here, but I think the adults are worse."

"You could have escaped all this. You're supposed to be over in cow heaven."

"Don't think I'd jump right to heaven. Now this . . ." His cool lips slid over hers. "Is a lot closer to heaven, even if it is under a picnic table." He rolled her on top of him, the snow crunching under him. Laughing in spite of the pandemonium she kissed the end of his nose. How many times had she thought about them being together in the snow like this, though a picnic table in a snowball fight was a new twist.

"This is my idea of goodwill to man, at least this man." His fingers slowly tangled into her hair as if she belonged to him and no one else. His even breath was warm and seductive on her cheeks, then her ear and neck as she planted kisses along his jawline, the stubble against her sensitive lips a real turn-on. Then again, everything with Case was a turn-on.

"How long can we count on the snowball fight lasting? I think under here is the only secluded non-nutty place in town."

"Except it's cold."

His eyes lit with passion that ignited too easily between them and she could feel his erection against her. She wanted more than pressing between layers of clothes. She wanted skin to skin, him in her and not just for a third time. She wanted him with her forever. But how? And since there was no answer, couldn't she just get over him?

"I can think of a terrific way to generate serious heat. Probably melt the snow right from under us and it's a lot more fun than shoveling it out of the way."

"Anything exposed to this weather is sure to shrivel."

His eyes devoured her. "Oh, sweetheart, with you around there's never any chance of that happening." He kissed her again, the sweet sensation of his tongue suggesting what he wanted.

A snowball skimmed under the table smacking Holly on the side of the head. "We have to leave. They're closing in."

He exhaled a deep breath. "Seems that leaving is all we ever do. I want us to be together. I hope you believe that. And I know you want it, too. I just have to figure out how to make it happen."

She put her fingers to his lips. "Destiny takes us in opposite directions. Or sometimes it's a Cessna 172 that does the taking. If we choose each other instead, how long would we be happy with that decision without becoming resentful? We can't live a life of compromises and ditch all dreams."

A snowball landed on Case's face and she swiped it away then kissed the remains from his eyes, cheeks, and lips, memorizing every detail that she'd have to live without. "We're going to get out of here and you're going back to the hotel, right?"

"And what are you going to do?"

"Lament the fact that Christmastown doesn't have riot gear? This place is bozo!" She pointed to the flashing red and green strobe lights mounted on the front of the sleigh that served as a police cruiser as it made its way down Jingle Bell Lane. "He knows if you've been bad or good so be good for goodness sake" blared from the speakers. "Look, they stopped throwing snowballs."

"Guess no one wants to be bad for Santa!"

Holly crawled out from under the picnic table, her nose suddenly meeting one snow-encrusted leg, then another one. She peered up at a man who looked more like Bigfoot than a tourist. He said, "So, who wins the snowman competition?"

Holly stood and dusted herself off and the man nodded at the four snowmen and one snowwoman standing to the side. "You're the mayor. Pick one. Our family or theirs?" He pointed to the others gathering around. "Ours has real charcoal eyes and a carrot nose. Do you know what we had to do to get those things? Good thing Merry Market was unlocked. We left money on the counter."

"Well, the snowpeople are all great," Holly said in a hurry before the other families described the attributes of their snowmen and the battle royal raged again. "I'll award the prize tomorrow morning, Christmas morning, when we all gather back here for the a celebration starting with the Christmas Day parade."

"Santa will be here?" A little boy chirped, jumping up and down. "He's really coming. He's just late 'cause of the snow, right?"

"Well—" Holly stammered 'til all the children from the families jumped up and down, suddenly more focused on Santa coming and having fun together than bombarding each other with snowballs.

Case said under his breath, "Santa should be member of the UN."

"But it won't last when they realize we can't get Santa and a plane here unless it has skis," Holly whispered back then said aloud to the families, "There's great hot chocolate over at the Gingerbread House bakery. I bet you're all cold and need to get warmed up."

The families shuffled off and Buck climbed out of the sleigh and hustled over. "Have you seen that Brinch fellow and Dorothy? The scavenger hunt's over . . . well, not exactly over since the families are arguing about who has the best finds. But it's been nearly two hours and no one's seen either of them. The sheriff and I have been riding the streets and the town council has combed the rest of the town. Nothing. Think he got lost in a snowdrift or something?"

Holly put her hands over her face and groaned. "Great. REVIEWER FREEZES IN CHRISTMASTOWN is not the publicity we need."

Buck added, "Especially when added to the headline that reads Santa Skips Christmastown. More proof that we should have done Halloweentown. No one would know if a ghost came or not."

Chapter Four

No more ghosts, Case thought as he caught sight of Savannah Sue perched on the edge of the snowy picnic table, legs crossed, puffing smoke rings into the air. She pointed to her fuchsia wheeled suitcase and said, "I'm all packed and ready, flyboy. Did you get my ashes yet? Last time I checked they were still sitting on the mantel. What are you waiting for? Christmas? Well, Christmas has done arrived. Time to get with the program."

"I'm working on it," Case said.

"Working on what?" Buck asked.

"Finding Brinch, that's what I'm working on. Do you have a list of the stuff needed from the scavenger hunt? That might give us a clue where he is."

Willa pulled a paper from her jacket pocket. "The answers could be a million things."

Sue puffed another perfect *O.* "Don't know what all the fuss is about. That snooty Brinch guy and Dorothy are at the market in the soap aisle."

"No kidding," Case said and Buck said, "No, I'm not kidding. This is the list, right here in front of me."

Case took a paper. He had to think of some way to link it to the market because telling everyone he was communing with a ghost and that's how he knew where Brinch was wouldn't do. "Number seven says *something from a Christmas song*. Bet they went to the market for . . . for Tide. Like tidings of good cheer."

Sue said, "That's two soaps, Tide and Cheer. Good work, flyboy."

"Tide like laundry detergent?" Buck asked and Holly added, "I think it's tidings of comfort and joy."

"Close enough. Let's give it a try." Case grabbed Holly's hand and said to Buck, "Get the sheriff and Harry. It's his store. And find the rest of the council. They're all out looking for Brinch. This is one situation tonight that's going to turn out okay and they all need to be there. I want to make up for some of the trouble I caused."

Sue gave a little finger wave. "Don't you go forgetting my ashes now, you hear?" And Holly plodded after Case saying, "You seem awfully confident of something that's really a long shot. Why the market? Tide . . . tidings. What in the world? Not much of a connection."

"I got a feeling he's there. And when we all find the old boy, he'll realize we take care of each other in this town and watch out for each other. It's a perfect theme to go with his Christmas article and get his brain off the Santa scenario."

They crossed the street, the sheriff sleigh following with bells jingling. Willa, Harry, and the others of the council joining the procession through the snowy night. If a bright star suddenly appeared over the market it wouldn't have surprised him at all. Holly said, "But why is Brinch gone so long? Two hours?"

"You heard the man, he's the master of this scavenger stuff and the market is perfect scavenger territory. Probably looking for just the right things. That snowman guy found coal and carrots."

They tramped up onto the wood porch and Case tried the doorknob. "See, it's open."

"But the lights are out," Buck said and Case added, "He probably doesn't want to give away his perfect scavenger finds."

They all paraded inside with Harry flipping on the fluorescents and Case calling, "Eugene? Dorothy? We're all worried about you. Where are you?" He headed for the aisle with the string of detergent bottles perched on the top shelf. "The hunt's over. Are you two ready for—"

"Yikes!" Dorothy yelped as she jumped up naked from an inflated sled in a Christmas display. She snagged a plastic elf to hide behind while Brinch scrambled to his feet grabbing a wreath that flipped a switch. Santa and the elves jerked into action, and lights strobed as a tooting train circled overhead to a chorus of "Rockin' Around the Christmas Tree."

Brinch held the wreath at his waist, attempting to hide his obvious condition. The man needed a tanning bed bad and the gathering crowd at the window probably thought that, too, plus a little more. Parents plastered their hands over kids' eyes and hustled them away.

Dorothy tried to make herself small behind the elf. "We were looking for chestnuts for the scavenger hunt then the chest and nut part sort of got the better of us and . . . Well, here we are and I think my reputation's ruined." She looked adoringly at Eugene. "I just couldn't resist the man."

Eugene plucked his coat off the floor and shrugged it on without letting go of the wreath. "How did you know where we were?"

Savannah Sue suddenly appeared sitting in inflatable Santa's lap. "Because I told them, you knucklehead. I knew this would be all kinds of fun and heaven knows this place could use a little."

Holly took off her jacket and handed it to Dorothy and Case said, "We had the scavenger paper and figured a lot of those items could be found here."

Eugene gave an arrogant snort. "I know what this is and it

has nothing to do with games, it's an underhanded trap to discredit me as a reporter. It's a ruthless trick."

"Eugene," Dorothy said. "It was just the two of us in here alone. Why would I trick you?"

"To get me to withhold my article, of course. You all come here and find me in a compromising position and intend to use it as blackmail unless I change my review." He stood tall, holding his coat tight around him. "Well I can tell you right now that's not going to happen!"

"What!" Dorothy's face reddened and her eyes went to thin slits. "I am not a compromising position, Eugene, and this town is not into blackmail. I thought we had a special connection and not just the kind we did in the Christmas display. I thought we meant something to each other and now you're saying I tricked you and planned on us getting caught? How can you think I'd plan this?"

She grabbed the wreath and whapped him over the head with it then scooped up her clothes and stomped down the aisle to the back of the store. "I'm getting dressed and I hope you rot in hell, Eugene," she called over her shoulder. "You're nothing but an arrogant pig!"

Brinch held his coat tighter, bits of plastic holly and evergreen tangled in his hair. "You all will be hearing from my lawyer."

"About what?" Holly folded her arms.

"Entrapment."

"I hate you, Eugene Brinch," came Dorothy's voice. "I really do. Next time you have sex I hope you freeze your balls off and they get eaten by the cat."

Case wasn't about to touch that line but he added, "I don't think you need any help in the embarrassment department, Brinch. You're doing a fine job on your own."

He snarled, "You all just wait till you read my review of this little town of yours in my magazine. No one will ever come here again; I can promise you that."

"And I know just how to give your article some real local behind the scenes color," Holly said. "Christmas Eve in the town poky. That should make an interesting addition."

"What?" Eugene's eyes bulged and his jaw dropped.

"You heard me. I think you should be jailed for indecent exposure. It will make your article more of a revenge piece than actual fact."

"You can't put me in jail. I'll press charges. I am the press! I demand my freedom."

Holly shrugged. "I think the town's doing the pressing because you're the one without clothes on and half the people here witnessed the event." She nodded to the picture window, which had more noses pressed against it than before.

Sheriff Tate snagged Eugene's hand and snapped the cuffs on one wrist then the other, enjoying the ritual way too much. "Your sleigh awaits, Mr. Reviewer." Case gathered up Eugene's clothes and took them to the checkout stand. "Paper or plastic?"

"I'll get you all for this!"

Case stuffed the wads of material into a paper bag. "Merry Christmas and remember to recycle."

Brinch jammed his bare feet into his boots then Tate ushered him out of the store and into the sleigh, the crowd dispersing as the sleigh jingled off. Seeing someone hauled off to jail was business-as-usual in the city.

Case said, "So much for the scavenger hunt. Not exactly what I planned."

"To tell the truth," Buck said. "That's the whole damn trouble, you planned it and the situation in Christmastown's gone from bad to worse. In fact every time you have an idea things get more complicated around here."

"It's all my fault," Dorothy said as she shuffled down the aisle. "I let Brinch get to me. We liked to talk about writing and books and travel. I thought he truly cared for me. All he cares about is himself and that stupid magazine. I'm a love struck idiot."

Willa said, "You're not the only woman bamboozled by love around here." She cut her eyes to Holly. "Case is the one to blame. First he brings us a coffin, then his ideas of an old-fashioned Christmas turn into more trouble, and now that reviewer guy is in the poky and going to write even worse things about us." She waved her hands in the air. "We're ruined, I tell you, ruined." She said to Case, "Your parents would be mortified if they could see what you did to this town."

Savannah Sue said, "Oh, Willa, for crying out loud, put a sock in it."

"Hey," said Holly. "Our problems are not because of Case. He was trying to help and he sure didn't bring on the snow storm."

Case turned to Holly. "I'm doing more to ruin your credibility than help. I'm butting out of your life and this time it is for good. I didn't come to cause you problems."

"There!" Holly said as Case walked off. "You got what you all wanted. Are you happy now? I hope so but I'm so mad at you I could spit!"

"Because we ragged on your boyfriend?" Willa huffed.

"Because he came up with good ideas while you all sat around whining and bellyaching." But the real reason was because they ragged on her boyfriend. The two of them may not ever be together but she cared what happened to him and wasn't about to have him lambasted by the council because they were looking for a scapegoat.

She said, "I'm still the mayor around here and here's what we're going to do. It's nearly midnight so we're getting the townies together and having candlelight caroling at the town square just like we did back in the day when life was hard and before we got to be Christmastown. If the stupid tourists don't want to take part, well, that's too damn bad. They can stay in their rooms and watch Letterman for all I care. This is still our town and we live here and have families and we'll celebrate any way we want and for sure we don't need a guy in a Santa suit to make it happen. Never did before, don't need him now."

"Jingle bells, jingle bells, jingle all the way" mixed with swirling snow as Case pushed open the sheriff's office door. No one was around except for Brinch pacing his cell. "What the hell do you want? Wanna cause more problems for me and everyone else around here?"

Case took the keys from the sheriff's desk. "That's no way to talk to the guy who's springing you from incarceration." Case opened the door but Brinch just stood there. His beady eyes beadier. "Why are you doing this? Give that Sheriff Tate fellow another reason to add to my rap sheet?"

"Around here it's naughty-or-nice sheets." Case took out his wallet and slapped bills on the sheriff's desk. "I cleared you getting out with Tate. That money's for the fine. Now you get to do your part. I've known Dorothy all my life and she likes you for some reason none of us can comprehend. Go apologize and tell her that you care for her and want her in your life."

"Apologize? Me? I'm Eugene Brinch and I don't need anyone, especially a country bumpkin from Virginia." His brows rose to his receding hairline and Case grabbed the lapel of his coat and hauled him out of the cell.

"You were a horse's ass back at the market and Dorothy is the best thing that's ever coming your way and you know it in spite of all your blabbering. Doing the wild ride in the market storefront is not something Dorothy does every day. She's a fine, respectable woman who happens to be crazy about you. Go find her, be nice and set things straight before it's too late."

Brinch stuck his nose in the air. "And if I refuse? Are you going to beat me up?"

"I don't have to because you'll be doing that to yourself for the rest of your life. So, what's it going to be? Stay here and wait to call your lawyers so you can make Christmastown look bad or go after Dorothy and get some of that Christmas spirit you write about?"

Case let Brinch go and he folded his arms. "I can still do a scathing report *and* get Dorothy."

"This is her town and you dumping all over it will tell her that being vindictive is more important than she is. Trust me on this, Eugene. Choosing your job over your woman is not the way to be happy and once you make the wrong decision making it right is damn tough, maybe even impossible."

"But—"

"You've got one last chance here." Case stepped aside and pointed to door. "Go, dammit, before I lock you back up, bury these keys in the snow, and they don't find them 'til spring! Could get real lonely in that cell. Aren't you tired of being lonely, Eugene?"

A spark of understanding slowly lit Brinch's eyes and he snagged his hat and dashed for the door. When it closed Case felt a cold breeze at his back and caught a whiff of cigarette. Sue sat on the corner of the sheriff's desk. "Well now, honey, that was just about the most precious thing I ever did see." She blinked moist eyes. "Makes me long for my Percival all the more." She gave Case a sideways look. "So when are you getting my ashes and when are we getting the blazes out of here? I want to be ready to go as soon as the snow stops."

"After waiting twenty years a few more hours can't hurt."

"Now those are the words of a man who's never really been in love."

"Hey, I was engaged." The *was* part making him feel sick at heart.

"Well, it must not have took like it should. Every minute's a terrible hurt when you're not with your darling man." She winked at Case. "Or woman. From what I've seen you need to think about that long and hard. Just do your thinking after you deliver me and my urn to Savannah." She took a puff of cigarette, her form fading into the swirl of smoke.

"Damn, I'd wish you'd quit doing that, gives me the creeps. And if you don't give up those cigarettes you'll . . ." He swallowed the *croak* word. Holy crap, he was giving medical advice to a ghost . . . a ghost who had better instincts on being in love than he ever did.

Case skirted the expanding crowd of candlelight and carolers singing "I'm dreaming of a white Christmas." Well that dream sure as hell came true in spades. Looking more beautiful than ever, Holly stood next to Buck. Brinch had Dorothy at his side and gave Case a subtle thumbs-up and a wink. Wink? Brinch? Wasn't there a story about someone's heart growing three sizes at Christmas?

Dang it all. Brinch had Dorothy, Sue had Percy, and he had a Cessna 172 and a hitchhiking ghost. Something was wrong with this picture. He approached Holly's house from the back so as not to draw attention to his urn snatching. He gazed at the second floor to the cracked bathroom window where he was headed when he went flying off the roof the first time.

"Holy Hannah," came Sue's voice beside him. "Do I have to do everything around here? Forget the window, Jungle Jim. Key's under the third plastic snowman on the left. Just lift his foot."

Case let himself in then took off his boots. The Christmas tree—in the corner where the Greens always put it—sat dark, the train he'd given Holly parked on the track circling the bottom. He plugged in the lights and set the train in motion, listening to the familiar clickity-clack of the cars.

Sue said, "I remember the night you two got engaged here. Christmas Eve just like now. You put the ring box on the train and stopped it in front of Holly. A little corny for my taste but it sure enough got the job done."

Sue plunked herself down next to her urn and pointed to it.

"Okey-dokey. I'm all twitterpaited. Here we go. All you have to do now is pick up this here thing, put it in the plane and we can get our ashes out of here." She giggled. "A little urn humor."

"Savannah Sue, out of this world comedian and bossy female all rolled into one."

"Who's a comedian?" came Holly's voice from behind him.

He spun around. Oh shit! "Uh . . ."

Holly's brows drew together into one long pissed-off line. "And who's Sue and do you mind telling me why is she suddenly making your life so good? What's wrong with *me*? You've never told *me* I'm out of this world."

"Nothing's wrong with you . . . babe." Maybe the babe thing would help.

"Don't you babe me. You have a woman in here. Another woman! In my house!"

Case shook his head. "No, absolutely not. I didn't bring her, she followed me all by herself—"

"Oh my God, there is a *she*!" Holly ground her teeth. "Did you think I'd be out all night taking care of things and that's why you brought her here? Moo room not good enough for you and your bimbo? I'm going to kill you within an inch of your life, Case McGill! When I said move on I didn't mean move on here right now this very minute. I'm not sure I meant move on anywhere."

"Well, that's damn good news."

"No, it's not. I'm trying to kick you to the curb and it's not working and now you have another woman." She puffed out a big breath. "Well, now that I think about it, maybe it is good in a pathetic sort of way. Maybe now I can get over you."

Sue wailed, "Heavenly days and Lord have mercy! I don't believe this. Another minute and we would have been out the door and on our way with the urn tucked under your arm. But are we? Pity sakes, no! I'm still here, the urn's still here, and nothing's changed. How in blazes did Rome ever get built? I can't get a freaking urn off a mantel."

Case looked at Sue and growled, "Will you just shut up for a minute."

"Shut up!" Holly yelped. "You're telling me to shut up!"

Case said to Sue, "Go take a walk or whatever mode of transportation you use but ship yourself out of here till we get this straightened out."

Holly slapped her palm to her forehead. "Now you're tossing me out of my house? You're making this getting over you easier and easier."

Case said to Holly, "Not you, the ghost! She's sitting on your mantel."

"Oh, for the love of Christmas! And I'm Grandma Moses sitting in a rocking chair!"

Case held up his hands and pulled in a deep breath. "Just listen to me for one lousy minute without going ballistic. There really is a ghost, I swear. That's who I'm talking to. Her name is Sue."

"Sue? That's all the better name you can come up with? This is the most pathetic explanation I've ever heard in all my life. I thought ghosts were named Albert and Harvey and Marley."

"Albert was an angel and Harvey an imaginary rabbit."

"Close enough! And which ghost, tell me that? Christmas past? Christmas present? Tiny Tim on Sue's shoulder?"

"I think she said something about the future because she wants to spend her future Christmases with Percy, he's her lover, and she has a pink feather boa thing on her shoulders."

"What have you been smoking!"

Case raked back his hair then pointed to the mantel. "That urn that you think is your beloved uncle Duke is really Savannah Sue. Best I can tell she's a stripper from Georgia who came here to entertain the squirrel boys and croaked and—"

Sue said, "Do you have to go and use the *c* word? I hate the *c* word. Dearly departed works just fine, thank you very much."

Case ignored her and continued, "When the morgue burned, her urn got switched with Duke's and he's in Savannah now on some mantel there."

Holly gave him the you-think-I'm-stupid eye roll then yanked back the curtain. "You've got a woman stashed around here somewhere. I know it. I can smell her. She's a smoker."

"See, that's her. That's Sue."

Sue floated down from the mantel. "I am plum tired to death of this. Everything is Holly, Holly, Holly. What about me? My urn? My Percy? Did you forget I have unfulfilled needs that require tending to?" She waved her cigarette in the air. "Well, piss and vinegar. The only way I'm going to get my problem fixed is to fix yours. If I don't get you and Holly together you'll be fretting over each other and I'll never get home. You'll fly off and leave me and my urn here for another twenty years. So get on with it, flyboy."

"Get on with what?"

"Leaving!" Holly said then Sue said, "Take Holly in your arms and kiss her, and for crying out loud do it like you mean it so we can get this show on the road. I get you two together, I get Percy and me together. That's the way it is."

Case glanced at Sue and he gave her a little grin. "Good idea about the kissing but it's not going to work in the long run." And before Holly could say another word he snagged her into his arms, his mouth devouring hers. She tasted of peppermint and chocolate and he thought about the first time they kissed under the mistletoe and how much he didn't want this to be the last time.

Holly gazed up at him, mouth parted, her lips warm and wet from his. Bells from the town hall rang out loud as his lips grazed over hers again, slower this time, more seductive. "Merry Christmas, Holly." He scooped her up into his arms.

"That's it, keep going," Sue encouraged 'til Holly said, "No! This is not happening again and with me there always seems to be an again with you."

Sue moaned, burying her face in her boa. "Love is so wasted on the young and alive."

Holly pushed at Case's chest and he nearly dropped her. "I can't keep doing this."

Sue said, "Oh, sure you can, honey. And I'm betting you do it really well. Actually, it's easy for women. They just show up and men take it from there."

Holly slid out of Case's arms. "You confuse the hell out of my life. I say I'm done with you and then you kiss me and my knees go weak and my eyes cross and my brain melts to a blob of goo and I forget everything but your kissing me and holding me and—"

"I do all that with one kiss?"

"Yes, blast it all." She stood straight. "I'm going to be strong. Besides, you've already moved on. You have another woman!"

Sue said, "When it comes to good sex, strong is vastly overrated. Just don't stand there, flyboy. Come up with some way to keep your woman."

"I'm thinking, I'm thinking," Case said and Holly replied, "What about? Your darling Sue?"

Three-way conversations sucked. "I'm still trying to figure out a way you can be mayor, I can have my business, and we can be together."

"You say that just to get into my pants." She hitched up her jeans. "Well it's not working, the pants are staying on. You're going back to your cow room and I'm going with you to get another wreath for the market since Dorothy demolished the last one over Brinch's head." She peered up at Case. "You're staying with your ghost or cute cupcake or whoever she is and I'm leaving with my wreath and that's the way it's going to be."

"Okay, if there was another woman, and I'm not saying there is, where is she now?"

"How the heck should I know? Out the back door, up the chimney, whatever." Holly threw one of his boots at him, barely missing his head. The next caught him square in the chest. She tramped out the door and Case sat on the edge of the chair. "Her aim's getting pretty good. If I stay around long enough she could go semi-pro."

Sue said, "You kissed her right nicely but she's a stubborn one. So I guess desperate times call for desperate measures."

Case cut his gaze to the mantel but Sue was gone. Okay, that was a good thing. He was ghosted-out for one night, had his fill of illogical explanations that got him into tons of trouble with no way out. He yanked on his boots and headed for the inn. The streets stood empty, his footsteps crunching snow the only sound. Everyone was cuddling in their beds and probably not with visions of sugarplums so much as with significant others they loved. Except, for him there was no cuddling, no Holly, not even a damn sugarplum, whatever the hell that was, and a lonely and really ugly bed.

He entered the inn to a fading fire in the stone hearth, snuffed candles on the mantel, and the lingering aroma of cedar and pine cones. Least it was quiet . . . until he heard Holly scream from upstairs.

Fuck! A missing ghost and a screaming woman in the dead of night were never a good mix. Melanie ran to the counter. "Holy Mary, now what?"

"Kids playing hide-and-seek. Nothing to worry about."

Melanie banged her head on the desktop. "Will this night never end?"

"Not soon enough." Case walked down the hall and when he got out of Melanie's sight he ran to his room and tore open the door. Holly stood dead still, white face, huge eyes staring to the top of the stack of boxes. He drew up next to her.

"Couldn't find the wreaths? Is that what's got you upset?" He hoped but knew better.

Holly pointed. "Woman. Big hair, pink boa. Cigarette. Great silver shoes." Holly cut her gaze to Case. "And then she suddenly wasn't there at all! I need therapy, Case. Lots and lots of therapy."

"Don't waste your hard-earned money, no one will believe you and you'll spend next Christmas in the loony bin. I've thought about this."

The door slammed shut behind them and Holly jumped into his arms. "I'm having a heart attack." She shivered. "You planned this, didn't you? Maybe . . . I hope. Is my hair standing straight up?"

"Just a little patch in the middle, the rest is pretty tame."

"There really is a ghost?"

"Cross my heart and hope not to die." He backed to the door and tried the knob.

"Locked?"

"Like Fort Knox. I'm betting this is Sue's little way of getting us together. She thinks if that happens I'll stop obsessing over you and get her and her urn home to Savannah and Percy."

Holly rested her head on his shoulder and he enfolded her in his arms. "We're locked in a cow room by a hostile ghost on Christmas."

"Don't know if I'd go straight to hostile but cantankerous, pushy, a little horny, and a first-rate buttinski works and her singing strips wallpaper. Don't ever get that woman singing." He stroked Holly's back, loving the feel of her close to him on Christmas, just like old times.

"We could pound on the door till someone comes and lets us out."

"And tell Melanie what? A ghost locked us in here? If Brinch catches that it'll be another nail in the Christmastown coffin. We're meant to be together, Holly. Even a ghost knows it."

"A ghost with ulterior motives and I can't believe I just said that. Every time I swear you off something happens to put us back together, though I got to admit this is a little extreme."

"It's a sign of some kind. We want to break up and can't seem to make it happen. And now we have a whole night locked together in a room. A really ugly room, but a room." He kissed her, longer this time, and the really great part was she kissed him back.

Chapter Five

Holly's body melted into his, making him warm as a sandy beach in July.

"I must be crazy to want you this much. It doesn't make sense and you ruin me for other guys, you know. You're always ready for me, wanting me, making me feel as if I'm the only woman in the world who can make you happy. No other man does that, Case. Not even close."

"Because you're the only woman for me, Holly," he whispered in her hair while he peeled off her sweater and kicked off his boots.

He backed her to the bed. "This thing is going to look a hell of a lot better with you on it." He sat on the edge and tasted her nipple though the red lace of her bra. The hard bud against his tongue reassured him she wanted this as much as he did. Her body quivered and she tangled her fingers into his hair, her soft moan of pure pleasure filling the room and his heart. "We're going too fast, Case."

He took her other nipple and he felt her sag against him, her arms trembling. "We were never good at slow. Better at charging full steam ahead."

She tipped his head. "And you give great steam."

He laughed then tugged off his jeans, watching Holly do the same. "You've got the best Santa suit in North America."

"Case, I got news." She flashed a wicked smile and twitched her hips, the white fur accenting all her terrific attributes. "It's about to get better." She flung off the bra and garter belt, leaving only the fishnets. She threw her arms in the air and did a little dance on her tip-toes that made him laugh. "Ta da!"

"Damn, you are the sexiest woman alive."

"Since the other woman in your life right now is dead I'll take that only as a sort-of compliment." She laughed and slid her arms around his neck, knocking them back onto the bed. "I've never felt more desirable in my life than right now laying naked across you in only my stockings."

"My woman. Remember that. Only for me." He rolled her over and kissed her neck then the little place behind her ear that drove her wild. He grabbed his jeans from the floor and fished a condom from his wallet then covered himself. "Hold on to me, Holly. Make love with me."

Her eyes went to dark emerald. "I'm just trying to hold on period," she gasped, her face flushed as she wrapped her legs around his middle, the silky fishnets on his skin tantalizing as hell.

"Oh, God, Case!" Her head tipped back and her breasts strained against his chest, the sensation making him climax with her as she yelled his name. No matter what happened for the rest of his life or who else he met, he'd never be this consumed by the love of a woman again. It was impossible to care for anyone more than he cared for Holly.

"How can it be so great all the time?" she panted, her breathing far from normal. "I keep thinking, oh this time will just be so-so, no fireworks or sizzle, just sex." She swallowed then peeked up at him. "It's never just so-so. Lovemaking with you is . . . earth-shattering."

"Just think what it would be like if we practiced. Damn, I'd like to practice with you, for about fifty years or more or until we both died from exhaustion."

She studied him for a moment, her eyes suddenly sad. "All day I've hoped the snow would stop but now . . . The sky around here should be all snowed out soon. And then . . . I don't want to think about then, Case. How are we going to let go all over again?"

He rolled off her and flipped onto his back, staring at the cow Christmas tree painted on the ceiling. What was there to say to Holly? *Hey, baby, we're together forever. I know how to make this right.* Except that was a damn lie, he hadn't a clue how to get them together. He went into the bathroom, the motion-activated light sending out a long low mooooo. He could hear Holly giggling and he laughed too, breaking the tension. He came back to Holly wrapped in a blanket all soft and warm and too inviting for a guy and gal with no future. "Maybe I should go."

She gave him a lopsided grin. "To where? We're corralled in this pasture and if we break down the door Melanie will have a lot of questions we do not want to answer. So, what ever shall we do with the rest of the night, Case? What was that about practice?"

He sat on the end of the bed. "And how do we get over all this tomorrow? Wave some magic wand and everything goes back the way it was before I landed?" He leaned forward resting his forearms on his thighs. "I'm messing up your life, Holly, not only by us getting involved but that I've made things worse in town, the town you helped build, the town my parents loved. If Brinch gets his way, Christmastown's going belly up. He may be a jerk but he has a lot of influence."

"I don't feel worse, and this was not your doing. I'm happy, Case. Right now I'm really happy and even Eugene Brinch can't ruin that." She sat up, opened the blanket she'd wrapped around herself then wrapped it around him too, her warm sexy body snuggling close to his. The hair on his chest rubbing against her arms, getting her all hot again, his back against her breasts turning her on more. "It's Christmas Day. Anything's possible on Christmas Day. And we're together now. Nothing can be better than that."

Morning sunlight streamed in through the Guernsey curtains but Holly lay on her side in the cow bed trying to get up the courage to look over at Case . . . or no Case. She did the chicken thing and felt for him but there was no warm body, just winter-cold sheets. "Damn," she muttered into the empty room feeling a hole the size of Virginia in her heart.

"At least he left a note."

That voice! That cigarette smoke! "Yikes!" She pulled the covers over her head. "Go away." Holly lifted a corner and peeked out at Sue sitting on top of the boxes. "Are you really a ghost or a reaction to too much sex?"

"Now I ask you, honey, is there really such a thing as too much sex?" She waved her cigarette holder. "You need to shake a leg and get yourself up. The note Case left says *I'm still thinking*. What in almighty Georgia does I'm still thinking mean? We need action here, girl, not cerebral down-time. Go get your man. I didn't do all this for my health." She laughed. "Too late for that."

"I like the boa. Goes great with the sequin dress."

Sue fluffed her hair. "When you become a member of the dearly departed society you get to choose one outfit. Except for Cleopatra. That little hussy can talk her way out of anything and she keeps using up all the blue eye shadow. But we're losing focus. You need to find Case and have him put my urn on his blasted plane that's still here. I told him I removed the fuel pump but I lied. Wouldn't know a fuel pump from a kidney operation."

"That means he's not gone?"

"And that would be the correct take on *still here*. Now go

and find him and tell him you want him forever. That should free up some of his brain cells drowning in testosterone overload and then he just might remember my urn!"

Holly flipped onto her back, moaned and put the pillow over her face.

"This is not shaking a leg, girl. What in tarnation are you doing now?"

"Nothing's solved. Me saying I love Case is only part of the situation. Case isn't staying in Christmastown; I'm not going to Savannah."

"You know, you'd love Savannah. No snow. Trust me, this white Christmas thing is so overrated. We have palm trees, pralines—"

"Palmetto bugs the size of small dogs."

"But the important thing is you'd have Case." Sue sat at the end of the bed. "Isn't that what really matters most or is it being mayor here in nutville?"

Holly gave her an evil look.

"So, who do you love, girl? The town or Case?"

Holly wrapped the sheet around her, stood on the bed and grinned like a Christmas elf. "Well, when you put it like that . . . I love Case!"

Sue puffed a smoke ring into the air. "As the young people say . . . duh! Pardon me if I don't go cross-eyed with surprise. Now for the love of Percy, just go find Case and let's get going."

"I need to drop off my resignation as mayor then pack. I'll wait for Case in the plane."

"With my urn! Lord have mercy, don't forget the urn. If I ever get to Savannah it will be a bloomin' miracle."

Holly never threw clothes in a suitcase so fast in her life. She ran down the steps of her house, bouncing the luggage behind her on each riser. She had her hand on the front doorknob and heard, "Wait!"

Looking to the living room she spied Sue perched on the mantel. "Forget something?"

"Right, the urn."

Sue faced south. "Percy, my love, I'm coming, baby. It ain't easy but I'm getting there."

Holly went into the closet and tossed out shoes, boots and an old tennis racket till she came to—"Dad's bowling bag. That should work." She dumped out the ball with a solid thud.

"No . . . you can't mean . . . After twenty long years in the wrong place I'm returning home to Savannah in a red bowling bag? It smells."

"I'll use Frebreze. It's the best I can do on short notice." Holly dropped in the urn and zipped. "If Dad sees it, he'll want to know what's going on. I'll have to think of something." She looked around. "Where is Dad, anyway?"

"Having coffee with his cronies over at Sweets and Treats. They spent the night helping Dodd get his place back in shape and then de-stressed with their good friend Jack Daniels. But right now they and the rest of the town are congregating at the square." She pointed out the window. "Look, see. I swear by the saints, if they're off to sing one more Christmas song I'm going to puke."

"Maybe Case is there." Holly hoisted the bags and opened the door. "Holy cow . . . except I've had enough of cows . . . there are snow plows and salt trucks pulling up to the square. That's where everyone's headed."

"To kiss the drivers for getting them out of here. I can relate, too, except I think they're really going for the red van behind the trucks where Santa's passing out presents."

"It came! Oh my gosh, it really came. The Santa Express got here on wheels instead of wings, I don't believe it! This is fantastic." Holly tried to jump up and down but the bags were too heavy.

"Yeah, peachy. I'm going to let you deal with the guy in red. It's Millie's fiftieth d-day, that's dead day, and she's throwing a shindig down in the old morgue but, whatever you do, do not let that bowling bag out of your sight."

Sue faded into a swirl of a snow drift as Brinch crossed the street and Holly hauled her bags from the porch. Brinch said, "Well, little lady, you did it, you really got Santa here. I didn't think you could."

What she could do is whack him over the head for calling her little lady.

Dorothy hugged Eugene's arm. "I told him we had it planned like this all the time. Intended to make Santa's coming a surprise to everyone. Something special each year, that's what we're doing in Christmastown." She gave Holly a go-along-with-me-on-this look.

Brinch laughed. "I owe you and your town a huge apology." He swept his hand across the square. "It's just like you advertised. Wonderfully impressive in my book. My readers will love my glowing review and your lovely town." Brinch nodded at the bags. "More Christmas secrets." He eyed the bowling bag. "Mind if I take a little peek?"

Oh that would be interesting! "But then it wouldn't be a secret." She faked a toothy grin and crinkled her nose in a mischievous elf way.

Brinch laughed again then sauntered off with Dorothy as the sun broke through the clouds, making the snow dazzling and the town a winter wonderland like some Christmas card. It was the image she had in her brain when she first conceived Christmastown and now here it was in the flesh except for the snowplows, salt trucks, and urn-toting bowling bag.

She watched Santa hand out toys to the kids, CDs for the teens, scarves for the women and hats to the men. Not exactly from the list of things-wanted that every person turned in when they made reservations at Christmastown for December twenty-fifth but no one seemed to mind. They actually were enjoying the spirit of Christmas. Another big surprise compared to the antics of the night before.

After Santa handed out the last present Holly went to him and said in a low voice, "I can't believe you got here. Rent-a-Santa is like the post office with their neither rain nor snow nor gloom philosophy. Following the snowplows was complete genius."

Santa's eyes danced and he winked, crinkling a thin scar at the corner of his right eye making Holly gasp and drop both bags. "Case?"

"What do you want for Christmas, a new bowling ball? Who would have thought?"

"You did all this? How? When?"

"A little Christmastown redemption for the messes I caused."

"If kids weren't around here I'd tackle you to the ground and kiss you senseless. Instead I'm going to Savannah with you. Look." She held up her luggage. "All packed and ready to go. I love you, I want to be with you always. I resigned my position as mayor and—"

His eyes rounded. "No, no! Don't do that. Very bad idea."

Three little girls in pink hats and matching mittens ran up to Santa Case. "Come build a snowman with us, Santa." They tugged on his arms and he looked from Holly to the girls. "Uh, sure."

The kids dragged him off as Holly said, "You don't want me to go with you to Savannah."

"Absolutely not. It won't work; we both know it. Just enjoy the moment. This is all great. I have to go build a snowman. I'll catch up with you later," were his final words as the girls dragged him to the middle of the square.

What the heck? She wanted to say eat dirt and die, McGill, but that was not the thing to say to Santa with the whole town looking on. How could he not want her in Savannah? She was willing to give up Chistmastown, being mayor, her friends and family for him and to him this was all about making things right with the town!

Seething, she stomped her way to the mayor's office to get back the resignation letter when Buck burst through the door right behind her. "Wow, oh wow! This is some terrific day, little girl. Case is a blooming genius. Got the snowplows to clear the way here and not just down on the four-lane like they usually do."

"And what did he promise them? That they'd be together forever?"

Buck gave her a look that suggested she lost her mind. "I think he promised them a big Christmas breakfast over at the Sleigh Bells Inn. He saved the town, Holly. Brinch is smiling ear to ear and rewriting his whole blasted article. The council's thinking about naming a street after him . . . Case, not Brinch. Case McGill Lane. Should make his parents proud as all get-out. He hitched a ride with the snowplow boys and got to Christiansburg. One of his buddies from high school has a shop there and Case bought all the stuff with his own money then drove it here behind the plows. Genius, pure genius."

"A street, huh? Well, it's sure going to make his day."

Buck took her by the shoulders and looked her right in the eyes. "He did this all for you. It's you he loves."

"Guess again. I was going to go to Savannah with him, give up everything, even being mayor." She waved her resignation paper. "He turned me down. This is about him and this town and family pride. Not me."

"He's got something cooking, I know it. He did all this for you, Holly. It's what brought him here. I know you have reservations because he walked out on you but he's back. Yesterday, he could have taken a different flight path down the coast to get to Savannah but he didn't, he flew over Christmastown . . . Diehard. He could have landed in Tennessee but he didn't do that, either. He landed here to see you. To be with you."

Buck kissed her on the head. "You got a good guy in Case. He's here to make things right and not just with the town but you. Have a little Christmas spirit, girl. That's what you built this town on, isn't it?"

"I think I'm all spirited out in more ways than you can imagine."

Buck left and Holly sat on the edge of her desk and picked up the last wise man. Why couldn't she have been a wise woman and never gotten mixed up with Case to start with? She should have locked him in that hotel room and swallowed the key and avoided this whole thing! Except he was her guy, the one she thought of each night before she fell asleep and the first person she thought of when she woke. She loved him.

"Holly," Case said as he shoved open the door, tramping in with his big black boots, red hat perched on the back of his head and shoving his fluffy beard out of his mouth. "Why'd you leave? You're the mayor, you need to make a speech about Christmas and how wonderful it is that everyone's here, blah, blah, blah. You know the drill. Why aren't you on the square celebrating? Everything's perfect, just the way you wanted it. The way I wanted it to be for you." He came closer. "Except you don't look like everything's perfect."

"You're leaving and not taking me with you to Savannah. Doesn't sound too perfect to me, sounds like a rerun of past experiences."

"I'll be back."

"When? Two years, two months, and eleven days from now? When another snow storm hits?"

"I'm thinking closer to tonight. I have to get Billy Ray to his family and Savannah, Sue home to her Percy, but then I'm all yours."

"We've had this discussion 'til we're blue. There's nothing for you here. Running a shop is so not you, little model airplanes, plastic cows. And you told me straight out you don't want me in Savannah."

"Because Savannah is so not you. This is your town, you

saved it. And now I'm going to make a little stretch of it my town too."

"Land your plane on Jingle Bell Lane?"

"I was thinking more like using the Santa Express landing strip and opening up a branch of my transport business here. It came to me when I hitched a ride with the plow boys and talked about all the things to do in the area that I miss most like whitewater rafting, fishing, hiking, rock climbing, antiquing. Well, that was one of the other guys but you get the picture. There isn't a landing strip in the mountains and now there will be. I don't want you in Savannah because I'm making Christmastown my home base. I can fly out of here, do charters to and from here, maybe even open an outfitter service for camping and hiking."

"So this is a business decision?"

He pulled her into his arms, his fluffy face making her sneeze. "It's you, Holly. All for you and us. I'm going to make this work because I want to be with you and I think I found the way to make it happen."

He took off the beard and smiled down at her, his eyes dancing. "Marry me now, on Christmas Day, in the town square next to the singing reindeer and flashing lights, in front of all our friends. Make all my dreams come true."

"And mine!" Sue added from the desk. "If you two get this settled, Savannah's a great place for a honeymoon."

"You did it, you really did it!" Holly threw herself into his arms, slamming them both against the wall like she did yesterday when he first got here. "I love you, Case McGill."

"And we are going to be together forever. Like Sue and Percy. Nothing can keep us apart now."

And here is a bonus story—
a Christmas present to you—
from Karen Kelley.
Please turn the page for

Thank You, Santa!

Chapter One

"How do I let myself get talked into these things?" Charlaine mumbled as she tried to straighten out the computer for the umpteenth time in the last four days. "Damn ghosts."

It was probably the spirit of that Elvis impersonator. He'd always given her trouble. And he loved screwing around with the computers. Putting people in connecting rooms tickled him to no end.

And she didn't know how many times he'd had couples scattering what they thought were his ashes, but were actually ashes from the hearth, to the four winds at midnight. It was a wonder they didn't freeze to death and their relatives sue the inn.

She scrolled down the page, then right clicked on Nathan Windstrom's arrival date. Yep, there it was, December twenty-fifth.

"Who in their right mind books a room on a holiday just so they can write a review of the inn? A guy without a life, that's who." She snorted. He'd fit in perfectly with all the ghosts. As though her parents didn't have enough to worry about with the snowstorm and an influx of guests.

A couple walked by. Charlaine looked up and smiled at them. She'd wondered about those two. Both songwriters. It had been easy to see the woman was in love with him. Apparently, he'd decided she was pretty special, too, because they looked all lovey-dovey. She sighed, wishing she had a man in her life who would look at her like that.

She returned her attention to the computer and the reviewer who should've already arrived. "Maybe the old codger got caught in a very deep snowdrift far, far away from here and will at least stay away until things calm down." *Okay, maybe I don't want him stranded in a snowdrift*, she thought as guilt washed over her.

She clicked on the screen. Nothing.

Click! Click! Click!

Great, now it wasn't doing anything. She really hated computers. Okay, she could do this. She wasn't about to let a machine beat her.

Take a deep breath. Move your finger off the mouse. She waited a couple of seconds. Very calmly, she clicked again. Nothing. Terrific, it had locked up.

A throat cleared behind her. She whirled around in her chair to face the person.

Her gaze zeroed in on the man behind the check-in desk. Oh, wow. Santa had thought to bring her a very nice present, and oh, baby, she really liked the way he was packaged. Yum.

"May I help you?" she asked, her words breathless. Good Lord, she'd sounded like Marilyn Monroe. She cleared her throat and sat a little straighter, trying for a professional look.

He returned her smile with one of his own. The kind of smile that made her toes tingle and her heart beat a little bit faster. The kind of smile that had her practically melting in her chair. If they didn't have any rooms left, he could certainly bunk with her.

Hot didn't even come close to describing him. He was tanned—and in the middle of winter, no less. And he had the kind of hair that made her want to run her fingers through it: thick, jet-black hair. It just brushed the collar of his jacket.

Thank you, Santa!

"I have a reservation," he told her, his words raspy as they scraped across her skin.

She drew in a deep breath.

His gaze dropped to her chest.

She wanted to tell him that she hadn't done that on purpose. Yeah, she liked what she was seeing, but she didn't want him to think she would jump his bones if he made one false move. Because she wouldn't. Pfffft, she didn't even know his name.

She cleared her throat. "Your name?" Might as well get that out of the way.

He didn't seem in any hurry to raise his gaze. Heat enveloped her. The kind of heat that made her want to hug herself so she could hold on to it. The kind of heat that made her want to tear off her clothes and say, 'I'm yours, take me!'

This guy had sinner written all over him. She could think of at least two commandments she'd like to break with him—maybe three—but for the life of her, she couldn't remember what the other eight were.

"Windstrom . . . Nathan Windstrom."

Splat!

The critic? No! That wasn't right, not right at all! "Damn." When she realized she'd spoken aloud, she quickly whirled around in her chair and faced the computer. "Yes, of course, Mr. Windstrom."

"Call me Nathan."

Heat traveled up her face. Talk about making a bad first impression. She'd practically drooled all over the desk.

Damn, damn, double damn.

And the computer was still locked up. She didn't need this. Computers hated her. Everyone who knew her was aware of that. She was technologically illiterate, but Sue had called and said she'd be about an hour late so she'd offered to cover for the admitting clerk.

"I'm sorry. I'm having a bit of trouble here," she said. What would he write about that?

Check-in is slow. Female at desk apparently horny and lusts after guests.

She could see her parents getting a bad review and it would be all her fault.

"Control, alt, delete," he said.

"What?" She didn't even look up as she clicked on the backspace key. Nope, nothing moving. She had hoped it would take her back to before the stupid computer locked up. It didn't.

His arms wrapped around her. Startled, she jumped. Oh, God, he was going to have his way with her. Throw her down on the floor. Take her right then and there.

Ohhhh, yesssss!

She hoped her parents didn't walk through the lobby.

Man, he smelled good. His woodsy fragrance wrapped around her, tantalizing her senses. Her love life was so in the toilet that the closest man she'd gotten to in weeks was her father and the Old Man cologne he wore. Bleh.

"Control, alt, delete," he said. His hot breath tickled her ear sending warm fuzzies down to the pit of her stomach—and lower.

"Hmm?" she murmured.

He pushed some keys on the computer. "Control, alt, delete. If you click on the mouse too fast, you'll lock up your computer. You don't want to do it very often, but pushing those three keys simultaneously will usually unfreeze your screen."

Hell, just his voice could unfreeze anything around her.

"See? Another window pops up."

She looked at the screen. Yep, there it was, asking if she wanted to end the program. She turned her head and looked at him. Their faces were only inches apart. He had the most beautiful green eyes she'd ever seen, and long dark lashes.

And then he smiled again. He shouldn't be doing reviews, he should be doing commercials. He could sell ice water to Alaskans in the winter.

But he was a critic and, from what her mother had said, a real hard-ass. She cleared her mind of *almost* all the sexual thoughts she'd been having—pfffft, she wasn't a saint. "Uh, thanks. I'll remember that."

"No, problem," he said and straightened, then walked to the other side of the desk again.

Back to business. Except she couldn't remember what the hell she'd been doing. Her mind was a complete blank.

"You do have a room for me?" he asked.

A room! God, he probably thought she was a moron. It was his fault. He shouldn't be so tempting. "Yes, of course, Mr. Windstrom."

"Nathan."

She scrolled down and saw her mother had put him in the old renovated morgue that had been added to the inn. What could her mother have been thinking? The spirit of that Elvis impersonator always hung out there.

Maybe there was something else available. She glanced through the list of rooms. The songwriters were checking out later, but their rooms would have to be cleaned. She drummed her fingers on the desk. No, it didn't look as if there was anything available.

She reluctantly got the key, then handed it to him. And the bellboy wasn't around either—of course. Neither were her parents. Her father was trying to fix a pipe that had burst, and her mother was helping the cook.

"I'll show you the way." She stood and hurried around the desk. They each reached for his bag at the same time. His hand was warm and strong as it enveloped her smaller one. She could imagine the heat his touch would create in other places.

"I think I can manage to carry my suitcase. I've been told that, for an old codger, I get around pretty well."

Busted. She bit her lip. "Oh, you heard that."

He laughed. "Yeah."

At least he had a sense of humor about it. "Sorry." As she walked toward the hallway that led to his room, she decided she couldn't make things any worse than she already had. "Listen, I hope you won't hold that against the inn. Usually it runs smoother than this. The blizzard has been hard on everyone and we've had a lot of guests and . . ."

"So, you've already been warned about the critic coming to town."

Another bad mark.

"I always write an honest review," he said before she could say anything more.

As though his writing an honest review told her anything.

"Here's your room." She unlocked the door and stepped to the side.

"There are drums everywhere," he remarked as he went inside, his gaze scanning the room.

She cringed. It was her parents' idea, not hers. "Twelve Drummers Drumming," she said. The base of the lamp was a drum, the writing desk was in the shape of a drum and painted red and gold with a white top, a drum footstool, drum tassels. At least he hadn't gotten the room with the molting hens.

"This is . . . different," he said.

She wanted to ask if he meant different in a good way or different in a bad way, but refrained from saying anything, afraid she might make things worse.

"I hope you'll enjoy your stay at the Sleigh Bells Inn."

He abruptly faced her. "I'll need a guide to show me around. Someone who can tell me a bit of the history surrounding the inn. Would the owners mind if you gave me the grand tour?"

She might be able to lead him in all the right directions to make up for her earlier blunders. "I'm sure it'll be fine. Is there any particular time?"

"I'll get settled in and meet you here in an hour, if that's okay."

"Sure." Strictly for the inn, she kept telling herself but couldn't stop the giddy feeling from washing over her.

"One more thing," he said.

She stopped at the doorway, looking over her shoulder. He really was a twelve on the one-to-ten scale of sexy men. "Yes?"

"What's your name?"

"Charlaine. Or Charlie if you like. Some of my friends call me Charlie."

"I'll see you in an hour, Charlaine."

She nodded, then left his room, letting her breath out. She'd never heard her name spoken the way Nathan had just said it. Soft, sensuous, like a caress.

"Wipe the drool off your chin, Charlie," she mumbled as she went down the hall.

"You and me both, honey!" a disembodied male voice spoke beside her.

She jumped and grabbed her chest. Her heart pounded so hard she thought it would jump right out and splatter on the floor.

"El, do you have to do that?" The dead Elvis impersonator could be a real pain in the butt sometimes.

"What's the fun of being a ghost if I can't scare anyone?"

"Well at least materialize, or something, before you start talking."

They went around the corner and his signature white fog began to take form. She shook her head. What a drama queen—literally. He couldn't just pop in like any normal ghost. No, he had to make a grand entrance. *Give me a break!*

"He's a hunka, hunka burnin' love, isn't he? I mean, absolutely dreamy."

Oh, no. If he . . . "Stay away from him," she warned.

"Moi?"

"Yeah, moi. I know exactly what you're capable of doing,

but this is serious. The guy is a critic." When he looked confused, she continued. "He reviews inns, bed and breakfasts, for some fancy-shmancy magazine. The guy has a rep for being hard as a rock . . ."

El snorted.

She stopped in the lobby of the inn, and frowned. "You know what I mean."

"Honey, you said it, not me, but it has been a long time since you've been around anything that could be considered hard as a rock."

She ignored his comment about her love life. "If he gives us a bad review, we'll lose customers. He could shut the place down. Then where would you be?"

"In that case, I promise to be good."

She warily eyed him. He was going for the innocent look, but she didn't buy his act for one second.

"Stay away from him," she warned.

He gave her a wide-eyed look. "Didn't I just say I would?"

"I don't believe you."

He slapped his hands on his hips and looked away from her. "I'm so hurt." He held his affronted pose for a good two seconds, then was gone in a poof.

"Drama queen," she muttered. It really wasn't a good thing to hurt El's feelings. Maybe he'd heed her warning. Yeah, like she really thought that would happen!

Chapter Two

Before Nathan closed his door, he'd glanced down the hallway. Charlaine had been talking to herself. Why he'd been surprised was beyond him. She'd been talking to herself when he'd arrived at the inn.

She was sexy as hell, though. She'd given him the once over, then gone back for seconds. Her gaze had slowly caressed him, her intimate perusal touching every inch of his body.

When was the last time a woman had looked at him like that? At least, one that had remotely interested him. Longer than he could remember.

He unzipped his suitcase, then just stood there, lost in his thoughts. He probably shouldn't have gone around the side of the desk. He could've just told her what keys to push. The move had been purposeful. He hadn't been ready for her to turn away after she'd realized he was the critic from the magazine.

He'd inhaled the heady herbal fragrance of her shoulder-length, deep brown hair. He'd wanted to do more than reach around her and hold down a few keys. And when she'd turned and looked at him with her soft, sensuous brown eyes, he'd had to force himself to move away before he did something stupid—like kiss her.

Damn, he got hard just thinking about her. Too bad she

might be crazy. Not that talking to oneself made a person ready for the looney bin.

He carried his shirts over to the dresser and put them inside, then went back to his suitcase.

It was the town.

She'd probably lived here way too long. This place could drive someone to the brink of madness. He had a feeling everyone here needed to be committed.

His first thought when he'd passed the 'You're Entering Christmastown' sign was that he'd taken a wrong turn. There'd been a glow of twinkling lights over the town as he neared—as though the place was radioactive or something. For one second, he'd almost looked in his rearview mirror to see if Christmastown spelled something demonic backwards.

Then there was the motorized Santa in the drugstore window. It should've been condemned for lewd behavior the way Santa rocked his hips. He wondered if they served more than sodas behind the counter.

And the costumes: snowmen, women in long dresses and men in capes and top hats . . . and did they have a sale on twinkling antlers? Maybe there'd been a big explosion at the North Pole and everything had landed in Christmastown.

The editor of *The Inns And Outs Of Traveling* was going to love this review. He almost felt sorry for the owners because so far it didn't look good. For them or for their daughter, Charlaine.

He'd known from the start she was the daughter. Before he'd left his apartment, he'd researched the inn. Charlaine was in a picture on the website. She'd been in the background of the photo, but he'd known it was her the moment he'd laid eyes on her. He wondered why she hadn't mentioned it.

Was she playing spy? His grin widened. If Charlaine had done *her* research, she'd have known he was a master at games, and he never lost. Nor did he plan to lose this time.

* * *

Charlaine grabbed a celery stick from the tray of veggies. She was a stress eater, she knew it, but she tried to munch on veggies rather than chocolate.

"What are we going to do?" she asked her mother, pointing with the stalk of celery.

Her mother, Melanie, didn't even look up from the pie dough she was rolling out. "Do about what, dear?" She glanced over her shoulder. "Abigail, what kind of pies are we making?"

Abigail's smile was as big and as bright as the town's Christmas lights. Charlaine didn't think she'd ever seen the woman frown.

"We're making four pumpkin cream pies and six coconut. If we run out, then I have that chocolate sheet cake with fudge icing."

Pies? Cakes? They were having a major disaster here and all they could think about was feeding the guests? "Mother!"

"Yes, dear?"

"Did you not hear what I said? The critic from that magazine is here. I have a feeling he's going to write a bad review."

"What does he look like, dear?"

A warm flush stole over her. What did Nathan look like? "Dark hair, kind of long." She sighed. "Green eyes . . ."

She got lost in the moment as she thought about him, fantasized about him taking her in his arms, lowering his mouth . . .

What was she doing? She was as bad as they were. "It doesn't matter what he looks like! What matters is the review he's going to write."

Abigail and her mother exchanged knowing looks.

"No! Don't either one of you go there." It was bad enough they had matchmaking ghosts floating all over the place, but did she have to put up with her mother, and Abigail, as well? Life really wasn't fair sometimes. "You know, you should be at least a little worried, Mother."

Her mother smiled. "When he gets a taste of these pies, I'm sure he'll write a wonderful review."

Her mother was so gullible. Nathan would eat her alive and spit her out. No, it was up to Charlaine to try to make a good impression. She bit her bottom lip. She'd better make a quick turnaround then because, so far, she hadn't done a very good job.

She glanced at the clock on the wall. Oh, Lord. She closed her eyes. Please, be wrong. She opened her eyes and looked at the clock again. No, she couldn't be ten minutes late. Oh, yeah, she was off to a flying start.

"I've got to go. Don't forget, I'm an employee like everyone else."

Her mother clapped her floured hands together, creating small white puffy clouds. "This is so exciting. Covert operations and all that."

Her mother watched way too many military shows. "Mom, I'm trying to save the inn."

Her mother sobered. "Yes, dear. Oh, and don't forget to wear your antlers. I just love the way they twinkle."

Abigail snickered.

Charlaine rolled her eyes. Did no one understand the importance of his review? She hurried from the kitchen. Of course her mother didn't. She was small town all the way and believed in truth, honesty and the American way.

Yeah, well, Charlaine had lived in the city, and she knew there were people in the world who would try to make a living off others' misfortunes.

She hurried through the lobby, barely glancing at the Christmas tree or the crackling fire. Usually, the warmth of the inn made her feel like she'd come home, but she just had too much on her mind. She waved at Sue, glad the other woman had made it in, then hurried down the hall.

When she came to his door, she took a deep breath, but before she could exhale, Nathan opened the door. His gaze immediately went to her expanded chest, then slowly made his way back to her eyes.

She let her breath out in a whoosh, heat creeping up her

face. *Ignore it!* "I'm sorry I'm late. Are you ready for the tour?" She smiled, hoping it came off sweet and not forced.

"Sure." He turned and grabbed a notebook and paper. "I like to jot down notes." He closed and locked his door, slipping the key inside his pocket.

Notes. Oh, she hated when people took notes. "Of course, that's . . . fine."

"This addition was added, right?" He looked down the long hallway.

How could he know that? Was he a contractor on the side? "Yes," she said. "It was once a . . . another building."

"What kind? I'm assuming it was a business?"

She shrugged, trying to sound casual while her stomach slowly tied into knots. "A morgue."

"Interesting." He flipped open his notebook and jotted something down.

Oh, another bad mark against the inn. This so wasn't good. "It was completely renovated, though." Her laugh came off a little shaky. "There aren't any dead bodies or anything if that's what you want to know."

Only a few ghosts, but she decided that she would only divulge information on a need-to-know basis, and he really didn't need to know about El or any other spirits.

He didn't even smile at her feeble attempt at humor. No, he was all business. But still sexy in a rough around the edges, *GQ* sort of way.

"What's down this way?"

"Storage. But you don't really want to go that way. There's nothing . . ."

But he was already headed in the opposite direction from the lobby. Oh, please don't go toward the embalming room. She hurried after him.

"My . . . the owners added this section to accommodate the guests. This inn is very popular. Did you notice the crown molding?" She pointed to where the ceiling met the wall.

He glanced up, but didn't slow. "Nice."

What? The man acted as if he was on some kind of mission. He rounded the corner at the end of the hall and went straight to a closed door.

Oh, no. Please, don't open the door. She hated this part of the old morgue. There was something spooky about it. Yeah, right, as if the ghosts didn't spook her enough.

"What's in here?" he reached for the doorknob and turned.

Nothing happened. Her heart slowed to a more normal pace.

"Just storage," she said. "Nothing at all interesting."

Unless he wanted to look through some dusty old jars that held things she didn't want to know anything about. If there were someone's remains or ashes down there, then she'd just as soon let them rest in peace. You couldn't pay her enough money to go down there.

"It won't open," he said.

"Locked," she said, even though she knew it wasn't, and never had been as long as her parents had owned the inn. No key, and they'd just never changed the hardware.

"Is that an Elvis song playing? Do you hear it?"

Thank you, El! He must be the reason why the door wouldn't open.

"Piped music," she lied. "Do you like Elvis?"

"Not really," he said, then jotted something down.

Crap! Double crap! El's anger was almost palpable. No one talked bad about the man he worshipped. She cringed. She wanted to ask Nathan if he'd ever heard of the saying, "Don't mess with Mother Nature." Multiply that by ten when someone angered a ghost.

Nathan suddenly turned, and stumbled. Oh, no! She threw her body forward to stop his fall. The next thing she knew, she was pressed against the wall, his body crushing hers. His very hard male body with sinewy muscles and all those delicious pheromones oozing from him.

His hands were on her shoulders. The heat emanating from him made her nipples harden, and her body ache with need. She looked up, met his gaze.

"Sorry." His breath caressed her face.

"No problem," she said when she caught her breath. "I'm just glad you didn't hit the floor. I'd hate for you to hurt yourself during your stay."

He raised an eyebrow. "Lawsuit? Bad review?"

She squared her shoulders but it only made her more aware of his hands on them. But he'd pissed her off with his insinuations so she'd ignore the warm fuzzies he'd caused inside her.

"No, that wasn't what I was thinking. I was just glad you hadn't hurt yourself. I'd feel the same toward anyone—critic or not."

"I'm sorry."

She frowned. Why did he have to apologize? She was just working herself into a good temper, then he tells her that he's sorry. And the worse thing about it, Nathan sounded sincere. He was playing dirty!

"Your eyes sparkle when you get angry." He studied her face. "I love the color. They're a golden brown—like caramel. I don't think I've ever seen eyes as pretty as yours."

And she was going to stay angry. She was . . .

She tried to swallow but her mouth was as dry as sawdust. *He's seducing you*, her head told her. *Who cares?* her body responded.

Her anger vanished. When he lowered his head, she knew he was going to kiss her, but she didn't move. Why should she when she wanted it as much, if not more, than he did? She wouldn't deny the chemistry that had been between them right from the start.

Her eyes drifted closed. The first touch of his lips sent spasms of pleasure through her and landed in the core of her being. This was good, really good. Her arms moved up, and wrapped around him, drawing him nearer.

She stroked his tongue with hers, he returned her caress. He tasted minty fresh—he was being very fresh. Yum. His hands slipped behind her, sliding down her back and cupping her butt, drawing her nearer. She could feel his need.

You don't even know this guy, her mind screamed. *Yes, you do,* her soul countered. *You've known he was out there, you've known him since forever.*

A shudder swept through her. She ran her hands down his back, beneath his suit jacket and finally she was touching him through the material of his shirt. She wanted to rip it off him, and explore at her will. She wanted . . .

He ended the kiss way too soon. She wasn't ready to step away. There was a lot more she wanted to know about Nathan. She wanted to know why she felt as though she'd known him all her life.

But maybe they did need to catch their breath.

"I didn't mean to come on so strong," he finally spoke.

"It was as much my fault as yours."

He pushed away, straightening his clothes. "Yeah, but you need to know a heated kiss won't change what I write about your parents' inn."

So, he knew she was their daughter. Still, it didn't give him the right to accuse her of coming on to him for a better review.

"That's what you think? Let me tell you right now, Mr. Windstrom, when I kiss a man, I kiss him because I want to. Besides, you were the one who kissed me, not the other way around." She turned on her heel and marched away. The nerve!

Chapter Three

Nathan knew he'd really been an ass and more than deserved Charlaine's scorn. "Wait," he called out, then hurried to catch up with her, grabbing her arm so she would stop. He wanted to apologize, needed to apologize.

"What?" She pointedly looked down at his hand on her arm.

He had no idea what to say. The kiss shouldn't have happened. But what was he supposed to do when she'd been right there, her lips so inviting?

"I'm sorry?"

"For which time? Kissing me, accusing me of using my body to get a good review? Or maybe it was when you refrained from mentioning that you knew I was the owners' daughter?"

"Yeah, that was a pretty lame apology." Damn, she looked hot when she was angry. The gold in her eyes sparkled with indignation.

He'd apologize for everything except kissing her. It would only be a lie. "I'm sorry I implied you would use your body to get a good review."

She arched an eyebrow.

"Hey, you should've told me you were the owners' daughter. It made you guilty by omission."

She looked liked she was thinking over what he'd said. "Okay, I accept your apology."

"But I'm not sorry about kissing you." His gaze strayed to her mouth. He was still holding her arm; he slid his hand down in a slow caress. He liked the silky smoothness of her skin.

She opened her mouth, then snapped it closed. He knew he'd made her forget what she was about to say. Her expression was easy to read and right now, she looked confused. She had the kind of face that couldn't hide a thing. His little sister was like that. She'd hated it when they were growing up. She couldn't get away with anything, while he could.

"Do you want a tour or not?" She jutted her chin out and squared her shoulders before she pulled away from him.

"Of the hotel?" he asked, feeling like sparring a little more.

"The hotel is the only thing I'll show you." She arched an eyebrow.

He had a feeling they were just words. He liked the chemistry between them, and he had a feeling she did, too. There was something going on between them. They'd both sensed it right from the very start. That instant attraction that only happens a few times in a person's life. He wanted her, and she wanted him. He had a feeling before all was said and done, they'd end up in bed together.

"Then lead the way," he said, bowing and waving an arm in front of him so she could pass.

She walked ahead of him. He didn't mind that she took the lead. The view was just as nice from this angle. Her hips had just the right amount of sway.

"This side has the themed rooms," she told him in a stilted, museum-tour-guide voice. "They represent the twelve days of Christmas."

Okay, Nathan would play it her way, for now. He jotted down notes. "Did the morgue close down?" He wondered why she'd stumbled just a little. Interesting.

"There was a fire."

"And?"

She looked over her shoulder. "There were bodies in the morgue."

Oh, yeah, great tourist attraction. People flocked to places that were supposedly haunted. Personally, he thought it was all a load of crap. He'd stayed in so-called haunted rooms and never even felt the chill of death hovering over his bed.

He hadn't seen anything on the inn's website, though. Odd they wouldn't advertise the fact there were ghosts if that was the marketing angle they were going for.

"So, you're saying the inn is haunted."

She stopped. "It *is* haunted. El tripped you. That's why you almost fell."

How convenient. She was damned attractive as she told the undoubtedly rehearsed story. But he wanted to know more. See how far she'd play this new game. Besides, she was damned cute. "I did stumble. But who or what is El?"

"El is Elvis."

He snorted. This was priceless. "The ghost of Elvis. You really expect me to believe that?"

Her frown deepened. "No, I don't. And he isn't Elvis. He was an Elvis impersonator and died on his way to do a gig. Now he's stuck haunting the inn."

"You mean no one told him to walk toward the light?" He was so good at keeping a straight face.

"You think this is funny, but you ridiculed his idol and that made him mad. If I were you, I'd watch your step."

"Am I going to trip again?"

"This is the lobby," she said as if he hadn't spoken.

"Nice tree." He'd decided to quit taunting her for the moment. Besides, it was a nice tree. His parents always put up a tree. Except this year.

Charlaine relaxed, his words breaking past the stiff demeanor she'd adopted. "Yes, it is." She closed her eyes and inhaled.

Man, he really wished she wouldn't do that because it was giving him all kinds of ideas.

"I love this time of year. The candles, the crackling fire, the decorated tree . . . coming home." She bit her bottom lip, lowering her gaze.

"What?"

"I didn't mean to bring up family."

Now he was puzzled. "Why? Are you ashamed of them?"

She raised her eyes. "No, of course not. My parents are great people. I just thought since you were here that maybe you didn't have any family, and I guess I felt sorry for you."

"My little sister and I sent them on a cruise they'd been dreaming about for years. It was our Christmas present to them. My sister is spending the holiday with her in-laws. When my parents return, we'll be at their house waiting for them with a fire in the fireplace, a decorated Christmas tree and lots of presents."

"Oh. Well, that was nice of you and your sister." Darn, she'd misjudged again.

"Did you think I didn't have a family? Maybe that I was hatched from an egg or something?"

And he was a smartass. "Of course not. I imagined the stork had brought you—possibly a drunk stork that might have dropped you on your head a few times."

He chuckled. Okay, so he had a nice laugh. Kind of deep. And it sent sweet shivers down her spine.

She cleared her throat and continued on her tour. "This is the dining room." Her mother chose that moment to step from the kitchen.

"Oh, hello." She beamed a smile. "You must be the critic for the magazine. Is . . . our employee giving you a good tour of the inn?" She winked at Charlaine as if Nathan wasn't even there. Her mother wasn't known for being subtle.

"Mom, he knows I'm your daughter."

She shook her head. "You should watch more spy movies.

I didn't think you'd be able to pull it off." She turned to Nathan. "Welcome to the Sleigh Bells Inn."

"Thank you, Mrs.—" Nathan extended his hand.

"Oh, just call me Melanie. We're not that formal here in Christmastown." She vigorously shook his hand.

"I can see that."

Now what did he mean by that? As if she didn't know the answer. His opinion didn't matter. Charlaine liked the town and all the fuss about Christmas.

"Is your room to your liking?"

"It's very unique," he said.

A very ambiguous answer. She'd seen the expression on his face when he'd been looking around. At least he hadn't told her mother right out that it was beyond bizarre. Charlaine supposed that when his review was out, she could make sure no copy came into her mother's possession.

"Don't let me stop you two from the tour." She looked between them as she wiped her hands on her apron.

Charlaine's gaze went from her mother's flour dusted hands to Nathan's, then to the streak of white on his suit coat.

"Charlaine, be sure to show him the sitting room. It's very cozy in there." She hurried back to the kitchen.

Show him the sitting room? Oh, Lord, her mother had just offered her up like the proverbial sacrificial lamb on the alter.

She looked at Nathan who only seemed amused. "I am so, so sorry."

"For what?"

She waved her hand. "You now have a streak of flour on your jacket, and my mother has shoved me under your nose like I have no hopes of catching a man on my own. I'm so embarrassed."

"Don't worry about it. My mother's been trying to get me hitched for years. It's not enough that my little sister has given her two of the most adorable grandchildren that anyone could ever ask for—and one of each sex."

"At least you have a sister to take some of the brunt. I'm an only child." She realized that it was nice talking to him. So, he was more than a sexy face and a delicious body. Sometimes she was so bad. "Come on, I'll show you the rest of the inn."

She took him around to the rest of the rooms, even to the sitting room, which at one time had been a library. Most of the inn had been turned into rooms, so the rest of the tour didn't last long.

"And that's about it, unless you want to go outside to the gazebo but it looks as though it's snowing again."

"I'd just as soon stay dry."

"Not the outdoors type, huh?"

"I enjoy warmer climates."

"Is that why you're tanned?" Open mouth and insert her size seven shoe. "I mean, it's obvious you've been either out in the sun or on a tanning bed." She couldn't help but wonder how much of him was tanned.

"I don't do artificial tans. I just got back from the tropics. A little sand and surf."

"A vacation from a vacation."

"I enjoy my job."

She only prayed he enjoyed the inn enough to write a good review. "I hope you'll enjoy the rest of your stay at the inn." She started to turn away.

"You didn't show me the kitchen."

Yeah, and she was hoping he had forgotten about that room. She didn't want to take him in there when she knew her matchmaking mother was still hanging out with the cook.

"How about I take you to dinner instead? My treat, and I can show you the kitchen later."

"Is this a bribe?"

He'd asked in a way that his voiced caressed her, slowly and sensuously. All she could do was shake her head. "No, not at all."

He smiled and she was totally lost in the green depths of his eyes. He was like a magnificent puzzle with every piece in the right place.

"Then I'll let you take me to dinner."

She started to draw in a deep breath, but then thought the better of it and glanced at the clock instead. "An hour and a half? I'll meet you here, in the lobby?"

"Don't be late. I'm hungry."

The way his gaze swept over her, Charlaine wondered if it was food he hungered for.

Chapter Four

Nathan sat in the chair by the window. He was already dressed for dinner, but it was still too early to go downstairs. He found he was eager to see Charlaine again. A few times during their tour, she'd had him laughing.

He tapped the eraser of his pencil on the tablet he'd been writing in.

But there was one problem. A big one. She apparently believed in ghosts. He wondered if there was something mentally wrong with her. Damn, it was a shame because he really did like her.

Of course, he knew there were people who believed in ghosts, and other than that, there was nothing else wrong with them. In every other aspect, Charlaine seemed fine. . . .

Man, was she fine. He closed his eyes and easily pictured her in his mind, could feel again the silky, smooth texture of her skin.

His gut told him she liked him, too. That, and her body language. Every time he was around her, she thrust out her chest. If that wasn't an invitation, he didn't know what was.

But it didn't change the fact that she believed in ghosts. Had she been traumatized as a child? He sighed, knowing he probably wouldn't ever discover the answer.

"There are no such things as ghosts," he muttered.

An Elvis song began to play across the piped-in music system. He frowned.

"That's going to get irritating." He'd have to find the OFF button before he went to bed or it would drive him crazy.

A chill swept over him. He shivered. That was the only thing about staying in renovated inns; they could be really drafty.

He glanced down at the notebook before tossing it on the bed and coming to his feet. He was still writing his notes from the last hotel where he'd stayed.

That one had been a real dump. They'd had a daughter that reminded him of how Lizzie Borden must've acted. Put an axe in her hand she'd be her to a T. He'd cut his stay shorter than he'd planned.

This review wasn't looking great, either. A shame. Charlaine's mother had seemed nice. A little odd, perhaps, but nice. Hmm, maybe that's where Charlaine got her mixed-up notions that ghosts do exist.

He'd work on his reviews later.

After making sure he had his key, he left in search of the warmth from the fire in the lobby. He'd make sure he asked for extra blankets tonight, unless someone else decided to keep him warm. Nice thought, but he needed to remember this was a business trip and not pleasure.

Charlaine poked her head through the neck opening of her dress, her arms in the sleeves, and wiggled it over her hips, skimming the palms of her hands down the sides. She reached for the black and silver watch that she'd left on her dresser—except her hand went right through El.

"Ehhhh! I hate when you do that!" She rubbed her hands up and down her arms. "It's like sticking my hand into a bowl of ice water, and it's just plain creepy."

"You did tell me to show myself first, didn't you? I'm only doing as you asked."

She narrowed her eyes. "No, you're being obnoxious."

"El is never obnoxious." Just as quickly, his mood changed. "Ohh, I love that little black number." He waved his arm at the same time he snapped his finger. "It screams, 'I want to have sex with you.'"

She glanced in the mirror. Screaming sex wasn't her intention. Whispering "I want to have sex with you," maybe. Screaming wasn't good.

Her gaze went to her reflection in the standing mirror. The black dress did cling to her curves before flaring out just a little at the hem and stopping at the top of her knees. The neckline was rounded, not too low, but not spinsterish, either. No, El was wrong. Her dress looked fine.

"You should see what he's wearing," El told her.

She worried her bottom lip. "You didn't do anything, did you?"

"Of course not. Unless you count ogling as doing something. He took a shower, and oh, baby, that man is packin'."

She covered her ears. "No, I don't want to hear about it. Na-na-na-na-na-na."

He sniffed. "Fine."

She slowly lowered her hands. She wouldn't put it past him to give her all the details. If she wanted to know more, she'd find out for herself.

"Just don't materialize in front of him," she warned as she went to her closet. "Or talk," she added, just in case.

"I said I wouldn't. Don't you trust me?"

She was in the process of digging around for her strappy sandals but poked her head out of the closet long enough to frown at him. "You're asking me—someone who has known you for how many years?—you're asking me to trust you won't interfere?"

He tugged on his white cape, not meeting her eyes.

Oh, the drama. She moved back inside her closet. There they were. She wiggled backwards until she was out of the closet and straightened. El was gone. Probably to go somewhere and pout.

She sighed as she sat on the side of the bed and slipped first one foot, then the other into her shoes. Okay, now he'd made her feel guilty.

"I'm sorry," she said, but there was only silence.

El wasn't so bad most of the time, and he really tried to do good deeds. But at the same time, he loved being just a little ornery. Like having people scattering his so-called ashes at midnight, in the dead of winter. The poor victims would come back in shivering from exposure to the harsh elements.

There wasn't anything she could do. As long as he kept his distance, maybe they would survive, and maybe Nathan would write a good review.

She slipped the delicate pearl necklace around her neck that her mother had given her for her sixteenth birthday, and fastened it. A brush through her hair, a dash of color on her lips, and she was ready. She grabbed her black shawl as she went out the door.

Her heart began to pound the closer she got to the lobby. Was she early? She looked at her wrist, but realized her watch was still on the dresser.

When she reached the lobby, Nathan was there, standing in front of the fireplace. The fire crackled and danced as he stared down into the flames.

She had a side view of him, and for a moment unabashedly stared. He was handsome in a black turtleneck, black pants and jacket. Her body trembled as she looked her fill.

Nathan glanced up. Had he sensed her presence? His gaze moved slowly over her. As she walked closer, she could see the appreciation in his eyes.

"You look beautiful," he said.

She grinned. "So do you."

"Somehow, I feel like it would be worth staying here just to look at you."

She worried her bottom lip. "I know I've been giving you a tour of the inn, and now we're having dinner together, but I still don't want you to think I'm trying to influence you."

"I never let anything stand in my way of writing an honest review."

She nodded. "Good." At least, she hoped it was good. She truly didn't want to think she was trying to bribe him or anything. Maybe he would give her just a hint about what he planned to write.

"Are you ready?" he asked before she could say anything.

"Yes, of course." Maybe later he would give her a hint.

They made their way to the dining area. She hoped Abigail had cooked most of the food. The cook had that magic touch when it came to food. Her mother was good, but no one came close to Abigail.

Alvin seated them at a table next to the large picture window that faced the town. Pristine white tablecloths draped the tables and in the center of each, there was a flickering candle in a red vase. The dining area was dim, romantic, and suddenly she felt uncomfortable. It wasn't as though she and Nathan were dating.

He pulled her chair out, and she sat down, then he went to his side of the table and sat, looking around.

"This is nice."

She breathed a sigh of relief as Alvin handed them each a menu, then silently left, but not before he discreetly winked at her as if to tell her that he, at least, knew the importance of putting on a good face for Nathan.

Alvin was a godsend. Mature, mid-fifties, and an asset to the inn. He used to work in a five-star restaurant but wanted to retire to a smaller town. He stopped here on the way to a job interview, fell in love with Christmastown, and stayed.

"What do you recommend?" Nathan asked as he perused the menu.

She smiled. There were only a few selections, but she knew he couldn't make a wrong choice. "That's one thing about the inn, everything tastes good."

"Then I'll have the steak."

He closed his menu and laid it to the side; she put hers on top of his. Alvin seemed to materialize with a bottle of wine.

"Compliments of the owners," he said, and poured them each a glass, then took the menus. He took their orders and left just as silently as he appeared.

So far, so good. No one could ask for better service than this.

Nathan raised his glass, swirled the liquid, then took a drink. When he opened his eyes, he smiled. "Wonderful."

She relaxed and took a drink, then set her glass back down. "I love this spot. You can see all of Christmastown from here."

"You really love this place, don't you?"

She nodded. "With all my heart."

"You don't find it all a little . . . garish?"

The night *had* been going well. "No, I don't. I think it's very quaint." She gazed out the window. "This town almost died. People were leaving, businesses closing. If they hadn't come up with the Christmas theme, there wouldn't be anything left. Can you even imagine what it would've been like for the ones who couldn't afford to move? The elderly on fixed incomes?" She raised her chin. "You can call it garish, but I call it salvation."

"It would seem I'm always saying 'I'm sorry' to you. And I am. I guess I looked at it from a tourist industry side."

"But it's so much more. A lot of retirees come here. Because of the tourism, taxes are low. It's a chance for them to enjoy the rest of their lives without being forced to watch every penny they spend."

He looked out the window. "And it gives them the chance to feel like a kid again."

"Maybe it gives us all a chance to feel like a kid again. If there's something wrong with that, then I don't care."

"Touché." He held up his glass, then took a drink. "My sister said I have a tendency to get too serious sometimes."

"Your sister is very smart." But she smiled to soften her words. "How can anyone not enjoy the twinkling lights?"

"They do twinkle."

He was being sarcastic again. "They say the astronauts can see them from space," she told him.

"Really?" He looked surprised.

"No, but I thought I should lighten the mood. I think we were getting way too serious."

"And would that be a bad thing? I think I'd like to get serious with you."

She swallowed, opened her mouth, but no words came out. She should feel . . . affronted or something. But he'd only said what she'd been thinking since the moment they'd met.

"I'm moving too fast. Believe me, I never come on this strong." He grimaced. "That sounded like a really bad line. Let me try again." He cleared his throat. "Tell me about yourself."

She didn't know whether to laugh or what. She did know the same charge of electricity apparently flowed through him that flowed through her.

Her grandmother had once told her about meeting her first husband, Charlaine's grandfather. All it had taken was one look and they knew there was something between them. Though he'd died after thirty years of marriage, and her grandmother had remarried, she'd told Charlaine that she'd never experienced the same kind of closeness with anyone else.

Surely, this wasn't what they'd felt. What her grandmother had told her about was rare—almost unheard-of nowadays.

No, she and Nathan would have a good time, she was

almost certain of that, then they'd part ways. So maybe it was better if they talked about something generic, like work.

"I don't lead as exciting a life as you do," she said. "I worked in the city, but my boss retired, so I'm actually between jobs. I've been helping my parents out, and enjoying Christmas. I may move back home, though."

"You're tired of the big city?"

"I like a quieter lifestyle. Long walks in the country, knowing my neighbors." She shrugged. "I guess the old saying is true that you can take the girl out of the country but you can't take the country out of the girl."

"You wear country very well."

She could feel the heat rise up her face. "Tell me about your work," she quickly changed the subject. "Do you like traveling all the time?"

Their food arrived. Nathan waited until Alvin had set the plates in front of them and left before he answered.

"I think I have the perfect job. I get to take vacations all year long, and I never have to pay for them." He cut into his steak, then took a bite. He closed his eyes, and she could've sworn he moaned.

It was all she could do to breathe as she watched him savor the taste of that one bite of steak. His expression was sensual as hell. Would he enjoy making love just as much?

When he opened his eyes, she could breathe again. But she remembered not to take a deep breath. There was already enough sexual fire building between them without her fanning the flames more.

"Good?" she croaked.

"I don't think I've ever tasted steak this fantastic."

"The fish is just as good."

He looked at the trout on her plate, then at his steak. "Want to split?"

She eyed his steak. "Sure." She laughed as she cut her fish in half and passed it to him. He did the same with his steak.

She dipped half of her tartar sauce out of the little white ceramic bowl and plopped it on her plate, then handed him the bowl. After he took it from her, she reached for the steak sauce, and dumped half the contents over her meat.

He looked at her as if she'd just desecrated a holy shrine. "You put sauce on this perfectly cooked steak?"

"It enhances the flavor." When he shook his head in remorse, she laughed.

He smiled, his eyes telling her that he'd reluctantly forgive her for ruining the steak. She realized that she'd never felt this relaxed around a man this quickly. And she knew they *were* moving way too fast.

And then again, it didn't seem nearly fast enough.

Chapter Five

"I can't believe I ate all my food and the rest of yours as well." Nathan scooted back a couple of inches from the table.

"I think it was the pumpkin pie with whipped cream that did you in," Charlaine said.

His stomach tightened. "Did you have to mention dessert? Not that it wasn't good. It was fantastic, but man, I'm so stuffed right now."

She grinned. He really liked her smile. It bewitched him, intrigued him.

"I have the perfect solution." She came to her feet, and held out her hand. "Exercise."

"You've got to be kidding." He could barely move.

She laughed. "Come on." She looked him in the eye. "You do know how to dance, don't you? I mean, I would think anyone from the city would be at least tolerable on the dance floor."

"Is that a challenge?"

"Yes, I believe it is."

"You're asking for it now. I once won a dancing competition. I even have the trophy to prove it."

"Really?" She bit her bottom lip.

"Yep, I beat Billy Curlin out with my fancy footwork. My teacher said I was a natural."

"Teacher? You've taken dance lessons?"

He nodded. "Third grade. Mrs. Lee's class."

She chuckled. "That was so not fair. You scared me."

"I know."

"Have you ever heard of revenge?"

"I have a feeling I might be in trouble."

"I would say so."

He let her lead him to the bar, sliding into one of the booths when they got there. Only one other couple was in there, but they were in a back corner. Nathan had a feeling they didn't even notice the arrival of two more people. They were too absorbed in each other.

"The songwriters," Charlaine whispered. "I guess they decided to stay another day."

The bartender, who didn't look old enough at first glance to serve drinks, came over to the booth.

"Hey, Charlie, what'll you have?" he asked.

"I feel like living dangerous, Chris. How about a hurricane," she said.

His eyes widened. "You sure?"

She nodded.

"Okay, but don't blame me if you have a headache tomorrow." He turned to Nathan. "And you?"

"Just a beer. The lady has warned me that she's going to dance my legs off tonight."

"She can do it, too. Okay, two drinks coming up."

"Got a quarter?" she asked.

"I thought the going rate for someone's thoughts was a penny."

She grinned. "For the jukebox in the corner."

"Ah." He fished four quarters out of his pocket and handed them to her, then watched as she strolled over to the jukebox. Man, he liked the way she moved. She had a natural walk, just a slight sway of her hips to say she was all woman.

He wondered what songs she would pick. Slow songs so he

could hold her in his arms or would she play it safe and go for a faster tempo?

She didn't waste time as she quickly punched in four tunes. As the record dropped, she straightened and crooked a finger in his direction. He smiled as he stood, and sauntered toward her.

The soulful voice of Michael Bolton singing "When a Man Loves a Woman" came over the speakers. She met him midway across the small dance area, and then he was taking her in his arms, and doing what he'd wanted to do all night—hold her close.

Her body was warm, her moves seductive, as their bodies blended, becoming one in fluid movement. He inhaled, his senses assaulted with a light scent of gardenias and something else that he couldn't name, but it made him want to press closer and breathe in everything she had to offer.

"You smell good," he whispered close to her ear.

"I was thinking the same thing about you," she murmured, running her hand along the back of his neck.

Excitement leapt inside him. "I want you." He spoke without thinking.

"I know. I want you, too." She stepped back, putting about a foot between them, and looked into his eyes. "You feel it, too, don't you?"

He nodded.

"It's not just my imagination?"

He shook his head. "If it is, then we're both imagining the same thing."

"Maybe we should sit for a while."

He let go of her, felt a moment of emptiness as they went to the booth. The bartender had brought their drinks. Condensation formed on the outside of the glasses. Maybe the cold drink would cool him off.

No, he knew there was only one thing that would cool him off and, even then, he had a feeling he would want more.

His brain kept telling him things were moving way too fast. Sure, he'd had his share of one-night stands without any regrets, but he sensed this time would be different. He didn't want Charlaine to get hurt. No matter how she acted, he knew she wasn't the type for a one-time-only deal.

Relationships for Nathan didn't last long. His job took him to different places, which could be exciting, but he also didn't have roots. He liked it that way, and didn't want to change.

But he already knew where this night would end, and there might be regrets afterward.

A tall glass of courage? Charlaine looked at her empty glass. She wasn't drunk, but she certainly wasn't feeling any pain, either.

She finished the story she'd been telling. Her blunder about getting on the wrong bus when she lived in the city and being four hours late for work on her very first day.

He laughed, then followed with a story of his own. Something about the last inn he'd stayed at. Her mind was elsewhere though as her thoughts moved to what it would feel like to be held in his arms, his lips on hers.

"Did you want a refill?" Chris asked, drawing her out of her musings.

She shook her head, then looked at Nathan.

"Nothing for me."

"Are you ready to go?"

He glanced at his watch. "I didn't realize it was so late." He stood, dropping some bills on the table. "Merry Christmas."

"You too." Chris went back to cleaning off the bar and preparing to close up for the night.

When Nathan slid his hand to the small of her back, tingles of pleasure swept over her. "I'm not ready for the night to end," she said.

He stopped just outside of the bar area. "Neither am I,

but you know what will happen if we spend more time together tonight."

She nodded. "I think I've known what would happen from the first moment I saw you. Don't say you didn't feel it, too."

"I don't stay in one place very long."

"I'm not asking you to marry me." She laughed.

She knew he'd leave, and she'd be left with only a memory of what they'd shared. She had a feeling it would be a damn good memory, though. She swallowed, knowing she was about to cross an invisible line. She took a deep breath. "I'm not wearing panties."

He looked at her, some of the color drained from his face. Oh, Lord, she hoped he wasn't about to have a coronary. What if he had a heart condition or something. "Are you okay? I know CPR."

He visibly swallowed, then grabbed her hand and took off in the direction of his room. Good, he wasn't about to fall over dead, although she did know CPR. But she was thinking of a different kind of mouth-to-mouth.

He didn't say another word until they were standing outside his door. He was fumbling as he tried to insert the key in the lock. "I don't normally act like a virgin on my first date."

"I'm nervous, too, if it makes you feel any better."

He rammed the key into the slot and shoved the door open, pulling her in behind him, then kicking the door closed. She almost laughed in the face of his eagerness, but she was just as impatient.

And then she didn't have to wait any longer as he pulled her into his arms and lowered his mouth. Ah, God, he tasted like heat and beer and lust. She met each thrust of his tongue. He ran his fingers through her hair; she pulled him closer, slipping her leg between his.

He ended the kiss, burying his face in her hair as he slid his hands beneath her dress and cupped her butt, pulling her closer.

"Oh, man, you weren't lying." His hands caressed her bare skin.

A shiver of pleasure ran over her as her sex rubbed against his leg and he massaged her bottom. Her thigh nudged against his erection. "There are way too many clothes between us." She moved away from him so fast that he stumbled, falling on the bed. She laughed.

"You think that's funny," he said, pushing away from the mattress. He came toward her, stalking her.

"Yeah, I do." She grinned as she reached behind her, unzipping her dress, but moving behind the only chair in the room. He stripped out of his jacket, letting it fall to the floor, then unbuttoned his shirt and tugged it from the waistband of his pants.

"What are you going to do about it?" She shoved her dress off her shoulders and let it slide to the floor. She stepped away from it and sauntered to the window. When she turned to face him, Charlaine knew the picture she presented.

"Right now, I'm going to just look," he said.

All she wore was a black lacy bra that pushed her breasts up and barely covered her nipples. A black garter belt, black hose and her three-inch black heels.

And she could tell Nathan liked what he saw as his gaze slowly roamed over every inch of her.

"Is that all you want to do with me?" she teased.

He unfastened his pants and kicked out of them. His briefs followed. He stood there completely naked, like a Greek statue, and he was about as hard as stone right now. Her legs began to tremble.

"No, I plan to do a lot more. Like kiss every inch of that delicious body."

"Do you have protection?" she asked, her words breathless as she imagined just where he'd kiss her.

He nodded.

"Lots of protection?"

He grinned. "Yeah, I have plenty."

"Good." She sauntered toward him. "I want you so badly I hurt."

"No more than I want you." He pulled her to him, her breasts crushed against his chest, but rather than hurt, it had the opposite effect and only aroused her more.

His mouth slid across her cheek, his tongue delving inside her ear. Hot and wet, he stroked and caressed, nibbling on her earlobe, tugging with his teeth.

She moaned, clutching his shoulders.

"You like that." It was more of a statement than a question.

"You know I do. Just like I know that you like this." She snaked her hands down his back, lightly scraping with her nails, then cupping and squeezing his butt. "Am I wrong?"

He chuckled. "I like a woman who knows what she wants, then goes after it."

She stepped out of his arms. "You're right. I want you." She traced his nipple with her fingers, then flicked across it. His nipple tightened. She leaned forward, licking him, then sucking. He drew in a breath. But Nathan hadn't seen anything yet. She reached down, encircling his erection, sliding the skin down, then back up.

Nathan grabbed her shoulders. "You're killing me."

"No, I'm just torturing you a little." She laughed. "Death comes later when I taste you."

He sucked in a breath. Before he could stop her, she'd already moved to her knees. With a wicked smile, she looked toward the cheval mirror. They were positioned just right that she could watch his expression when she licked up his length. He clenched his jaw.

He looked at her, then toward the mirror. "Double torture."

"But sweet torture."

"Oh, yeah, sweet. Very sweet."

She took him in her mouth, knowing he got pleasure, not

only from her mouth on him, but from being able to watch her in the mirror. An interactive sensuous movie.

She found the area on the underside of his penis and lightly massaged, knowing he would get even more enjoyment at the same time she ran her tongue over the tip of his erection loving the soft silky feel against her mouth.

"Enough," he moaned. "If you keep doing what you're doing, I'm not going to be able to give you pleasure." He tugged under her arms and pulled her up. "And I want to pleasure you."

She stood in front of him, ready for him to do whatever he wanted with her body.

"Nice." He lightly caressed down the center of her chest.

She arched toward him, but he moved away. "Ugh."

He laughed. "Turn about is fair play." He pulled the chair closer to the mirror.

Her pulse quickened. The chair had no arms, but it was cushioned. They'd be able to see what the other did. She liked a man who enjoyed sex.

She sat in the chair, then watched his face as she slowly spread her legs, letting them hang off the sides as she leaned back, drawing the cushion behind her so that her chest thrust forward.

"Let's see what you've got," she challenged.

"I thought that was obvious."

She chuckled. She hadn't thought a critic would have a sense of humor. She'd been wrong.

"Damn, you're magnificent." He straddled the chair, bringing her legs over his so he could move in closer. He massaged her breasts, tugging on the nipples before leaning forward and taking one in his mouth. He rolled the tight bud around with his tongue as he sucked.

"That feels incredible." She clutched his head, pulling him closer.

He moved back, but continued to fondle her breasts. "Do

you feel it all the way down to here?" He touched between her legs. She jerked.

"Oh, God, yes. Right there. Just like that."

He tugged on the fleshy part of her sex. "I'm going to take you with my mouth. I'm going to kiss you and lick you until your whole body trembles, and I want you to watch me."

She whimpered, practically having an orgasm just listening to his words. He slid down, lowered his head and began to work his tongue over her sex. Fire pulsed through her body.

"You taste sweet and hot."

"Nathan, I think I'm dying." Her body trembled from head to foot.

He chuckled, moving away long enough to slip on a condom. When he came back, she started to get up but he shook his head. "Scoot to the edge of the chair." He took the pillow from behind her and slid it beneath her bottom.

Her head was lower than the rest of her body. Her lower half completely exposed and elevated for him to feast his eyes upon.

With any other man, she would've been embarrassed to be in this position, but she saw the way Nathan looked at her, as though she was the most beautiful female he'd ever seen, and it was all right. He made her feel beautiful.

He stroked down her sex once, twice. Her thighs quivered. Then he entered her. He slid inside her body, letting her adjust. God, he was big. She gasped.

"I'm not hurting you, am I?"

"No."

He sank deeper, then waited.

"More."

She took all of him, but soon her body grew warm and she wanted more. As if he sensed she was ready, he began to move. Slowly at first, then he picked up the pace.

She watched him, then looked into the mirror. It was erotic, sensual, and beautiful all at the same time. The mirror image distorted as she got caught up with what she was feeling. She heard herself moan as the heat began to build inside her. She contracted her inner muscles. Heard him groan.

She lost herself in the motion of their bodies coming together, then moving apart. He leaned forward, squeezing her breasts, tugging on the nipples.

Her body began to tremble as wave after wave of release washed over her. God, the sensations were incredible. Her body shook and trembled. He jerked, gasped, grabbed her thighs as he came.

The seconds ticked by, their ragged breathing filled the room. She groaned when Nathan pulled away from her body.

"Sore?" he asked.

"A little."

"I'll be right back," he said, and headed for the bathroom.

She slid around on the chair so she could watch him. He had a nice butt. Besides, now that she was satisfied, she was embarrassed that she'd acted a little slutty—okay, a lot slutty, but, Lord, it had paid off big time. It had been so worth it. That was the best sex she'd had in a long time—if ever.

She smiled. Nathan was a hunk. She stood, going to his closet and borrowing his robe. It might have gotten hot a while ago but now she was chilled.

The bathroom door opened and he stepped out as she was belting the robe. He wore the one the inn provided.

"My robe doesn't do that gorgeous body justice," he said.

She laughed. Maybe that was what she liked about him. He made her laugh. "But it does keep me warmer."

"True." He walked toward her, stopping when he was only a few inches away and pulling her into his arms. "You're something else."

"I thought the very same thing about you." She rested her head against his chest, heard the steady beat of his heart. She closed her eyes and for a moment, wished they could stay this way forever.

They couldn't, though. The light of day would come streaming through the window tomorrow, and everything would be different. She didn't want him to regret bringing her to his room.

"I think I'd better go," she said, wanting to end it now rather than wait until morning.

He held her just a little tighter. "Stay. Tonight."

She was tempted. She frowned. Why shouldn't she stay? So what if it ended. Life should be fun. No recriminations. But for some strange reason she felt a prickle of pain stab her in the heart.

She met his gaze, and nodded. She could tell herself that she didn't want any ties in her life, but her convictions didn't ring as true as they once had.

Chapter Six

Charlaine always woke early, but when she glanced at the clock, she saw it was almost seven-thirty. Fantastic—not! Her mother would wonder where she was and eventually go to Charlaine's room to check on her. Her mother would probably get hysterical, get her father involved, call the police . . .

She rolled out of bed. Nathan moaned.

"Shh, go back to sleep."

"What time is it?" His words were slurred.

She grinned. He was so damned cute that she wanted to crawl back in bed and snuggle against his warm body. She sighed with regret. They would end up doing more than snuggling, and she knew that for a fact. They'd snuggled at least three times during the night. Oh, man, had they snuggled.

She had to quit daydreaming. "It's barely past seven. Go back to sleep," she told him. "I'll meet you for coffee later."

He dragged his eyelids open. "Kiss me good-bye."

Laughter bubbled out of her. "I fell for that line once already. I'll see you later." She began scooping up her clothes.

"Spoilsport." But he was already drifting off to sleep.

She hurried to the bathroom, shutting the door behind her before she turned on the light. She was still smiling as she set her clothes on the counter. When she looked at her reflection, her smile disappeared. Bleh, she looked rough.

She wet a rag and quickly washed, promising herself a hot shower as soon as she made it back to her room. When she grabbed her dress, something clunked to the floor. A small notebook—Nathan's.

She looked at the closed door, then reached down to pick it up. It was her parents' reputation on the line, and he shouldn't have left it out.

Taking a deep breath, she opened it and began to read: *the place is a dump, and the daughter is scary. She reminds me of Lizzy Borden.*

Her eyes narrowed. Is that what he thought of her? That she was an axe murderer? If only she had an axe handy. Apparently, they wouldn't be getting a good review from him since he said their relationship would have nothing to do with what he wrote. But did he have to be so cruel?

She jerked her dress over her head, then her feet in her sandals, and marched back into the bedroom. Nathan slept like a baby. She aimed the notebook at his head, but stopped herself from throwing it at him—just barely. Instead, it clunked against the headboard.

"Go to hell!"

He jumped, jerked to a sitting position. His hair stuck out at odd angles and he looked wild-eyed. "What?"

"I'm Lizzy Borden?" She planted her hands on her hips and glared at him.

He rubbed a hand across his eyes. "No, of course not."

"Then I guess sleeping with you did pay off."

"What are you talking about?" He glanced at his notebook, then looked at her. His eyes instantly cleared. "No, you're wrong."

"I don't think so!" She turned on her heel and hurried out of the room, slamming the door as she left, but it didn't relieve an ounce of her anger.

* * *

Nathan knew he had to do something to fix everything back to the way it was before Charlaine read his notebook. So far, he'd only caught glimpses of her. Every time he thought he was close enough to talk to her, she'd skitter away.

So now, he was back inside his room. He'd never felt this empty. What the hell had she'd done to him? He'd always been able to handle one-night stands, as had the women. But everything changed when he met Charlaine. He didn't believe in love at first sight, but there was definitely something between them.

He missed her. That was the plain and simple truth. And he didn't want it to end like this—with her thinking the worst about him.

With a deep sigh, he sat down on the side of the bed. "I don't know what to do," he said to the empty room.

"I could help, but then, you don't believe in ghosts, do you?"

Nathan jumped, whirling around in a circle. "Who's there?"

"You can call me El."

Charlaine was doing this. Getting even. "Okay, Charlaine. You scared me, we're even, now let me explain about my notes."

A fog appeared in the corner.

"Come on, Charlaine. You've carried this far enough."

A man appeared from the fog. At least, he thought it was a man. He looked like a poor imitation of Elvis. He had the costume down pat, except for the wig. It was black, but that was about as close as it came to resembling Elvis.

"Boo."

A blast of cold air swept over Nathan. He took a step back before he realized he'd almost bought into Charlaine's little game.

He raised a sardonic eyebrow. "I guess you're going to try to tell me you're the Elvis impersonator ghost."

In the blink of an eye, the hologram or whatever the hell it was, moved from the corner to the top of the dresser.

"There are no such things as ghosts." Damn, his words didn't hold a lot of conviction. But ghosts weren't real, were they? No, there was no such thing.

"You might be a hunka burnin' love, baby, but you upset Charlaine."

He eyed the hologram or whatever the hell it was. Elvis eyed him right back, except more like Nathan was a juicy steak. Damned uncomfortable. He took a deep breath. "She's doing this. Man, she's good, too."

The so-called ghost moved to the bed. "An unbeliever."

"Yeah, I am and there's nothing you can do to convince me you're a ghost."

Elvis vanished. Charlaine should've known not to pull a stunt like that.

"Don't Be Cruel" began to play. She'd already told him there was piped-in music. "Not funny, Charlaine, and I wasn't cruel. The notes you read were about a B&B in another state."

Elvis appeared again. "Is that the truth?"

"Yes."

"Then I'll help you get her back. I'm good at that, you know."

"I'll play your game. What do I have to do to win you back?"

Elvis laughed. "Why don't you try me on for size?"

"Yeah, whatever."

A burst of cold air seized him and suddenly he wasn't alone in his body.

"What's happening?" He faced the mirror, turning one way then the other.

"What I could've done with a body like this. Uh-huh, baby, hot doesn't even begin to describe you."

As if his hand had a will of its own, he slapped his butt. The cold air whooshed out of him and the apparition reappeared on the bed.

"That takes so much out of a ghost." He waved a hankie in front of his face.

"What—"

"I just borrowed your body for a bit. Now do you believe?"

Nathan stumbled to the chair and sat down. He might be able to rationalize everything else, but he couldn't explain that. He'd felt the . . . the spirit inside him.

"You're real," he mumbled.

"If you can call being dead real—then, yes."

He closed his eyes, rubbing his hand across his forehead. He didn't want to believe in ghosts. "Charlaine hadn't been talking to herself."

"Actually, she does. Sometimes she's talking to me. Not that you should worry about it. It looks like she won't be speaking to you anytime soon—if ever."

"If I explain, she will understand."

The ghost examined his fingernails. "Good luck. She's leaving in the morning."

"Leaving?"

"Going back to the city. I doubt you'll ever see her again."

Nathan glanced toward the clock on the bedside table. It was almost ten now.

"She's leaving very early."

No, he wouldn't let her leave until he'd spoken with her one more time. "You've got to help me. Tell me where her room is."

"I can't."

He came to his feet. "Then I'll knock on every door until I find it."

El chuckled. "Oh, I'm sure if you create a major disturbance in the hotel she'll definitely be in the mood to listen to you."

"Then what can I do? I've got to see her again."

"Well, there is one thing you can do."

"What? I'll do anything."

El smiled. Nathan didn't think he was going to like what he was about to hear.

Chapter Seven

"You have him doing what?" Charlaine snapped the book closed that she'd been reading.

El sat on the dresser. "Scattering my ashes."

She frowned. "Why would Nathan do that? He doesn't even believe in you."

"He does now, darlin'. God, I'm so good that I amaze myself."

She looked out the window, then at the clock as she jumped out of her chair. "I'd kill you if you weren't already dead. It's freezing out there, the wind has picked up, and he could be frozen stiff by now."

His expression turned thoughtful. "Frozen stiff and dead. Hmm, it has possibilities."

Sometimes she . . . No, she wouldn't waste her energy thinking about what she wanted to do to El. Instead, she pulled on pants over her nightie, a thick sweater, then boots. She grabbed her coat as she rushed from the room.

Dammit, she should've handled things differently. But she'd been mad—no, furious—with him.

"Why would he go to the trouble to scatter stupid ashes at midnight?"

"Because he cares," El's voice came from right beside her.

She knew he would be close. He hated to miss the scattering of his ashes. Such a drama queen.

"He doesn't care. Why would he refer to me as Lizzie Borden if he cared?"

"Those were notes on another inn. A real shit-hole."

She stopped and looked in the direction of his voice. "And you couldn't have just fixed everything by telling me this?"

"But then you would've had great sex, and parted ways. You had to know just how much you cared for each other."

"I don't care about him."

"Yeah, right. Now tell me again why you're rushing outside in freezing weather?"

"Because there are enough ghosts here without adding another."

She came to the door and tugged it open. A blast of freezing air made her gasp, but she resolutely made her way outside, tugging her hood over her head, then pulling the door closed behind her.

She stomped to the back of the inn, knowing that was a favorite place of El's. She was right. There Nathan was, holding up the same old urn. She thought it might have actually held his ashes at one time but they'd been scattered to the four winds long ago.

Lord, it was freezing out here.

Nathan's voice carried to her on the wind. "Take El's spirit and set him free!"

She rolled her eyes. Nathan tugged off the top of the urn and shook out the ashes. The wind blew them behind him. She quickly closed her eyes.

Splat! Right in the face.

Bleh. She coughed, spit and spluttered. This was so not funny.

"It worked!" Nathan yelled. He ran to her, brushing the ashes off her face.

"You just dumped the ashes from the fireplace all over me."

He shook his head. "No, they were El's ashes. I set his spirit free."

"We should be so lucky."

"I like you a lot. My notes were about another inn."

"I know, El told me."

"Don't leave tomorrow morning. Not before we have a chance to see where our relationship is headed."

She had a feeling El had told a bunch of lies since she had no intention of leaving tomorrow. But she couldn't be mad. Not when there was always a happy ending, and she was sure her and Nathan's relationship would have a very happy ending.

"I like you a lot, too," she told him.

He pulled her into his arms and lowered his mouth. This was where she belonged. It felt as if everything was finally right in her life.

This had been the best Christmas ever. *Thank you, Santa!* As she snuggled against Nathan, she heard the faint sounds of . . . "Burnin' Love?"

Sheesh.

Such a drama queen.

Nail-Biting Romantic Suspense
from Your Favorite Authors

Romantic Suspense from
Lisa Jackson

See How She Dies
0-8217-7605-3 $6.99US/$9.99CAN

The Morning After
0-8217-7295-3 $6.99US/$9.99CAN

The Night Before
0-8217-6936-7 $6.99US/$9.99CAN

Cold Blooded
0-8217-6934-0 $6.99US/$9.99CAN

Hot Blooded
0-8217-6841-7 $6.99US/$8.99CAN

If She Only Knew
0-8217-6708-9 $6.50US/$8.50CAN

Unspoken
0-8217-6402-0 $6.50US/$8.50CAN

Twice Kissed
0-8217-6038-6 $5.99US/$6.99CAN

Whispers
0-8217-7603-7 $6.99US/$9.99CAN

Wishes
0-8217-6309-1 $5.99US/$6.99CAN

Deep Freeze
0-8217-7296-1 $7.99US/$10.99CAN

Final Scream
0-8217-7712-2 $7.99US/$10.99CAN

Fatal Burn
0-8217-7577-4 $7.99US/$10.99CAN

Shiver
0-8217-7578-2 $7.99US/$10.99CAN

Available Wherever Books Are Sold!
Visit our website at www.kensingtonbooks.com

Say Yes! to Sizzling Romance by

Lori Foster

Say No to Joe?
0-8217-7512-X   **$6.99US/$9.99CAN**

When Bruce Met Cyn
0-8217-7513-8   **$6.99US/$9.99CAN**

Unexpected
0-7582-0549-X   **$6.99US/$9.99CAN**

Jamie
0-8217-7514-6   **$6.99US/$9.99CAN**

Jude's Law
0-8217-7802-1   **$6.99US/$9.99CAN**

Murphy's Law
0-8217-7803-X   **$6.99US/$9.99CAN**

Available Wherever Books Are Sold!

Visit our website at **www.kensingtonbooks.com**

He grinned, his teeth white against the dark night. "Won't tell a soul, promise. I don't know your name so your secret's safe. I'm out of there tomorrow too, no reason to hang around."

Then he kissed her again and she ran her hands through his hair and around his strong neck and she sure felt a lot better than she did five minutes ago. He touched her face, his erection pressing into her middle. Been months since she felt one of those and . . . well dang . . . they really did come in sizes.

"What do you want?" Moonlight danced in his eyes. "Tell me and I'll make it happen. It's the code of the dumped. We hang together, gotta be there for each other."

She swallowed. "I think I want what you want but I could be wrong."

parties should be outlawed." He reached for the mug. "Miss your guy?"

"Miss the sex." She slapped her fingers to her lips. "Can't believe I just said that. What's in that cider?"

"Apples." He chuckled then nodded at the crowd. "The natives are leaving, probably to go home to lovers and warm beds." He took a long drink. The carolers finished up their last song, kettle fires got extinguished, and the gazebo suddenly went dark, leaving a sliver of moon, the faint glow of streetlights and the quiet of falling snow. She let go of the railing. "Guess this is our cue to go home."

She slipped on ice, stumbling against Handsome, making him lose his balance too. They both fell onto the wood bench in fits of laughter. LuLu buried her face in his pea coat. "This is the most fun I've had in two months. Gives you a clue how great my life's been lately. Thought twenty-five was going to be the best year ever."

"I was hoping twenty-nine would do it for me." His eyes darkened as he stared down at her and then, slowly, as if giving her time to stop him, he kissed her. It was one of those mutual kisses—the kind that said I really want this and hope you do too.

And she did, a lot. He tasted of cider and cinnamon and smelled like fresh snow and one totally delicious man. His tongue touched her bottom lip, her mouth opening as if she'd been waiting for him and this kiss all her life. Amazing what a little cider can do to brain cells. Then their lips mated more than kissed and her brain cells sizzled.

"I needed that," he whispered, his breath hot on hers, his voice low, a little rough and a lot sexy. Where'd this guy come from?

"Glad I was here for you." She nodded for emphasis. "I think I'm horny and tired. Good thing I'm leaving tomorrow. If I ever ran into you after saying something like that I'd die of embarrassment."

LuLu Cahill looked out from the gazebo to the falling snow, Christmas lights and carolers on the corner and knew with absolute certainty that she wanted to be anywhere but home for Christmas! Too many couples, smiling faces, families, and total happiness when all she felt was totally pissed-off. She grabbed the railing and growled like a poked dog.

"Not exactly the joyous sounds of the season," said a guy who walked up next to her. "Anything I can do to help?" He handed a travel mug. "I'll share my apple cider."

"You can help wring my cheating ex-boyfriend's neck who maxed my credit cards then left me." She took a sip, then handed back the mug. "And you're here alone because you're a stranger in town?"

"That and I was dumped at the altar, have guests without a Christmas Eve wedding to attend and had to get out of the house and away from their pity party. If your ex shows up, I'd be glad to help with the wringing idea. Course then we'll be sharing a jail cell instead of cider."

He was tall with buzzed dark hair, clean shaven, a little lonely and a whole lot of handsome. "Can't believe a good looking guy like you got dumped."

"Lost out to the drummer for blue Sticky Notes. Bachelorette

Keep an eye out for I'M YOUR SANTA,
A sexy anthology from Lori Foster, Karen Kelley, and
Dianne Castell,
Coming in October from Brava.
Here's an excerpt from Dianne Castell's
"Home for Christmas" . . .

happened between them. His mind went up in a blaze of need, possessiveness, and passion as he deepened the kiss.

She let him. Damn! She was leading now, holding him, letting her tongue curl and caress over his, as he basked in her warmth and breathed her scent in the night.

He pulled her even closer, holding her tighter in his embrace, never wanting this to ever end, wishing to stay here forever, lost in the dream and the sheer and utter wonder of Alice Doyle's kiss.

alive and no doubt dead by the time they dug them out. You saved their lives."

"I didn't do it alone. Sergeant Pendragon . . ."

"Is an old man. You went down into the cellar, he told me that. You went looking for them, not knowing if you'd be able to get out again. That, Mister Watson, is courage in my book." He ought to tell the truth, but she'd think he was out of his mind. Perhaps he was. "Thank you," she went on, "and I look forward to working with you."

She offered her hand.

He took it.

His earlier impression had been dead on. Her skin was warm, even in the chilly night, her grasp strong and he might sense rather than see her smile, but he just knew it crinkled the corners of her blue eyes. Which must sparkle with life and beauty and . . .

Oh, dash it all!

Holding hands was nowhere near enough. Why waste the night and the moment?

He put his arm on her shoulders, drawing her closer. To his utter amazement and delight, she stepped into him, looking up at him. This close he could almost see the soft curve of her lips. He felt the warmth of her breath as he lowered his mouth and brushed her lips with his.

That was all he intended, a reckless, stolen kiss that they could both forget in daylight.

If they had any sense.

Which they obviously didn't.

Instead of stepping back, she leaned into him, warm and soft against him, and tilting her neck, opened her mouth and wrapped her arms around him.

His lips pressed hers and dash it, she was kissing him back. Hard. With a little sigh, she came even closer, pressing herself into him and reaching up to pull his head down. His tongue touched hers. High explosive wasn't the word for what

Ignore the blackout, their exhaustion and the injured child sleeping in the car, and they might have been returning after an afternoon spin across the Surrey Hills, stopping off for a picnic by some river and now he'd be getting ready to ask her in for coffee.

He almost laughed out loud.

Seemed stress and fatigue made his imagination run riot.

". . . er . . . excuse me . . ."

She'd been talking to him, or trying to, while he was verging on impure thoughts. "Sorry."

"That's alright. I'm the one who needs to apologize." She leaned the bicycle against the side of the house and looked up at him. Her face was a pale shape in the darkness. "I'm not good at apologizing. Never have been. But I owe you one. That first afternoon, I made some very rude, unjustified comments. I'm sorry," she paused as if to catch her breath. "You're not a coward. Tonight proved it and I had no business to make such a sweeping judgment without knowing a thing about you."

He shrugged, unsure how to reply. "Tonight, I just did my job." With a lot of help.

"Without you, those two brothers would have been buried

Don't miss Rosemary Laurey's
SUPER NATURAL ACTS,
COMING IN November from Zebra . . .

Silence.

He looked at her. "See, no ghosts."

If there were any in the old hotel, he'd probably pissed them off. One thing she hated more than a skeptic was a pissed-off ghost. They could get really nasty when they were riled.

"I wouldn't do that if I were you," she warned.

had been on television. His shoulders were wider up close and his eyes more green, the color of finely cut emeralds.

The kind of eyes, and the kind of smile, that could talk her right out of her clothes and have her naked on a bed before she realized how she'd gotten there.

Oh, yes, he was a clean-shaven devil in an expensive suit and if she wasn't mistaken, wearing designer cologne.

But she wasn't stupid and she wouldn't fall for his charm. He'd figure that out soon enough.

Trent was a skeptic. Her enemy. He'd made jokes about her column. She could very well lose her job if she didn't change his opinion about the supernatural by the end of their stay.

Lust could not enter the equation.

She faced him once again, tilting her chin and looking up at him. He was very tall, too. "You said some pretty ugly things about me on television. Do you always take potshots at people you've never met?"

"Nothing personal."

Was he serious? The bangles on her wrists jangled when she planted her hands on her hips. "Nothing personal? You're joking, right?"

She gritted her teeth. She would *not* stoop to losing her temper. But she'd to wipe that sardonic smirk right off his face!

His smile turned downward and it was like a thundercloud hovered over him. Well, she was the lightning bolt that would strike him down.

"I go after all cheats, not just you," he said.

"Now I'm a cheat?" *I won't lose my temper*, she told herself.

"You're bilking the public when you feed them a line of crap about ghosts being everywhere and that you can talk to them."

"And how do you know they aren't?"

He swung his arm wide. "Do you see any?" He looked toward the second floor. "If there are any ghosts here show yourselves," he yelled.

A shame because he could've looked at Selena James' legs a lot longer.

"I don't scare so easily." He casually leaned against the balustrade and crossed his arms in front of him.

"But then you've never stayed in a haunted hotel," she said.

"I can't stay in a place that's haunted since there are no such things as ghosts."

As she stepped closer, he could see her eyes weren't different colors after all. No, it was worse than that. They were a deep, haunting violet.

Her features were pure, patrician, and she was tall. Maybe five-eight. For some reason he'd pictured her much shorter.

When she breezed past him, he caught the scent of her perfume. It wrapped around him, begging him to follow her wherever she might lead. She was definitely a temptation, but one he'd resist.

She faced him and his heart skipped a beat. She was alluring and sexy. Probably the reason she had so many followers who faithfully read her column. She was like a spider, weaving her web for the unsuspecting fly. But he knew her game and wouldn't be drawn in. No, Miss James had finally met her match.

Definitely tempting, though.

Man, he'd been spending way too many hours closeted away in front of his computer while he finished his last deadline, then been consumed with promotion for his current release. Dating hadn't been top priority.

Maybe two weeks alone with Selena was just the time off he needed.

Selena watched Trent. The changing emotions on his face that finally steeled into speculation.

Would she or wouldn't she? She'd seen that interested look before in men's eyes.

Trent wasn't bad himself—even better in person than he

"Boo," a woman said in a very dry, sultry voice from behind him.

He whirled around. For a split second he thought the place might actually be haunted. But if he was looking at a ghost, he hoped she didn't vanish anytime soon because she looked pretty damned sweet as she stood in the open doorway.

No, not sweet. Nothing about her looked sweet. She was earth, wind and fire all rolled up into one magnificent woman. The combination was sexy as hell.

Slowly his gaze traveled over her. Past long black hair that draped over one shoulder to kiss a breast. She was like nothing he'd ever seen with her loose white skirt, bangles at her wrists, and a multicolored full skirt.

Selena James looked even better in color than she had in black and white.

He wondered if she knew that with the sunlight streaming in behind her the skirt she wore was practically transparent. He didn't think he wanted to tell her. He rather enjoyed the view.

"Did I scare you?" she asked in a mocking voice, one eyebrow lifting sardonically. She swept into the room and shadows blocked the view of her legs.